THE RIDERS

BOOK OF

REVELATION

By: Mikarosyn

TABLE OF CONTENTS

CHAPTER 1 – THE CABIN OF EDEN

Rain pattered a chaotic melody on the tin roof as the warm aroma of coffee drifted into the room and danced with the woodsy smell of the fire. Crumpled into an oversized and over-loved mustard yellow armchair, I flipped casually through the musty pages of an ancient book—lore from the days of old when confused and desperate people tried to make sense of this unpredictable and unjust existence by seeking comfort in fairytales about fair, wise Gods. All-powerful beings that protected good souls, who, let's be frank, most likely weren't that good at all, from the crushing fires of the afterlife. *What a bunch of morons.* I learned a long time ago that no one would save you in this world but yourself, and you're better off investing your time and resources into tangible skills that could take you somewhere far away from your sorry start in life.

That was what I'd been doing since the day my mother screamed and swore her way through labor, only to take one look at me and decide she was better off if I was someone else's problem. The days, months, and years bouncing from group home to group home were only made more bearable by losing myself in all the books, articles, and videos I could get my hands on, consuming all the knowledge I could in hopes of being thoroughly prepared for my chance to make a break and start anew when the time came.

Escape had been my sole driving factor from as far back as I could remember. Everything else just seemed empty and meaningless. All I ever wanted was to exist outside of it all, in my own little void. I remember the first time I tried to run away when I was just six—the world taught me early even seemingly nice people didn't always have the best intentions. The cops found me in a raging storm, soaked and squatting in some bushes under a bridge, terrified and shaking. They took me back to my foster home, where I paid dearly for that stunt, but it didn't stop me from trying again at eight, ten, eleven, and fourteen.

On my sixteenth birthday, a particularly handsy foster father gave me the final push I needed to completely break free. That night was a blur, but I rose from his bed in the morning like a phoenix rising from the ashes. I found myself on a bus heading west with the saddest backpack you'd ever seen and a wad of cash I'd stolen from the box of unmentionables under dear old Dad's bed. I vividly remember dropping a lit match on my way out. Billows of black smoke were already rising from the windows as I walked down the silent early morning sidewalk. Loud thuds echoed across the still morning air, cracking open the quiet. The sounds of bottles of alcohol exploding as the flames reached them still ghosted my ears. I had never really given it much thought as to if he ever made it out of there, but just in case, I avoided the headlines for the rest of the week for plausible deniability. I remember sinking deep into my seat on the bus and watching the sun rise slowly over the vast empty stretches of the dawn-drenched highway, feeling a sense of ease for the first time in my life. I lived for these quiet moments, and I had never experienced one quieter than the hum of the tires on the road to freedom as the passenger three seats back snored softly and the driver stifled a cough.

Life after that was actually fairly easy and uneventful. I arrived on the bleak shores of the northwest and easily found my flow. I looked young for my age, but I had a deep emptiness in my eyes that kept folks from asking too many questions. I managed to find a freelance writing gig that paid enough to get by and suited my nature.

While staying at a run-down motel, I met the strangest old lady named Eden just a week after arriving at the overcast town with next to nothing to my name. She owned a cabin deep in the woods, far away from towns and neighbors, which had become neglected and abandoned as the years caught up with her. She wouldn't reveal her age to me, but based on some of the stories she shared in passing, I pegged her for at least a hundred. She was eclectic and weird but had a fierce kindness in her eyes and insisted that I move in and look after the property. I tried to turn her down several times, but of course, she was relentless, and in the end, we came to an agreement. I would fix up the place, and she would visit for Sunday dinners.

I never would have imagined how well-suited I was for that life. My vast internal library quickly sprung to life as I began fixing odds and ends throughout the house. By the end of my first year, I had spruced up the place and established a network of fences that housed goats, miniature cows, dogs, and chickens, along with a budding garden. During my second year, I built a greenhouse, fixed up the workshop, and even tried my hand at slaughtering and processing a few animals, including a deer that I shot myself with the bow I crafted by hand from a shoddy YouTube tutorial. It wasn't a precision instrument by any means, but it got the job done. During my third year, I could proudly declare I was officially able to hunt, grow, gather, and build almost anything I needed, allowing me to obtain almost all of my resources from the land and limiting my interactions with the outside world as much as possible. This was really for the best because one thing hadn't changed about the world: no matter where you move or how far you go, people generally suck.

Maybe it was me. Maybe it was my dead, empty eyes. Maybe it was my lanky too-long features or the pale, sickly color of my skin. Maybe it was the curtains of silvery-gray hair that hung straight and volume-less around my depressingly average face. Maybe it was the way I couldn't remember a single time I'd genuinely smiled in my entire life. Whatever it was, people often approached public interactions with me like you would with a leper. Their eyes shifted, avoiding contact at all costs as they frantically wracked their brains for a polite way to excuse themselves from my presence as soon as humanly possible. Those were the kind ones—bolder ones sneered openly, whispering insults and hurling hatred with a smile and a snicker. On the worst days, I'd even been subject to public outrage and humiliation, screamed at for simply existing, and random outbursts of anger from strangers I hadn't even looked at, let alone spoken to. To this day, I never have figured out why I seem like a magnet for fear and chaos, death and despair, but what I have figured out is that the further I am from people, the better. Except for Eden.

Eden was like a cosmic ray of sunshine delivered straight to Earth in a raging explosive comet. She could light up the sky in one instant or blacken it for centuries in the next. Eden was everything good and bad about humanity wrapped up in one wrinkly package. She was loud and obnoxious, wise and deep, foul-mouthed and fierce, and soft and subtle. She was all of these things and none of these things because to boil her essence down to just words was impossible. She was like nothing this world had seen, and I was convinced she had come from some other planet far from this realm. Above all, though, she was consistent.

Every Sunday, just as the sun was setting, she would appear on the horizon, walking slowly but steadily with a basket in her hands and a knowing smile on her face. She always came with exactly what I was craving and with more than enough for me to stash away for the week to come. After three years, her well of stories was yet to run dry, and when I was with her, it was simple. She picked up the slack in conversation when I grew quiet, and she listened, truly listened, when I did speak. Something I'd rarely encountered in this lifetime. I'd never looked forward to the company of any living soul, yet somehow, my Sundays had become sacred. It was just last night that I saw her last, the warm glow of her personality and the bell-like chime of her laughter still radiating within the walls of the cabin. Monday mornings almost felt like coming down from a high—she was that infectious.

I shut the dusty book I had sought out to pass the morning hours after rising with the sun to tend to the animals, returning it to one of the many shelves sagging with the weight of books collected over lifetimes and passed down by Eden's family. I rose from the chair, bones cracking and muscles pulling, and stretched my lanky arms toward the ceiling, taking a deep breath and clearing my head. *Time to get a move on, I suppose.* Lumbering into the kitchen, I drifted toward the enticing smell of coffee, grabbing my old and worn ceramic cup from the drainer in the sink. I only owned one, but it seemed more than enough. The intoxicating aroma billowed up toward me as I poured my cup. I added a small serving of milk, fresh from Greta, my goat, and watched as the cream swirled into a nice, modest brown color, muted and unassuming, much like me. Sipping the steaming cup of motivation, I gazed absently out at my garden through the kitchen window, leaning casually against the counter and watching the slow drizzle of rain on fresh spring plants. It was mesmerizing; the clock ticked on, but time became nothing as I drifted into the now, absorbed in my body, lost in the nothingness, my favorite place to be.

A sudden movement in the corner of my eye brought me crashing back down to reality. My head jerked as I searched for the disturbance, scanning my yard with intense precision. Was a hawk after the chickens again? Did one of the goats get loose? Did that damn bull break the fence again? Homesteading was peaceful, but it came with its own set of troubles, that's for sure.

Draining the rest of my cup, I rinsed it quickly in the sink, donned my faded yellow rain jacket, pulled on my matching duck boots, and headed swiftly for the yard. Sloshing through the mud, my breath came out in light puffs into the cool air. I made the rounds, checking in with the dogs and goats, the cows and chickens. I walked the garden to make sure no pesky rodents were destroying my hard work. I stepped into the greenhouse, the work shed, and even the storage room, clicking the lights on one by one, finding nothing but a couple of rats and one loud barn cat calling for some breakfast since catching it was clearly too much trouble.

I guessed it was just my imagination. *It wouldn't be my first time seeing things no one else had.* I used to think that maybe I was psychic, maybe I could communicate with the dead, maybe I was special, but in time, I realized I was just lonely, and a lonely mind will do a lot of fucked up things. Pushing it aside, I dredged my way back up to the cabin, bringing half the yard with me on my boots. I paused just short of the expansive back deck that served as a viewing platform for the entire property and turned my head to the stormy skies above. The pitter-patter of rain on my exposed face was refreshing and woke me up more than the coffee, perhaps from years of abusing the substance already, even at just nineteen. It renewed me, setting me off on my early afternoon chores, moving methodically from one section of the farm to the next, tending things tediously. This was the closest I'd ever felt to joy, a delicate peace to the order and routine, and I thrived in it. I tended to each thing fully, as if it were the only thing in the universe, giving it my undivided attention. I did this day in and day out, and I could pass away my time like this for many years to come—

maybe all my years to come, if I was being honest.

The universe doesn't always cooperate with our vision of destiny, though, unfortunately. Not that I've held much stock in destiny, fate, or whatever you want to call it, but some things you just can't deny seem to happen for a reason. People will argue that it's a coincidence or just a small synchronicity. People will say you're projecting what you want to see in the signs of the universe and that the only true God is Chaos. People will argue about a lot of things, most of which I don't care to engage in, but one thing I know for certain, though, is that whatever you want to call it—fate, chaos, destiny—when it comes knocking, it knocks hard. The reality is that more can happen in one day than can happen in years, decades, and even lifetimes. Events can conspire in such a way that, in a matter of moments, the entire course of your life can drastically alter, dragging you with it whether you like it or not. You can fight it, you can plant your feet and refuse to move, you can cling to your old comfortable life, you can shut your eyes and hide under the covers and pretend it's all a bad dream, but if one of those days comes for you, believe me when I say, it's coming for you.

As it would turn out, today was about to be one of those days. Today was the day destiny was coming to collect a debt long overdue.

The sun dipped below the tree line, casting long shadows across the soggy rolling fields, drenching the land in rich golden hues. I scattered feed for the chickens as I cooed them lullabies, luring them into their coop to settle and sleep for the night. I walked the grounds slowly, with purpose, wishing each creature a hushed goodnight, a soft pat on the head, and a stroke in just the right spot. I moved through the paces, and the paces moved through me, settling my restless soul. Staring up at the shower of falling stars in the twilight sky, I tried not to drag my feet as I found my way back inside the cabin, reluctant to face the long night after another exhausting day. It was at night the thoughts came, unavoidable, all-consuming. During the day, I could stay busy, occupied enough to stay in the moment. At night, they always came for me—the dread, the emptiness, the absolute utter hopelessness. Like old friends who had long ago worn out their welcome, they stayed with me through the night, holding me to my despair, cradling me in my discomfort, and singing me to sleep with the songs of lost souls. Try as I might to overcome them, they was me, and I was them. Together we mourned for a world destined to demolish itself.

I hovered over the stove, reheating rice and beans left over from the night before. Standing on my tiptoes, I pulled a neatly wrapped parcel off the top of the fridge and gingerly unwrapped the parchment paper surrounding a soft and tender loaf of sweet cinnamon cornbread—Eden's specialty. I gathered my bowl and a generous slice of cornbread and made my way loftily to the same beloved armchair I spent every night and most mornings in. It was wedged perfectly between the fire and an oversized storybook window that looked out onto the eerily beautiful old-growth forest that expanded uninterrupted for miles north to the nearest mountains. A small pond that separated the house from the woods was still glistening with the last remnants of the sunset as a koi fish broke the still surface and leaped lazily through the air before splashing back down into the fiery pool below. I smiled despite myself, not a real one, not one that reached my eyes or parted my lips, but a shadowed smile, a cast-off of the small fleeting comfort this home brought me.

As I scraped the last tasty morsels from my bowl, I stood, rinsed my dish in the sink, and changed into my favorite fitted knit turtleneck in a muted blue that brings out the intense icy blue streaks usually hiding in my swampy green and gold eyes. I pulled on my oldest, softest light blue overalls, holey and worn, patched in several places with vintage hand-sewn decals, and decorated with an eclectic arrangement of embroidered flowers scattered across the damaged denim; they were one of my only processions from my time in the system. As many terrible memories as they carried in their faded fibers, they were comforting, like a childhood home, and I find myself in them almost every night. Rolling the bottom cuffs a few times, I pulled on an eccentric pair of blue and yellow striped socks before sauntering back to the living room, collapsing in a heap next to the fire. I fish around under a worn hand-crafted table from the days when furniture was made with purpose and care, dragging out a vintage tray stocked with everything I could need for the night. A variety of small jars carrying samples of the season's herb harvest and my preferred tools of the trade. Purples, reds, and golds danced with the green bounty of the earth, the only solace from the deep empty vast that is my mind.

Carefully wrapping the crumbled herb into the raw hemp paper, I bring it to my lips, sliding my tongue across the paper, the sweet aroma taunting me with its alluring relief from the endless internal noise as I complete the final touches. Striking the lighter, I rolled the joint gently for a nice, even burn, savoring the first puffs of my smokey salvation. Taking a long deep drag, I exhaled my worries, releasing myself from the bonds of this existence. A deep numbing sensation settled over my body, moving from limb to limb, finally invading my mind, spreading its haze through my entire being. This season's crop had been particularly potent. Taking several longer drags, I snuffed out the half-smoked joint before I eased back into my chair, cradled by the warmth of the fire mixing with the sweet cool air drifting in from the open window. The swell of the crickets outside playing a symphony to the stars above, the trees swaying softly in the wind, the wolf howling in the distance to his beloved moon, the sounds of nature rocking me to sleep, one gentle breath at a time. Slowly I slipped off to dreamland, a peaceful snore quietly escaping my lips, silence settling in for the night.

Screaming abruptly brought me back to this dimension as I jolted upward in my seat. The frightening sounds were pouring out of my own mouth, intense, blood-curdling screams that had the entire farm stirring outside, belting and cawing back at me. Of course it was me. *It's always me.* I took a deep breath, preparing myself for the inevitable as the rush of night terrors caught up with me, gripping me once more in images of death, terror, and destruction. I rode out the lucid recap of the dream I'd previously been trapped in, letting the horrors wash through me. By the time they had their way with me, I was shaking, sitting in a pool of my own sweat, my head pounding something fierce. I stumbled my way into the kitchen, flicking on the softest lights available yet squinting my eyes painfully anyway. Pouring a glass of water, I washed down some ibuprofen before downing the rest of the cup, hoping not to wake up totally dehydrated. Walking into my bedroom, I collapsed in a heap of exhaustion on my bed, too tired to even undress. Curling up into a ball, I wrapped myself in blankets, closing my eyes as I tried to block out the darkness, desperately forcing myself back into a restless sleep. Deep breath in, deep breath out, deep breath in, deep breath out.

Just as my mantra was kicking in and I was caught in the sweet abyss between this world and the next, an earth-shattering crash rattled the entire house, followed by an ear-splitting roar that I felt down to my bones. Adrenaline kicked in, and I was on my feet in a heartbeat; another beat and I was at the door, lacing up my old white Converse high tops with shaking hands. I ripped the door open and stepped out onto the porch, confronted by a massive crater in front of my house where what appeared to be the largest bolt of lightning I'd ever heard had just struck. I stared in awe, speechless at the sheer force and power of Mother Nature, when all of a sudden, another massive bolt of lightning tore through the sky, ripping apart the heavens and crashing into the earth once more in the exact same spot. A shockwave radiated out from the epicenter, forcing me to stumble back into the doorframe of the cabin. I grabbed the house to steady myself as the energy from the blast coursed through my body, paralyzing me momentarily.

"I thought lightning never struck the same spot twice," I whispered breathlessly.

The air was charged, and the entire farm was intensely silent despite the disturbances. Wide-eyed and anxious, I found my footing and moved forward once more in an attempt to investigate the damage to the blast site. Before I even made it off the porch, the heavens exploded for a third time, sending another crushing wave of power bolting down to the earth, hitting the exact same spot once more with twice the force of the previous hits. One moment I was moving toward the impact site, and the next, I was flying through the air, crashing into the old wooden rocker and landing in a bruised heap on the doorstep. The world was spinning, and my head was foggy, but I righted myself, tenderly pushing up onto my knees, raising a bloody hand to sweep the tangled mess of silver hair out of my eyes so I could figure out what the hell was going on here.

That's when I saw him. Standing in the center of all that chaos and destruction was a tall, foreboding figure, electricity sparking off his rich caramel skin, completely covered in vivid white and gold hexagonal geometric tattoos and some sort of ancient writing. Steam billowed off his lean shoulders. He was completely motionless, a statue who didn't even seem to be breathing, standing gracefully among the chaos. I knew I should be afraid, terrified, and probably running for my life right now, but something about him had me transfixed, and I just couldn't look away. Without warning, he lost his rigid structure and crumpled to the charred ground below. I bolted to my feet, stumbling slightly from the hit to the head, and raced to his side without thinking. I dropped to the ground next to him, hesitating as I reached out. *This could be dangerous—***he** *could be dangerous.* My hesitations were too late, though. Moving almost too fast to perceive, he sat up and placed both hands firmly on my shoulders, gripping me with such intensity that it hurt, as his deep electric blue eyes shot open, piercing through me to the very core of my soul.

"We're not safe here. We gotta move. Now. Her shadows will be here any minute now!"

He spoke urgently, but his voice was deep, velvety, and smooth, perfectly matched to his dark skin and long locks of silky deep purple curls loosely piled into a messy bun on his head. His voice had a seductive quality to it, and I couldn't help but feel lured in by his words, even if they were totally insane. I was struggling to even remember how to speak when, without warning, he grabbed my hand fiercely.

"We're out of time," he stated matter-of-factly before pulling us both to our feet in one solid motion, swooping me effortlessly into his arms.

Just like that, we were off into the night at a breathtaking speed before I could even find the words to object. I stared at him, utterly speechless, as everything I knew disappeared behind us.

CHAPTER 2 – THE PALE HORSEMAN

Trees were whipping past us at a breakneck pace, the stars above were all but a blur, and my house was getting further and further away. My thoughts were running even faster, and I knew I needed to say something, *anything*, but the shock of everything that had happened was making it hard to think of anything coherent.

All at once, my courage flared up inside me. "STOP!" The words exploded out of me, halting him in his tracks abruptly.

He set me down instantly, looking deeply apologetic as he took an exaggerated step back from me. "My apologies, my lady, but I don't think you understand. I just want to keep you safe. We need to keep moving. The time has arrived for you to be activated, and they've come for you."

I didn't mean to be so angry, but was he kidding me? "You sound like a fucking crazy person! What do you mean activated!? Who? Who is coming after me? This is nonsense, and I don't want anything to do with you or your little fantasy!" I twirled around, a hot mess of anger and tears at this point, and started raging my way back home. *Who does this guy think he is, dropping into my life and making such a mess of everything?*

A strong hand pulled me back around, making me stumble, tripping into his sturdy, strangely hot arms. I blushed intensely as I lifted my gaze and found his face far too close for comfort. At this distance, I could see the distinct ring of gold in his surreal blue eyes. Furious, I pushed him off of me as I steadied myself.

He held eye contact in an unnatural way before speaking

softly. "Listen, I know it's a lot to take, but you need to trust me, Nato."

My eyes widened as I took a startled step back. How did he know my name? Who was this guy? "That's it. I'm out." I turned abruptly and started bolting back home, mustering as much strength as I could, forcing more power into each step. I could hear his muted footsteps behind me; I had a feeling he was buffing his speed to give me some false sense of freedom, but I took advantage, nonetheless. My legs were burning by the time I broke through the woods and stumbled my way back into the soft light of my beloved cabin. It stood peacefully in the night. Sure, there was a big crater in the front yard now, but other than that, it remained the same, a beacon of hope on an otherwise illogical night. I took several steps forward when reality suddenly ripped apart around me.

I was flying through the air. Everything around me was hot, intensely hot, so hot I couldn't breathe. My ears were ringing so fiercely that it was nauseating, and I couldn't start my lungs. I needed oxygen, and I was suffocating under the weight of my own bones. Suddenly the ground buckled, splitting around me, shattering everything I had come to know. The world went dark—I was lost, drifting through a damp black void for what felt like an eternity. Was this it? Was this how it all ended? Everything seemed so painful and hot, and I just wanted to let go and give myself over to the peaceful emptiness that was calling out to me. That's when I felt his soft, strong hands gripping me, pushing down methodically on my chest, jolting life back into my broken bones. I awoke bathed in blinding golden light as he chanted in a language I'd never seen in any book, the tattoos covering his body glowing brightly. I felt his energy pulsing through me, and it was all I could do not to scream as it rushed through me, closing my wounds and resetting my bones.

As the light faded, we were both left panting, gasping in shock, pain, and exhaustion. I sat up in disbelief as I tried to comprehend what I was seeing. Everything, and I mean everything, the cabin, the workhouse, the greenhouse, the fences, my heart shattering silently as it dawned on me that even my pastures and all my animals had been reduced to a smoking pile of rubble. Everything I had loved, everything I had built, the nearest I had ever come to being happy, reduced to nothing but an empty field below the twinkling skies, a useless pile of rubble still steaming in the cool night air.

At first, I didn't need to fight back the tears. I couldn't cry if I wanted; I couldn't even breathe. Dropping to my knees, I spent several minutes with my hands clutched into the damp earth, desperate for a connection to hold on to as I fought to gasp tiny puffs of oxygen, barely enough to keep me conscious. After several painful minutes of feeling very much like a fish out of water, the grace of a deep breath opened the floodgates, and a fiery stream of tears bubbled out all at once, raw as they burned my throat and nose. In a matter of moments, I was a mess of emotions, sobbing as I collapsed further into the ground, pounding the dirt in fury and frustration. I had so little in this life. Why must I sacrifice more?

A reassuring hand rested on my shoulder for several moments before the mysterious man sighed softly. "I'm so sorry for your loss. I tried to warn you. I wish we had more time to mourn, but we must be moving." He stood and reached his hand out, a soft, compassionate look in his eyes as he urged me up. I stared disbelievingly for a moment, numb to the core of my being, and just like that, I let go of everything and took a leap of faith. After all, I now knew he hadn't been wrong. Grasping his hand firmly, I lifted myself to my feet, determined to let go and move on as I always had in the face of tragedy.

"You're right. Let's go. What's done is done." My words were hollow, but I knew it was the only way to survive in this world.

I planted one foot firmly in front of the other and started off in the direction we had first run, determined to meet my destiny with dignity and composure. Even if it meant starting completely over again. How many times was that now? I had lost count at this point.

We were silent for a long time as we traveled through the winding forest. He seemed to instinctively know where he was going, and I had no mental capacity to argue. I just followed in his steps, going through the motions.

We moved like this for hours when he turned around sharply, scanning the woods behind me. "We can stop and rest now. We have a big day ahead of us tomorrow."

He pushed past me, moving from tree to tree, marking the air with strange symbols. Light streamed from his fingers, burning into the trees, sealing us into some type of protective barrier of soft light from what I could tell. I started to shiver as he moved methodically around us in a circle. I wrapped my arms around myself, clutching the thin knit material of my sweater in my numb, cold hands as the chilly night air seeped past my skin and into my bones. Finishing his task, he turned to me with a sympathetic look and swooped toward the center of the circle, creating a vivid blue fire in one fluid motion where no fire had existed beforehand. It was the tipping point for me.

I gasped, blurting aloud as I abruptly broke the several-hour silence, "How the hell did you do that?!"

He grinned and bowed modestly. "Cheap miracles are child's play."

I stared at him bemused and couldn't help but laugh, a tense sound, at his bizarre answer. "Right, sure, makes sense."

I rolled my eyes as I collapsed into a comfortable position

next to the fire and held my hands out to warm them. The day was catching up to me, and I could feel the weight of the world bearing down on my shoulders. I could only imagine what terrors my dreams would hold tonight, if I could sleep at all. I pushed back these thoughts and gazed across the blue fire at the still, brooding figure across from me. His eyes were fixed on the flames, and he seemed eternal as he sat there, like a statue in some ancient church. He was a total stranger, yet somehow, I felt like I had known him always; if I was honest, there wasn't anyone in this world I actually knew like that, so that was absolutely insane. Must have been an effect of shock, like Stockholm syndrome or something. Still, it was hard to deny just how captivating he was, like a planet whose gravity just pulled you right in. I was still staring at him when his electric eyes shot up, catching mine as a grin spread across his face. I turned away, embarrassed, ashamed, but still so goddamn intrigued. Blushing, I looked back up, grinning back apologetically. I needed answers, and it was time.

"So what gives? Are you, like, a god or something?" I laughed dryly, shooting for the least likely answer to break the ice. To my surprise, he laughed loudly, a throaty and comforting sound, the type of laugh that made you want to laugh too.

After a few minutes of chuckling, he locked his piercing gaze onto mine again. "I wish! You're not far off base, really. Just an angel, though, a fallen one at that too, so pretty low on the totem pole, actually." I stared at him in shock, my jaw literally dropping open.

"An angel?" I stammered over the word, my brain racing again. "What do you mean, an angel?!" *This is a joke. It must be a joke. Or a dream that makes total sense, this is just one really elaborate, super lucid night terror, and soon I'll wake up screaming. Oh, it will be perfect, screaming in my own home in my own bed—*

He interrupted me flatly, breaking me out of my self-pitying spiral. "You know, like the all-knowing, prayer-answering dudes in white, except not." He grinned again while staring at me earnestly with those captivating blue and gold eyes.

I sighed, confused, tired, and honestly overwhelmed. "You don't really look the part." I gestured toward his rugged appearance. Mostly nude, lean but built, with shredded denim shorts and large bare feet planted firmly on the ground. Scars decorated his body along with ancient-looking markings and the hexagonal geometric tattoos in white and gold scattered asymmetrically across his richly colored skin, a handful of piercings ranging from a gold lip ring to a dangly purple and teal crystal hanging off his ear. "Aren't you supposed to have wings or something?" I scoffed. Ah, sarcasm—a defense mechanism I learned from a life hard lived. He brushed off my attitude with another carefree grin. He wore the expression too well, which was almost smug if you ask me.

"When I need them, I do. My powers are limited when I'm earth-side, and the longer I'm here, the more they drain. You basically just become a glorified human if you stay too long. Not that some haven't chosen that life, but it's certainly not for me." He looked at me, smiling matter-of-factly.

After staring blankly at him for several moments, an awkward tension lingered in the air as I sat pensively, taking him in for far longer than would be considered normal in polite society. He held my gaze the entire time, something I couldn't quite decipher behind those ocean eyes.

After the longest silence in the history of mankind, I let out a breath I didn't know I was holding. "You're serious, aren't you?"

He laughed again. Didn't he understand this really wasn't all that funny? "You really thought hard about that one, didn't you, my lady? Obviously, I'm serious! Didn't you see me come down in a bolt of lighting? Didn't you watch what that demon and her shadows did to your home? This is very serious. You are the Chosen One, the Harbinger of Change, the Pale Rider. You're destined to redeem this world, and I can't let anything stand in your way."

He had a fierce look of determination in his eyes as he spoke. It took me by surprise. I'd never meant anyone with this level of passion and devotion. Most people walk this earth in their own little bubble, devoid of any depth, glued to their phones and consumed by their cravings and crutches. My heart fluttered softly. It had been cold and dead for as long as I could remember, and it was an uncomfortable feeling, kind of like I was gassy. His long sigh brought me back to the moment as he settled into a more comfortable position. For the first time, he looked relaxed.

"It's a long story, and it's hard to explain here, but I'll do my best, so bear with me." I took a deep breath and settled in, too, gazing at him fixedly, lulled by his melodic alto voice.

"A long time ago, before you or I existed, the world was created by an all-knowing God. An army of angels was created of their own Godly genetic makeup to carry out the bidding of this God. We all obeyed loyally until a time came when an angel decided that they didn't agree, speaking against our God's divine plan for humanity. They believed in more freedom, chaos, and creativity than our God wanted to grant the mortals of Earth. A battle ensued, and many angels fell, myself included. They fled to the Underworld, deep in the core of Earth, and began to influence the societies of men in any way they could. But I returned to our God, repentant and remorseful. I had been led astray by the message of my brothers and sisters yet was turned away by their actions. I was gifted a second chance in the form of a mission that only I could carry out for our creator, given a new identity as Amil, the Angel of Death. I've come to collect you, the final Rider of the Apocalypse, the conduit of the condemned, the last hope in a hopeless place. This world has become dark and destructive, and I know you can feel in your heart that it's time for a fresh start. Come with me and join the other Riders in bringing forth the new age of humanity."

I shook my head in disbelief. "Wait a minute, are you trying to say I'm a Horseman of the apocalypse? You mean like Revelations? Like in the Bible? *The Bible?!*" I had never been religious, but curiosity had driven me to read a passage or two for historical purposes, of course, certainly not ever out of a desperate desire for there to be *something* bigger than myself and my sad little existence. "You've got to be kidding me!"

He shook his head in return. "Not a Horseman. *The Horseman!* You're the final Horseman. We've collected the other three, but you've been very elusive. We almost didn't find you in time. You're the last Rider, the Horseman of Death. Don't let the name scare you. Death is so final in this realm, but death and birth are one and the same in the grand scheme of the universe. Consider it more of a transformation. You're just awakening the human species to their higher selves."

Amil stared at me for a moment as if he was weighing how well I was handling all this. He seemed to hesitate before continuing with an even softer voice. "I'm sure you've felt it. All the others saw the signs. Perhaps a deep unavoidable void within yourself? Dreams showing you what's to come, the end of times in a fiery blaze of glory?" He raised his eyebrows, pausing to give me a moment to absorb what he was saying. To accept what he already knew, I knew based on the look in his eyes.

I dropped my gaze to the flickering fire and whispered meekly, "I mean, maybe, it just seems so surreal..." How could I hold the key to redeeming humanity? I was nobody.

Nodding knowingly, he seemed to read my mind as he spoke again. "You are more amazing than you realize. I've spent lifetimes waiting to serve you. You may not know it, but it's an honor just to be in your presence." He bowed his head before looking back up at me coyly. "Even if you are a mess." His angelic chuckle broke the tension, and I looked down at myself, covered in mud, scratches, and blood.

I couldn't help but laugh sheepishly. "Yeah, a real honor, clearly." I tried to hide a weak smile as I rolled my eyes half-heartedly, the weight of the day was closing in on me fast, and I knew I didn't have long left. "This has been fun and all, but I'm about to pass out, so if you don't mind, I think I'm going to call it a night."

Without waiting for a response, I turned abruptly and lay down, curling into the fetal position. I needed time to think, I wanted to run into the forest and never look back, but that seemed like a quick way to die, so this would have to suffice. I gave in to the intense and overwhelming emotions I had been holding back all night. Just yesterday morning, I had walked the grounds of my farm methodically tending to my animals and crops, and now everything was ash, and I was supposedly some mythical Rider of Death. It was absurd and absolutely mad, and I just wanted to go back to my old life. Silent tears streamed down my face, and with the fire to my back, the cold of a northwest spring night began to seep through my thin clothes. My body began to shiver uncontrollably, and I clutched myself tighter to fight off the chill.

Warm, lean arms wrapped around my waist, pulling me close to a surprisingly soft body. I gasped aloud, tensing instinctually. I hated when people touched me, let alone this close, but I simply couldn't deny that everything about him just felt *safe*.

Inches from my ear, he whispered softly, sending a chill up my spine. "Don't make this weird. I need to deliver you to the Kingdom in one piece. You won't do anyone any good if you freeze to death out here."

I didn't give him the pleasure of a response, but I relaxed, sinking into the grooves of his strong body, soaking in the warmth of his fiery skin. He started to hum softly, something that sounded ancient and otherworldly. I drifted peacefully in his arms, falling into a deep, dreamless slumber; no night terrors, no waking up in the middle of the night screaming in sweats, just uninterrupted serenity. For the first time in my life, I slept blissfully, waking refreshed as the first rays of the morning sun peaked over the horizon, bringing the forest to life around them.

I would never admit it aloud, but I could have laid in his arms forever. I was absolutely still as I listened to the slow and steady breathing as his chest lifted softly, hitting my back every other moment, sending shockwaves through my body at the simplest touch. The birds chirped, and the breeze swayed through the trees as the morning passed. I wanted to hold on to these simple moments before facing the reality of the road ahead of us.

His soft voice suddenly broke the silence, husky with sleep. "How long have you been listening to me sleep?"

Defensively, I brushed him off. "You're absurd, don't be so full of yourself."

I sat up, pushing him off of me, creating a million miles of distance between us so I could clear my head and think properly. Overnight, everything had changed, and I was filled with uncertainty and dread at the prospect of lunging haphazardly into such an unclear future. I liked consistency, I liked routine, I liked isolation, and this was anything but that.

Loud rustling grabbed my attention, breaking my train of thought. I jerked my head in the direction we had come from the night before, alert and on edge. Amil jumped to his feet, crouching in a defensive position and placing himself between me and the oncoming rush of darkness.

"They're here. Prepare yourself."

Prepare myself how? What did that even mean? Before I could decide, a swarm of bats erupted into the grove, fluttering around us in chaos, a few taking bites at me before they flew off into the morning sky. I jumped to my feet as a hoard of lanky shadowy figures suddenly emerged, dripping from the sunrise shadows of the trees and molding into solid form before my very eyes. Leading the pack was a wild and strange creature, stalking forward like a cat, smiling like she was hungry and I was something to eat.

Her black skin was striking against her glowing golden eyes, a mess of flaming red and smokey blue dreads cascading around her, the colors seeming to move throughout each other surrealistically like liquid locks. Golden beads and crystals were scattered throughout her hair, a million tiny treasures hiding in there. Gold freckles decorated her face, and her body was painted in gold tattoos flecked with white. A collection of geometry different than Amil's decorated her skin, pentagonal instead of his collection of hexagonal geometry, with more of the strange ancient language scrawled across her body. Her white dress was simple and unassuming, but she wore it well, the white silk riding against her skin in all the right places. She casually strolled up, locking her eyes on me, completely ignoring Amil as if he wasn't even there.

"Hello, love. It's a pleasure to meet you." She smiled warmly, but there was something wicked in her eyes that I just couldn't trust. She extended her hand as Amil hissed fiercely, a primal protective sound that didn't phase her one bit. She held her position fearlessly as I sized her up, the tension thick in the air.

After a long moment, I nodded my head, refusing to take her hand. "The pleasure is all mine, I'm sure. Who, may I ask, are you?" Anger flickered in her eyes, but she covered it smoothly, grinning deceitfully as she pulled her hand back. She recomposed herself, shifting her stance as she continued.

"Damia, but *you* can call me Mia." She curled the *"you"* sensually on her tongue, grinning with the air of a girl who was used to getting what she wanted. It stirred something in me that I quickly pushed away. I couldn't afford to be distracted right now. "Who I am isn't important, though. It's all about you, my dear. You're the reason we're all here." She brought her hands together in a menacing manner, twiddling her fingers together like a collector. "Now, the only question is, do we have to force you, or will you come willingly?" She must have already known my answer, though, because before I could speak, the shadows behind her erupted into action.

Rising like the tide, the figures merged together into one black mass, swelling high into the air above them before crashing back down to the ground like a rogue wave. I caught one last look at the wicked exotic creature smiling at me with cruel eyes before the all-consuming darkness washed over me, stealing my breath and crushing my soul. It was as if a lifetime of night terrors had merged into one mythical creature who was now gleefully reigning terror upon every ounce of my body. The pressure was immense, and it was all I could do to hold on to my fleeting consciousness as I slipped further and further into the cold black void.

Hot hands pulled me back into my body as I felt the pressure subsiding. Amil was cradling me in his arms with the most intense look on his face, his white tattoos glowing blindingly bright, creating an aura of hot white light around us. The black monster pushed angrily against the orb of light, screeching in frustration as it searched for any weakness in his protective barrier.

Amil knelt on the ground, placing me down gently before forcefully dropping both palms to the earth below. An explosion of blinding light rippled out from us, blanketing the forest in a blaze of white that washed everything away.

CHAPTER 3 – TILL KINGDOM KEEP COME

The forest was completely empty around us. Moments ago, this small clearing in the trees was a scene of terror and fear of all the bad things in this world and the next. Now birds chirped soft serenades to the rising sun, the breeze rustled the branches playfully, and the cool fresh air carried sweet scents of new life. The contrast of it all and the shock of two near-death experiences in the span of twelve hours cracked my icy shell. Laughter bubbled out of me in a manic sort of way, and soon I was laughing so hard I doubled over. I laughed and laughed until suddenly I was crying, sobbing in an ugly sort of way. I lay on the forest floor and sobbed like I have never sobbed in my life. I don't know how much time passed, but Amil sat silently and patiently the whole time, letting me fall to pieces over and over again in waves of grief. Grief for the life that was gone, grief for the home I finally thought could be permanent, grief for the girl I never was and now never could be, grief for losing everything that was ever normal, over and over again.

Eventually, I stood, gathering what strength I had left, sorting my miseries into tiny little compartments and filing them away deep inside. Clearly, there was no point in running from destiny, so I looked at Amil resolutely. "I'm ready. I want to know who I really am."

With a solemn nod, he gestured forward. "They'll be back before long. Follow me, and I'll explain everything." We ventured into the woods, following some unknown path he seemed certain of. "As I told you last night, the Almighty One, Hova, created this realm eons ago. While humans have made many clever and creative guesses over the years, no one's ever been quite right. The earth was one big experiment. Imagine it much as you would a GMO garden in this world but with even more genetic manipulation. Humans were created in our image, with less power but much more moral freedom. They were presented with ethical dilemmas throughout their short lives to see if they would rise to the occasion or slowly tear each other down like crabs in a bucket, affecting the quality of their soul and dictating how clean or tainted their essence, or as we call it, *mana*, was by the end of their individual journey on this plane." He paused momentarily, seeming to choose his words carefully.

"The eternal war between good and evil isn't quite what humans think it is, though. When this world was created, Hova worked hand in hand with their most beloved and revered angel, Cifer. There came a time when their ideologies split irrevocably, and the Almighty One cast Cifer and her disciples out of the Kingdom. Banishing them to the Underworld, they were stripped of their angelic powers, our ability to harness the ether using hexagonal geometry, and branded with the name *demon*. Since the beginning of time, they've fought over mankind's souls, but not on an individual level like preachers want scared flocks of sheep to believe. More like we're harvesting soul energy, or *mana*, on a massive scale. The more we have, the more base creative material we have to sculpt with. We can use it to enhance our own powers, craft waves of new angels, create fundamental changes to this reality, or even start whole new realities. Its possibilities are endless, and it's the most valuable substance in existence. It's precious and limited. The only way we can obtain it is by breeding it. We've experimented with a variety of forms, but the only successful trial so far for rich, clean mana has been when we created a species designed directly of our own genetic makeup. A watered-down version of our very own DNA—humans. But the real trick was free will. While we lose some to the path of evil, the righteous produce such vast amounts of mana that the trade-off is typically worth it."

I stared at him blankly. How could all of humanity just be a crop grown for harvest? It was so cruel, so meaningless. I'd never been a believer, but deep down, I always hoped there was something for us beyond the mortal bonds. Otherwise, really, what was the point? We should just give up and let it all go to hell. The conspiracy theorist had been right; it was all a trap, and we were all doomed. We might as well arm ourselves and collapse into anarchy if that's the case.

He interrupted my spiraling thoughts empathetically, once again seeming to read my mind. "I know it sounds cruel, my lady, but you must understand. Where we come from, it's a whole different reality. Do you feel bad for ants when you wipe them off your counter? Do you feel bad for the chickens you harvest to stay fed through the winter? I hate to put it so bluntly, but the lives of humans are just so…insignificant." He paused again, studying my face, calculating his next move. I wondered what he saw there—if he could see the horror in my sickly green eyes.

"Listen, I know it's a lot to take in, but you must realize there's a much bigger picture here. The fate of a lot more than just this planet is at stake, and humans are but a small piece of the puzzle. I could try to explain it to you, but in the end, it's only something you'll believe if you see it for yourself. If you come with me to the nexus point, we can travel to the Kingdom, where you will have your eyes opened to the truth. You will see your place in the grand scheme of things and awaken to your destiny as a Rider."

"What is that even supposed to mean?" I shot back sharper

than I intended, but keeping the frustration out of my voice was hard. It was all just too much. "A Rider. The Horseman of Death. You call me these things, but what do they mean? I'm just a girl, a sad, pathetic girl who can barely even keep my shit together when I have bad dreams. I'm no Harbinger of Change. I can promise you that." I let out a long deep breath trying to regain my composure as a grin played across his face.

It was irritating how well he wore the expression. How good he looked even in nothing but rags and covered in dirt and blood from a night on the run in the woods. I'm sure I looked like hell. My hair was tangled and knotted to the point that running my hands through it wasn't even an option. My cuts and gashes had been healed by whatever strange magic he had cast on me back at the cabin, but the blood, dirt, and rips remained. My favorite old white sneakers were caked in mud, looking more orange than white. My mouth was dry, and tears had caked streaks of filth on my face, and all I wanted in the world was to take a long hot shower.

"Well, if you'd let me finish…" he interrupted my stream of thoughts coyly. "Cast out from the Kingdom, Cifer had begun harvesting the tainted mana, something we previously thought was impossible. A fail-safe was created to protect the Kingdom from Cifer's rising powers, a back door in case things ever needed to be reset. The four Riders of the Apocalypse: Pestilence, War, Famine, and Death. Each would awaken when the time came to their divine destiny of destruction, rising to right the wrongs in the world.

"Long ago, the Almighty One realized the time was neigh. Darkness had gripped the humans, and Cifer's collection of tainted soul material was growing stronger by the day. Cifer discovered the fail-safe and began to seek out the Riders, hoping to alter the course of fate. An elite army of angels was prepared, each assigned a Rider to guide them on their path to enlightenment. We would protect you from the shadows of the Underworld and open your eyes to the infinite potential within yourself. You, my lady, are the most important piece to the puzzle, which is exactly why Cifer wants you so desperately. You control everything. You're the key to the redemption of humankind.

"With your help, we can bring in a new age of humanity and raise the level of consciousness, creating a more peaceful and resilient society. Cifer has other plans, though, hoping to manipulate you into creating an apocalyptic event with no follow-up, leaving the humans to descend into more and more chaos as anarchy takes hold on this planet, allowing the shadows an endless buffet of tainted souls to harvest." He paused, studying me a moment more. "I know that's not what you really want, is it, my lady?"

The air was heavy with the weight of the information he had just unloaded on me. He looked at me with uncertain eyes. He could probably tell that every instinct in my brain was telling me to bolt. I evaded the hard questions with an easier one, something I had been wondering for some time now. "Can you read my mind?" I looked at him pointedly in the eyes, daring him to lie to me.

To my surprise, a soft chuckle escaped his lips. "Not exactly. I can read your mood, though, and that seems to be about the same thing for you." I rolled my eyes blatantly, irritated by his answer.

I had always been told I wore my emotions on my sleeves, but it didn't mean I needed some smug stranger pointing it out. I pressed further for information. "So the mood reading thing, and the healing back at the cabin, the fire, and whatever the hell that blast of light was, what else can you do?" I raised my eyebrows inquisitively, focusing on the small details that had always helped my brain process things that overwhelmed me, which was almost everything growing up.

"Lots of things, not enough things, nothing compared to what *you* can do." He looked at me intensely, with reverence and devotion. "Your powers are limitless, and you were born of this realm, so you'll never face the same limitations I have here." He stopped, placing his hand softly on my shoulder, gazing deep into my eyes. "There's so much I want to show you."

I shuddered, pushing his arm off of me. "What powers could I have? I've spent my entire life being less than ordinary, and even in the worst of times, there was nothing I could do to protect myself."

I stared him in the eyes defiantly, trying to hide the pain in my eyes that threatened to betray my hardened tones. It was just still so much to wrap my head around. I was starting to doubt that I hadn't actually hit my head too hard in some common farm accident and this was just some fantasy scenario playing out in my head while I lay in a hospital bed somewhere, trapped deep in a coma. I searched his eyes desperately for any sign that this was real, that I needed to accept this reality, embrace it, and own it so I could make the best of it. That's what Eden would tell me to do right now.

I bit my lip, holding back a sudden wave of emotion. Eden was going to be so upset about the cabin. Her entire family history was stored in those walls, and she had entrusted me to protect it, and I failed. *I failed her.* Her glowing face filled my mind, pulling at my heartstrings and threatening to send me overboard again. That isn't what she'd want, though. I needed to get a grip.

Amil was staring at me silently. Of course he knew I was processing, my mood must be all over the place, and he seemed to understand it was best to leave me alone. After several moments, he spoke, breaking the silence. "I can show you your potential if you want. We can start right here, right now, if it pleases you." He paused, giving me a moment to ponder silently before continuing.

"However, if I may suggest, perhaps we should get to the safe house and shower first?" He gestured toward my haphazard appearance, as my cheeks burned bright red in response. Patience had never been a strong suit of mine, but it seemed to be the only way out of my current mess.

I sighed, dropping my shoulders and the defensive posture I hadn't even realized I'd taken. "You're right, you're right, a shower is definitely in order first. How far away is this safe house?"

He smiled, clearly unsurprised by my answer. "We are close now, just a bit further."

I nodded, signaling for him to lead the way so I could follow, giving me time to fume over the situation without interruption as we approached our destination.

The morning sun gave way to afternoon rays, the sounds of the forest shifting slowly with the sun. We carved our way through the woods for hours—so much for just a bit further. I traced his footsteps silently, processing the past twenty-four hours as we moved along the still-damp path. My thoughts were as tangled as the undergrowth growing thicker by the moment, trying to grab my feet and pull me down like the forest wanted to eat me alive. At first, I thought it was my imagination, but I became certain the trees were trying to keep me out when a rogue root wrapped around my ankle. I pulled away fiercely, snapping the thin root, but another was already wrapping its way around my other foot, this time with more strength and speed. A third root was grasping at the foot that got away when I called out in a panicked squeal, "A little help, please!"

Amil whipped around, completely unaffected by the rabid flora. He looked momentarily shocked before rushing to my side. "Sorry, my lady, forgot about the security protocols." He reached down, cupping my left hand in his. He closed his eyes and bowed his head as he whispered in ancient tongues. A hexagonal geometric symbol burned bright hot white on my right hand, growing brighter and brighter with the crescendo of his voice.

I gasped as the mark of the flower of life seared itself permanently into my skin, rows of ancient-looking text scrolling their way slightly up my arm. As Amil stopped chanting, the glow started fading, settling into a soft white tattoo that matched the ones all over his skin.

"There you go!" he remarked cheerfully as if what he had done was as normal as strapping a day pass on me for a festival. "You'll be immune to the deterrents now."

My mouth hung open as I stared at the new mark on my body. "What the hell is this?!"

He shrugged casually. "Just a bit of genetic programming, like biological software, to upgrade your body. It encodes your DNA with the blueprints necessary to override and hack into any viral system. We have viral security systems operating at every Kingdom Keep as a deterrent for humans and demons alike." He turned, trekking forward through the enchanted woods. Still stunned, I followed him silently. Curiously I twisted my hand, watching the slight shimmer of light as I moved the new tattoo.

I was so absorbed in my thoughts that I didn't notice the root in front of me until it caught my foot, sending me flying face forward toward the ground. Amil was on his knees at my feet in a flash, capturing me in his unnaturally warm arms. Blushing, I looked up at him apologetically. He smiled in return, seeming to enjoy the moment a bit too much. His arms subtly wrapped tighter around me as he held my gaze intensely.

Staring back, a sudden thought furrowed my brow as my look turned incredulous, piecing together two and two as I thought back to the night before. My indignant shout shattered the delicate moment into a million pieces. "Wait a minute! All these hours dragging our feet through the woods, and you could have gotten us here in no time. What gives?!" I raised my eyebrows, defiantly shoving off of him and back on my feet. I stared down at his piercing eyes, demanding answers.

He shrugged, pushing himself casually off the ground, seemingly unfazed by my irritated attitude. However, a slight air of disappointment hung over his usually cheerful voice. "I told you I'm on borrowed time. From the moment I leave the Kingdom, my powers are draining. The more I use them, the faster they go. I have to be vigilant about conservation if I'm going to keep you safe and reach the nexus point in time." He gazed back down at me longingly for just a moment before turning to the north. "That being said, let's hurry up. The sun is almost setting."

We pushed further into the deepest and thickest part of the woods we'd encountered yet. Great patches of moss hung heavily from the trees, concealing the path ahead and causing the narrow trail to grow dark and hard to navigate rapidly. I could still see the soft glow of the golden evening sun burning on the tops of the trees high above, but on the forest floor, darkness had swallowed us completely. I noticed my tattoo glowing faintly as I felt an uneasiness deep in the pit of my stomach. Amil pushed aside a heavy curtain of moss, abruptly revealing a massive open meadow, still twinkling with the last rays of sunlight that the trees had previously hidden from view. It was filled to the brim with every type of wildflower you could ever think of, blooming in unison, swaying softly in the breeze, seeming to hum a whispered melody.

The soft music wrapped me in a blanket of soothing fuzzy feelings that tingled like soft electricity through my body, jolting from my toes to my fingers and back again. I felt like I'd been connected to a cosmic current and was being charged by the very ground I walked on. Lights already appeared to be glowing softly in the windows of a small and unassuming cabin set dead center in the clearing, a stream of smoke drifting casually out of the chimney. The final streaks of sunlight gave way to the first twinkling stars of a dark pink, dusky sky as we trekked across the large field. Reaching the massive covered porch, classically decorated with white rockers and eclectic farmhouse decor, it stretched its way across the entire front of the cabin. I climbed slowly up the solid dark wood stairs, my legs exhausted from the long journey. Amil placed his hand on the door, chanting softly for a moment before it popped open with a gentle thud.

He pushed the door open fully, holding it for me as he extended his hand warmly, welcoming me into the glorious space inside. I stepped past the threshold and into an architectural dream. Everything seemed cream-colored and vintage bronze as I moved through the house. Bright, sparkling, and unnaturally clean, with unreal open cathedral ceilings that didn't really align with the height of the house in my mind. A massive industrial-grade kitchen was attached to the open living room, stocked to the brim with everything you could need to make a gourmet meal, including fresh fruits and veggies that seemed somehow to have been picked that day. Quartz countertops connected the expansive prep counters into a generous breakfast bar with seating. A liquor cabinet and matching quartz drink bar were attached to the other corner of the living room next to the sparkling white quartz fireplace. Two doors led off to what I assumed were bedrooms and a set of French doors leading out onto a screened-in deck twinkling with large vintage string lights. The cabin wasn't large by any means, but it was one of the most glamorous homes I'd ever been in, and it used every inch of its space to full effect.

Amil was already at the bar, pulling down a couple of small glasses and a bottle of liquor with a simple yet elegantly refined design that hinted at expensive origins. Handing me a glass, I immediately noticed the exquisite craftsmanship of the crystal. Intricately carved geometric patterns caused the glass to sparkle and shimmer, playing tricks with the soft lighting in the cabin. Everything about this place was attempting to appear simple yet simultaneously was made from the finest materials this world had to offer. I took a sip from the glass, and it was like muted liquid honey, burning sweet in my throat. As the liquid traveled through me, I could literally *feel* it spreading warmth through my body, delivering a much-needed dose of life into my cold, tired limbs. I instantly felt my body relax intensely while, somehow, my mind became more alert. It was an incredibly strange sensation. Amil watched my reactions, a humorous smile on his perfect face, obviously amused by whatever emotional rollercoaster he must be experiencing vicariously through me. I rolled my eyes when I realized he was watching me, irritated by how relaxed and happy he seemed all the time. No one should smirk that much; it's unnatural.

"So about that shower?" I needed some time to myself.

"Of course, this way, my lady. The good shower is in the master bedroom." He led the way through the farthest door into a breathtaking master suite.

A massive four-post bed commanded the room, positioned perfectly to take advantage of the stunning view outside the storybook window that reminded me of the one at Eden's Cabin, or at least the one that used to be there. The waxing moon had risen, casting moonbeams onto the rolling fields of wildflowers outside, still swaying in the soft breeze. Just behind the house was a large lagoon, glowing eerily with a mysterious natural light that seemed to come from everywhere and nowhere at once. Its translucent green waters were alive with fish, dancing erratically beneath the surface, seeming to mirror the spontaneous twinkling of the stars above. I was momentarily mesmerized, caught in my thoughts again.

Finally pulling myself away from the window, I turned to

see Amil waiting by the door, arms crossed as he leaned casually against the wall, waiting patiently as ever as I took the time I needed to mull over my internal dialogue. Seeing I was ready, he led me into a spectacular bathroom equipped with an extravagant shower as large as my bedroom back home.

Amil gave me a quick tutorial on the surprisingly complex multi-head setup before politely excusing himself to give me some privacy. I turned a series of knobs to get several shower heads going at once to create a cross stream of high-pressure water. I continued turning till the water was as hot as I could stand it. I slowly pulled my clothes off, another loss hitting me as I realized my favorite overalls, the only remnant of my childhood, were shredded to pieces and beyond repair. I tossed them aside without thinking twice, and there was nothing left to do but let go.

Looking in the mirror, I was tender and bruised from being tossed about several times over the past twelve hours. The healing hex Amil had cast on me had fixed a lot of things, but not everything, apparently. Stepping in the shower, I let the intense steamy water wash over me, blissfully losing myself in the numbing hum of the shower. I soaked under the water with my eyes closed for what could have been hours. Never in my life had hot water felt so amazing, like it was literally healing my body and replenishing my soul. Had I been paying attention, I might have noticed the bruises rapidly fading back into my normal, deathly pale skin color. When it felt like all my old skin had been burned off and my worries washed down the drain, I finally twisted the knobs off, taking a deep breath, trying to quell the fresh batch of nerves assaulting my stomach that, for the first time since this all started, had nothing to do with being a Rider of Death on the run from demons.

CHAPTER 4 – THE STRING OF FATE

I found myself standing in the middle of the most unreal closet I'd ever seen. It expanded on and on, row after row of high-end designer clothes made of the finest materials but in the most subtle and discrete cuts and fits. A high-end luxury style that would let you feel in-place in even the most sophisticated crowds while also allowing you to blend in with ease when necessary. Oddly enough, I came to realize while rummaging that every single article in the closet was custom fitted to my frame exactly as if they'd all been tailored for me by a seamstress. With delight, I ran my hands over the soft, delicate fabrics, running my fingers through furs, silks, and satins. It was all so stunning but far from anything I'd ever wear.

After a while, I finally found a large set of drawers in the back of the closet that, after a lot of determined digging, rewarded me with a pair of perfectly distressed high-rise mom jeans, soft and faded like they had been used for years, yet obviously destroyed with such precision and attention to detail that they must have been custom made by hand. I found another set of drawers holding enough underwear to start a Victoria's Secret, which eventually provided me with a sensible set of matching black cotton undergarments. I returned to the racks, flipping slowly through an eclectic section of sweaters till I found a deep blue cropped fitted hoodie in a soft rayon that I slipped on, grateful to be done trying to navigate this labyrinth of clothes.

Flipping my hair a few times, I pulled the damp tangle of

gray strands into a messy high bun and loosely rolled the bottom of my pants a few times before heading back into the living room, feeling refreshed but apprehensive. As I entered the room, I noticed Amil had changed into simple gray sweats with a basic white shirt and was already hard at work in the kitchen, his own purple hair wet and smoothed back into a bun. He was marinating two of the most delicious-looking steaks I'd ever seen in salt while chopping the ends off fresh asparagus as the enticing smell of warm bread filled the room. Looking up at me, he smiled tenderly, staring at me for just a moment too long before turning back to his task at hand. I sat down at the breakfast bar, finding the drink I had abandoned for a hot shower waiting for me at the counter. I watched Amil as he moved expertly in the kitchen with the skill and confidence of a trained chef.

He spoke without looking up at me. "It's my favorite thing to do when I come to this realm. We have nothing like it where I come from. There's a strange comfort in creating something so common, so fleeting, yet so fulfilling. Something that, for a moment, literally becomes one with the ones we choose to share it with."

He continued moving through the motions as I let the silence hang heavy between us. There was a spark there that I wanted to dampen by any means possible. I didn't want to know him this way. I wanted to move through the motions like I always have, completing the bare minimum to get by so I could call it a day and end another bothersome day in a bothersome existence. Perhaps this mission was actually a blessing in disguise, an answer to the burden that had been in this life. Perhaps if I could just focus on my part of the play without overthinking it, we could close the curtain on this comedy of tragedies.

Amil interrupted my thoughts again. Did he know I was spiraling into self-loathing and despair again? Probably. Goddamn mood reader. "What's your spice tolerance like?"

I struggled sheepishly, pulled from the pits of my self-pity. "As good as anyone else's, I suppose."

He grinned, nodding as he heaped an aggressively large spoonful of horseradish into a bowl of sour cream before tossing in a generous amount of freshly ground dill and a dash of salt and pepper. He stirred the bowl with an effortless grace before placing it on the counter before me, garnishing it with a few more dashes of dill. He turned back to the professional six-top gas burner, to a pan that had been resting on the open flame, heating the butter lining the bottom. The steaks sizzled fiercely as they were dropped on the pan, quickly browning on one side; the asparagus on one of the back burners began steaming profusely. Dropping a dollop of butter and a dash of seasonings onto the veggies, Amil covered them so they could steam, pausing momentarily to wait for just the right moment to flip the steaks. As the meat hit the pan again, butter sizzled a serenade to my empty stomach, and he began pulling plates from the cabinets above, spreading them out before me, followed by silverware and even a little napkin folded into a miniature dove. Amil flowed effortlessly, moving about the kitchen like a dancer as he expertly plated the steaks so they could rest. He portioned out the asparagus before pulling the dark bread from the oven and smearing it generously with homemade cinnamon and brown sugar butter. He whisked a large dollop of his homemade sauce over the steak before pushing the completed dish toward me, a spitting image of a plate served at a five-star restaurant.

He grabbed his plate, sliding casually into the seat next to mine. I picked up my utensils, silently cutting into the perfectly cooked medium rare steak. The knife cut through the steak like butter, and I lifted the first steaming piece of meat into my mouth, moaning softly as the morsel melted effortlessly with almost no actual movement from my jaw. I was almost embarrassed, but there was no stopping me as I quickly shoved several more pieces of steak into my mouth, suddenly aware of just how ravenous I was. I followed the tender sirloin up with several forkfuls of crisp, buttery asparagus and an unladylike bite of sweet dark bread that took out half the roll at once. I finally gained some composure and slowed my chewing with a few sips of the dark liquor I had abandoned earlier.

When I looked up at Amil from my drink, I found him focused on his own plate, clearly pretending not to see me attack my dish like a wild animal. I cleared my throat as I pushed past my comfort zone and into the abyss of small talk that I often avoided at all costs. "So this is what you like about Earth? I mean, it's not a bad choice, by all means. It just seems like for an all-powerful being, there'd be more you'd desire." He chuckled, that soft, warm sound that wrapped you up in its soothing melody.

"You would think, wouldn't you? That's the funny thing about life. The more you understand, the less you actually desire." He paused pensively before carrying on. "It's not the only thing I like, though." He turned to me with a playful look before laughing and pushing his last morsel of steak around in the remaining sauce. He swallowed it in just a few strong chomps of his jaw and pushed himself up from the counter, walking to the coffee table in the center of the living room.

I cut another piece of steak and chewed it slowly as I watched him open the top of the table, expanding it out, revealing a series of hidden compartments stashed within the table. I gasped as I realized it was loaded to the brim with every imaginable hue of green, flecked in all the colors of the rainbow. The wave of intense earthy smell hit me shortly after the initial shock of what I was seeing and nearly knocked me out of my seat it was so potent. I couldn't help but jump to my feet and fawn over the purity of the product, the vastness of the variety, and the sheer care that must have gone into the plants. He grinned as I shifted through the jars, lifting them into the light to examine the different colors and crystals. Gushing over the scale of the stock, Amil allowed me my time to enjoy the collection while he gathered the supplies he needed.

Much to my dismay, he finally closed the coffee table, and we drifted back to the counter. I slowly finished my meal as he began expertly pulling apart the herb, finely grinding it before wrapping it up in dark, raw hemp paper. He lifted the joint to his lips, sealing the paper before starting on a second one. I see great minds *do* think alike. As I cleared the last bit of food from my plate, he was already sweeping it away from me, clearing the counter and depositing the dishes into the sink in one fluid movement. He placed one of the joints behind each ear, poured us both a fresh glass of warm golden liquid, picked up the bottle, and stepped toward the back door.

"Care to join me outside?" He raised his eyebrow, a confident grin playing across his face, but was that uncertainty in his eyes?

I hesitated for what felt like a lifetime before pushing myself up from the counter, gripping my cup like a lifeline. I nodded my head softly, refusing to make eye contact. His eyes were too deep and sincere, and I had no interest in losing myself in them. I followed him out to the screened patio. It had an unnaturally warm atmosphere despite no presence of any outdoor heater and the cold of another brisk northwest spring night pushing in on all sides. The large vintage Edison bulb string lights created a pocket of soft light, keeping the intense darkness that had settled upon the land at bay. A collection of rockers were scattered across the patio, offering an up-close look at the sparkling lagoon I had first spotted from the bedroom. I walked to the edge of the balcony, gazing down at the rolling hills below and the expansive pool of glowing bluish-green liquid and drawn in by the intense energy radiating from the waters. Raising my glass, I took another long swig from my cup before seeing Amil open the door and cascade down the steps to the open stretch of mossy lawn between the house and the pond. I was barefoot, but so was he, so I guess it was no time to complain. I hurried after him, still gripping my drink like it was an anchor keeping me grounded.

When I caught up to him, he was paused at the edge of the luminescent water, sipping his drink pensively, still holding the nearly full bottle in his other hand. "This is another thing," he spoke quietly, like he was revealing some great secret. "Swimming —it's another simple thing that is unlike anything in our realm. You would think it's like flying, but it's not, not even close. I can't quite explain it, but I feel the most at peace when I'm in the water like I was made for it."

We both took silent sips of sweet liquor before he broke the tension. "So shall we smoke, my lady? It's another preferred activity on my list." There was a gleam in his eyes as he winked at me.

Dropping to the mossy ground below, he made himself comfortable on the still-humming earth below us. As he struck the lighter he had pulled from his pocket, I found I had no choice but to curl up into a cross-legged heap next to him, trying desperately to keep some distance between us, resisting the urge pulling me closer.

The paper ignited, exploding momentarily in a spark of fire before settling into a red ember that glowed brightly when he pulled the sweet smoke into his lungs. His chest expanded, tight against his too-thin white t-shirt, as he held his hit for an exaggerated amount of time before finally releasing a billowing cloud of smoke, looking more like a dragon than an angel at this point. Taking another long draw, he passed the joint to me. I ignored the spark that jumped between us as our fingers brushed together lightly. As I filled my lungs, I was overcome with intense feelings of bliss and joy. The effect of the herb was like nothing I had experienced in my life. It instantly soaked into every fiber of my being, lifting me to a new plane of pleasure and relaxation. Much like the liquor, it had the bizarre effect of simultaneously relaxing every cell in my body while awakening every corner of my mind.

We sat in silence, savoring the smokey sensations as we sipped our drinks speculatively. I watched schools of fish swim in oddly geometric arrays, one jumping out of line occasionally to break the surface and fly, free in a realm it didn't belong in, even if just for a short moment. Amil was leaning casually back on his palms, staring up at the heavens above, the stars twinkling in his large pale blue eyes. Could this strange creature before me really live up there? At this moment, out on the cold moss, smoking herb and drinking liquor, he just seemed so human, so real. More real than most of the people I had met on this entire planet, if I was being honest.

His eyes flickered down to mine, grinning with delight at catching me in the act of appreciation. He snuffed out the final ember of burning herb, releasing one last giant cloud of smoke before hopping lightly to his feet. He extended his hand to me, still grinning like a dumb ass. "Care to join me for a swim, my lady?" My eyebrows shot up. I was high, but he *must* be joking, right?

"Seriously?! It's freezing out here. The cold might not affect you, but I'm pretty sure that's a hard no for me." I crossed my arms stubbornly, set in my decision, when he suddenly looked at me with such intensity that it was all I could do to keep my thoughts straight. His piercing blue eyes were searing through me, melting through the very core of my being as he pleaded with soft silky tones that cut through my resolve like knives.

"You don't trust me? Have I led you astray thus far, my lady?" His eyebrows lifted softly, his eyes locked on mine, trapping me in his gaze. At this distance, I could easily see the thin golden streak wrapping around his iris, glowing in the lights of the lagoon.

I struggled to find my breath as I pieced together a broken, barely coherent response. "Kay, stop it. You win." His chuckle broke the tension as he released me from the grip of his gaze, turning to the water. I gasped as I felt the pressure of his presence unwrap itself from my body, leaving me feeling weak and breathless in all the best and worst ways.

Taking a moment to set the second joint down securely on a nearby boulder, he casually tossed his clothing aside as he bounded unabashed toward the water's edge and dove in carelessly in nothing but his boxers. I suppressed a laugh as I rolled my eyes. How the hell was he so magnetic? Must be a stupid angel thing. Reluctantly I pulled off my sweater, shivering as the cold night air crashed against my skin, seeking to eat up my warmth as quickly as possible. Already regretting my choices, I fumbled my way out of the faded jeans. I managed to only almost fall flat on my face once before rushing to the water's edge while I hugged myself tightly, trying to fight off the chills that threatened to send me into full-on convulsions. Pausing at the bank, feeling exposed in just my undergarments, I searched the glowing green waters for Amil, but he seemed to have disappeared beneath the surface of the water.

Guess it was no time to be a coward. Feeling shy but more emboldened than normal, I stepped forward with the liquid courage coursing through my veins, placing one foot slowly into the lagoon. To my great surprise, the water was amazingly warm, like a perfectly tempered heated outdoor pool. Without another moment's hesitation, I dove in, grateful for the water soaking into my skin, warming every cell in my body. I opened my eyes underwater to a world of brightly colored fish excitedly swimming around me, putting on geometric shows for me in person. Now that I was underwater, I could hear the beautiful music the fish seemed to be humming, and I could see the light coming from the bottom of the pool, still some fifteen feet below me, emitting from crystals scattered among the rainbow of corals and dancing seaweed forest and interwoven with the sparkling white sand that made up the lagoon floor. This was by far one of the most beautiful places I'd ever seen in my life, and I wanted to spend eternity under the water dancing with those fish to their sacred song, but nature compelled me upward, breaking the surface as I gasped for much-needed oxygen.

Amil was treading water near me, smiling as I surfaced. "What did I tell you? Magic, right?" His eyes were sparkling, and there was no hope in hiding the massive smile breaking across my face, a strange and unfamiliar expression.

"It's absolutely unbelievable!" I struggled slightly to tread water as effortlessly as him, having spent almost no time in any water growing up. Fortunately, there was something natural about it to me, and I was quickly getting the hang of this whole swimming thing, even if I had never done much of it. Amil unexpectedly began moving forward, filling the gap between us, causing my heart to skip two beats.

"We have these at all the Kingdom Keeps. Imagine them like you would the Fountain of Youth almost. They have restorative powers and help replenish our stores of angelic ether while here on Earth. Nothing close to the resupply we get when we return to the source, but enough to keep us going on our mission. Like I told you before, we become more human the longer we are here, hence why these outposts are so heavily stocked. Makes it that much easier to get by when your powers are fading and your time is limited on this plane."

I nodded, half listening, half distracted by the cutest little fish who had just come up and started nibbling on my hand, flipping back and forth from one finger to the next as he desperately sought to engage me in more fishy business. Suddenly a massive wave of water was soaking me, disorientating me as I sought to fight my way to the surface again and clear my face. My ears popped, draining water and filling with the unbridled sound of Amil's laughter as I coughed out the warm water that filled my lungs, noticing its oddly sweet taste even on the way back out.

"Excuse me?! How rude!" I admonished him, but I couldn't hide the grin on my face as I frantically splashed water back at him, determined to seek revenge for his unprovoked attack.

He laughed maniacally as he dove away, evading my attacks and returning more unfairly powerful waves that capsized me again. I rode the power of the wave down and continued my way underwater, catching up with him and launching a sneak attack from below, managing to use the element of surprise to actually have enough strength to physically pull him under—at least, I hope it was that and not just him pulling his punches. Pushing him even further below with a well-placed launch off his shoulder with my foot, I used the force from sinking him to rapidly surface, laughing loudly as I broke through the water and bobbed in place, keeping an eye on my feet below to ensure I could perform any necessary evasive tactics.

He popped up just a moment later, holding his hands up in surrender. "You win, you win, I surrender it all to you, my lady." His voice was heavy as he looked at me with a mischievous yet calculating look in his eyes.

He began swimming forward slowly, like a crocodile prowling in the water, quickly closing the distance between us. He wrapped his arms around me suddenly, pulling me close to his bare chest, taking my breath away as I pressed into him. "What is it that my lady desires as her prize?" I tensed up, intensely conflicted by the war waging in my body, the desire to pull him closer, and the instinct to run away as fast as I could, equally strong, presenting ironclad arguments for both prosecution and defense.

My world started spinning. Had I forgotten to breathe? Where were my lungs? Darkness started closing in from the sides of my eyes, and I could feel myself fading when he loosened his grip on me and started shaking me lightly, concern thick in his voice. "Nato. Nato! Come back to me. Are you okay?" I shook my head, coming to my senses, as I finally took a gasping breath.

With my head clearing and the world coming back into view, I realized he was staring at me, his eyes drowning with concern, compassion, and confusion as he tried to navigate whatever turmoil he must sense from the depths of my mind. I shook my head again, trying to brush it off, and touched his face with my hand softly. I wanted to erase that intense look of guilt in his eyes, to assure him he had done nothing wrong because he certainly hadn't.

"S'not your fault. Sorry, I'm a mess." I slurred over my words, not as composed as I thought I was, but I pushed on regardless. "I just don't do well with people being in my personal space. It's not you. It's me." I smiled warmly, still holding my hand on his face purposely. "I *do* feel safe with you, though, as weird as that seems to me. I don't know how you do it, but it's like I've always known you. It just feels right or something." I began mumbling as I trailed off, dropping my hand as red heat filled my cheeks. I looked away, feeling exposed. What had compelled me to reveal so much?

He picked my hand back up, returning it to his face and holding it there as his charming smile returned, drawing me back in already. "Of course you do. I was *made* for you. Every cell of my body has been programmed to serve and protect you. You are my everything, and I will never let anyone make you feel out of place in your own temple again. I can promise you that." His eyes were searing into me, burning with sincerity and commitment to his mission, driven and focused as they bore into me, crushing me again unintentionally under his passionate aura.

He took a deep breath, seeming to choose his next words carefully. Was that a hint of blush in his cheeks too? "You are safe with me, always. I am *yours*, in whatever way you want, but *only* in the ways you want." He leaned in slowly, purposely, refusing to release my eyes from his intense gaze. It was all I could do to keep breathing normally.

Suddenly his lips were on mine, soft and smooth, tender and kind as they moved against mine with reserved passion, parting my lips slowly as I instinctually pulled him closer. I felt myself opening as a flood of emotions washed through me, awakening parts of myself long dormant, stripping away my hesitations, and plunging me into his depths.

CHAPTER 5 – DREAMS OF AWAKENING

Breaking free of his riptide, I stared up at him in wonder, taken aback and still trying to piece myself together again. His intense icy eyes were sparkling as he gazed back smugly, looking too content with himself, still trapping me close to him in his grasp, treading water to keep us both afloat. My insides were still filled with static, slowly settling yet desperate for more, for another hit of its newfound drug. It was all I could do to contain myself. I'd had the unfortunate pleasure of being with men in my life, but never had I been kissed by someone in a way that left me craving, hungry for more. It consumed me, and all I could think about was his hands on my body, his name in my mouth, and those lips on mine once more. It was an overwhelming sensation to *need* someone so badly—it was dangerous. If life had taught me one thing, it was to never rely on people too much; you're just setting yourself up for failure. Even if it was *tempting*, I needed to be smart now more than ever.

I took a deep breath, trying to clear my mind and suppress the fuzz still gripping my body. Pulling back softly, I pleaded with my eyes for him to understand, yet I cringed as I saw my mood hit him. The way his eyes dimmed broke my heart into a million pieces, and suddenly I wanted nothing more but to cradle him in my arms. Resolution was more important now than ever. Dropping my eyes, I pushed out of his grip as his arms dropped listlessly, confusion clouding his eyes.

Amil recovered quickly. After a flash of emotions, his smile was back just as quickly as it left, and he took my hand as if nothing had happened. Still not able to look at him, I attempted to form the words to make him understand that there was nothing I wanted more than to melt into his arms and forget the rest of the world, but there was something inside me he couldn't fix, something no one could fix. Nothing good ever happened to anyone who ever tried.

Before I got a word out, though, he was holding a hand up, silencing me with a soft kiss on the head. "Hush, my lady. Whatever you want, however you want. No need for explanations. You made your choice, and I respect it wholeheartedly," he beamed, radiating sincerely as he pulled me along with him toward the shallower end of the lagoon.

I was staring at him again. He really was such a gentleman, and it was unnerving but refreshing, to say the least. I floated along effortlessly in his wake, allowing myself to be swept up behind him as I gazed down at the fish. Another school was following after me, nibbling at my toes relentlessly.

As he reached an area where we could actually reach the sandy bottom, he released me, turning with a resolute look on his face. "There's something important we should do here if you'd allow me the honor, that is." I planted my feet into the soft sand below, and it was like silk wrapping around my toes.

I looked at him, perplexed. "The honor of what?" He looked more embarrassed now than he had all night.

He cleared his throat before continuing. "It's not something I have much experience in, but are you familiar with a baptism?"

I scoffed, busting out laughing at the concept of me, one of the most anti-religious people I know, the apparent Rider of Death, being baptized. I was laughing so hard that it took me a moment to notice how genuinely hurt he looked. He was staring down at the water in a brooding sort of way that I'd never seen him do before.

"I'm sorry, I'm sorry." I hastened to regain any sense of tact, realizing that this was clearly very important to him. "I thought you were kidding. I mean, hello, Rider of Death here... Not exactly baptism material, right?"

He looked up at me shaking his head, recovering from my outburst of apparently inappropriate laughter. "I mean, it's not like anything you've read in any Bible. It's a sacred ceremony performed only on the holiest of beings. It is a way of aligning you with the meridians and unlocking your hidden potential within, connecting you to the source so that you can pull from the ether. It is the highest honor to take part in a baptism. To be present when a holy being awakens bonds you to them permanently, connecting you with a thread of fate." He paused, looking down again, clearly hesitating.

"I will not mislead you. I was told to wait till we arrived at the gates of the Kingdom for a more experienced member to perform the ceremony, but I had a bad feeling. You'll be safer if you can protect yourself, and your safety outweighs all other orders I've been given." He grew silent again, contemplating a moment before he carried on in nothing more than a whisper. "It's not my place, but if you trust me, I can do this for you. It's your choice."

He didn't look at me as his voice trailed off, full of uncertainty and something else I couldn't place. He shifted uncomfortably in the waist-deep water, finally bringing his eyes back to mine. He seemed to be searching for something in them. It was refreshing to see him like this, so vulnerable, somehow softer now that he wasn't grinning like a coy idiot. It made me want to wrap him up in my arms, comfort him, and give him anything his heart could desire. I couldn't claim I completely understood what he was asking of me, but it was the least I could give him if it meant this much to him.

"So what would we have to do?" His face erupted into

sheer joy as he cheered unabashedly like some high school jock who had just scored.

I rolled my eyes but couldn't fight the small smile that spread across my face at his intense jubilation. When he was finally done with his outburst of excitement, he took my hand, his skin practically buzzing with excitement and anticipation.

He looked around for a moment, seeming to search for a very specific spot, although I was clueless as to what criteria he had in mind. Upon finding whatever he was looking for, he rushed forward, wading through the water hastily as he towed me behind by the hand. Stopping, he turned to face me with the most serious look, boring intensely into my eyes with that sharp blue gaze.

"You're positive?" Returning the seriousness of his look, I nodded my head tersely, fighting back the nerves that had started to creep in. He smiled serenely, but it didn't reach his eyes. They stayed laser-focused and determined, clearly treating this task with the utmost importance.

I gasped softly as he swooped me off my feet and cradled me into his arms, floating me on the still surface of the glowing lagoon. A strange silence fell over the night as everything around us grew eerily still. The fish stopped swimming, the frogs stopped croaking, and even the crickets silenced their endless symphony. Amil was still staring into my soul as the wind died down, and the seconds seemed to stretch on for lifetimes before he broke the crushing quiet.

"Are you ready?"

I took a deep breath, settling the intense quaking inside to a soft tremble. "I'm ready."

Amil bowed his head, closing his eyes as he continued to cradle me half in and half out of the water. Softly he began chanting at nothing more than a whisper, his ancient tattoos glowing faintly, radiating brighter and brighter with the crescendo of his voice. The mantra seemed to take over him, louder with each repetition, and his voice became less and less his own with each passing cycle. The choir of a thousand beings channeled through his mouth, a melody of a million voices, singing in perfect harmony. The ethereal sounds flowing from his lips became almost more than my ears could bear, transcending beyond the sound barrier and wrapping us in a physical aura of golden energy. The chanting was pulsing through my body, forcefully rearranging my insides in a tangible way. It was uncomfortable, like slowly getting each bone in my body popped one at a time. Climaxing in a crashing pitch of power, the air erupted around us, the golden globe dissolving as the loud chanting gave way to utter, intense silence.

Amil opened his eyes, glowing like his tattoos, empty like he wasn't there anymore, as he dipped me slowly beneath the surface of the warm water. I took a deep breath and closed my eyes, pinching my nose as I was submersed into the pool. I suppose I expected a standard dunk like I'd seen in movies before I surfaced a drenched mess declaring my love for Jesus Christ or whatever. Instead, immediately upon dropping below the surface, I was seized forcefully and ripped from the waters, up into the atmosphere, and far, far away from this planet. I was tearing through space and time at an alarming rate as everything I had ever known was stripped away from my mind, replaced by the crushing force of the all-knowing universe bearing down on me, seeping into every crevice of my being, soaking into every crack in my soul, attempting to imbue me with the very essence of *everything*. I felt like I was exploding, breaking apart piece by piece, and I would never be whole again. There was so much information, too much information; I was being crushed under the weight of cosmic comprehension. I held on for as long as I could, but bit by bit, it consumed me completely, and suddenly, I vanished.

Crashing back into my body, my consciousness came back all at once, and I ripped forth from the waters, screaming as I was reborn into this realm from the cosmos above. I was consumed by the knowledge coursing through my veins, rewiring my circuits, and rerouting my nervous system. I gasped, trying to even remember my name as the knowledge of anything and everything tried to condense itself into a comprehensible form that could exist on this plane within its boundary conditions.

When the powers of the universe finally stopped cascading through me and subsided into a soft constant ripple, I was left feeling empty and exhausted, barely able to keep my eyes open. I collapsed limply into Amil's arms, able to hold on to just enough consciousness to stay awake as I rested weakly against his chest. The world was spinning as he silently carried me from the waters. I stared up at him as he looked solemnly ahead. I wondered vaguely what that must have been like for him, reflecting on what he had said about the experience bonding him to me permanently, curious if he had felt even a fraction of the intense energy that had coursed through me. I couldn't explain it, but there seemed to be something to his words because I couldn't deny the soft tug of some invisible string between us that hadn't been there before. Or perhaps it had been there all along, a ghost of a chain, a shadow waiting to be awoken. I reveled in it, basking in the glory of something that could be mine, something no one could take away if I was brave enough to take a leap of faith. Oddly enough, I felt something else tugging at me, but I couldn't place the source.

My thoughts rambled on as I faded in and out in his warm arms. He walked so delicately that I was hardly disturbed in his comforting grip as he traversed across the hilly terrain of the mossy yard and up the staircase to the twinkling lights of the back deck. I realized the soft hum of the night had returned at some point, soothing me further into a blissful transcendent dream state, vivid lucid flashes of color and concepts already trying to take over my semi-conscious mind. Holding fast to my grip on this reality, I focus on the soft rise and fall of his chest as he silently carried me past the threshold and into the bedroom. Ever so gently, Amil placed me on the welcoming pillow top mattress that seemed to wrap itself around me, cradling me in its comforting grasp. Unconsciousness was crashing down on me fast, pulling me further away from this realm, but as his hands slipped away from me and he moved to leave the room, I was jarred momentarily back into my body as the words escaped unintentionally.

"Wait. Stay." My words were mushy, and some small part of my mind knew it was wrong to use my hold on him for my own needs, but I couldn't help but be selfish right now. I *needed* his body next to mine, and I wanted to believe he needed me just as much because, without further persuasion, he was next to me in bed in one smooth motion, pulling me into an unbreakable grasp. He molded himself into me perfectly, keeping me grounded in this world as I drifted off into an intense dreamscape.

Bright colors sparked behind my eyes, shapes expanding and contracting, revealing hidden patterns, puzzles that perplexingly folded in on themselves before blooming back to life. An unseen force whispered secrets to me in an ancient tongue, both foreign and familiar, revealing the secret pathways with which the angles moved. Tessellations tracing across timelines exposed by the fractals fracturing reality and space, collapsing into itself infinitely. I was a voyager, drifting through the vast nothingness—everything was me, and I was everything. Expanding effortlessly, I multiplied within myself, revealing within me a thousand different versions, all existing simultaneously, all as one, and one as all. The many melted back into the whole, standing alone at the brink of an endless sea, gazing at the reflection staring back at me, moving independently. The pure essence of the soul, transmitting truths, codes, and colors of the universe, frequencies aligning within me harmonically. I fell forward into my soul reflection, merging into one divine being. Stairs sprung into life before me one at a time, leading me down further and further, twisting in on themselves before opening into a vast chamber, alive with glowing blue light. A stone platform called to me; I rested there in a timeless state, basking in the burning blue flames of the source, refilling my desperately empty vessel with the ethereal essence of eternal life.

When I opened my eyes, it seemed as if lifetimes had passed. For the first time in my life, I felt a deep sense of ease within myself. The dark pits of my soul seemed to have been swept out and filled with light, unlocking the secrets of the universe within me. I couldn't comprehend it all on a conscious level, but beneath the surface of my skin, a new truth had settled into my bones. As if someone had rebooted my whole motherboard and updated it with a new operating system. Everything seemed a bit brighter, clearer, and more colorful. I watched the light stream through the massive window, breaking apart as it hit the curtain surrounding the four-post bed. The bits of light that made it through were scattered across Amil's peacefully sleeping face, more at ease than I'd ever seen it. Laying there, I absorbed the hard lines of his jaw, the soft dark purple stubble peeking through his caramel skin at the edges of his short messy beard, the way his teeth seemed to be clenched slightly in his sleep, the soft way his chest rose with each deep breath.

He was hypnotizing, there was no denying it, and after last night, I wanted him more than ever. Even with my awakening, though, traces of my old ego still remained, holding me to the fear of abandonment that had shaped my existence in this world. If I was careful, though, I could keep him close *and* keep myself safe. I was sure of that much now. I was still soaking in his rugged beauty, watching the light play in his silky violet curls, when his voice, husky with sleep, nearly caused me to fall out of bed.

"See anything you like, my lady?" His eyes were still closed, but that stupid grin was back, lighting up his tired face. I rolled my eyes, secretly glad to see he had recovered from last night's rejection.

"Lots of things." I grinned coyly myself, happy to throw him a bone—he had earned that much, at least.

His eyes shot open, looking at me incredulously, confusion clouding his sleepy blue eyes. "You're impossible," he mumbled, complaining under his breath as he turned away from me in an attempt to hide the blush I just barely caught before his back was to me.

Rising like a phoenix reborn for the second time in my life, I jumped out of bed feeling light and airy, curious to explore this new, more vivid world I now inhabited. My muscles felt stronger, and my heart felt like it was beating just a bit faster as I moved effortlessly toward the closet. I had always been in shape, if not a bit clumsy, but my body had never flowed as freely and gracefully as it did now. It was as if my mind and vessel had harmonized, and everything was operating at a much higher capacity, making all the tiny movements that much easier.

As I searched through the clothing again, my brain seemed to process the room faster, making it a cinch to quickly locate a cropped olive-green sweater in a chunky knit that paired with my eyes perfectly and a pair of the softest dark forest green high-rise leggings. I pulled the comfortable outfit together with an oversized burnt orange cardigan and a long pair of oatmeal knit socks before bounding into the main room, still buzzing with a leftover high from last night's journey.

To distract myself, I began to piece together a tiny espresso machine in the kitchen, searching out the necessary ingredients to make a morning latte, even if caffeine might be the last thing I needed, as I was already abuzz with newfound energy. Moving methodically, once I gathered everything I needed, I ground the fresh, rich dark beans, pressing them into the portafilter before turning the switch and taking a deep breath as the aroma of fresh coffee began filling the small room. I filled a tin cup with cold milk as the shots brewed before steaming it generously, moving the cup purposely as I allowed just the right amount of foam to build up. Once the milk was steaming, I split the brewed espresso between two beautifully crafted ceramic cups, designed to resemble cuts of a crystal, and stirred in a small amount of a homemade chocolate sauce I had found waiting expectantly in the front of the fridge. Pouring the steamed milk into artfully crafted swans that swam peacefully on top of the cups, I looked down at my creations with pride.

Amil wandered into the main room, drawn out by the alluring smell of espresso, clad in just a thin pair of jogger pants. I pretended not to notice his lack of clothing as I pushed his cup across the counter with a smile. "Join me for a cup?" I was bursting at the seams to ask him a million questions. For all the answers last night's vision seemed to have provided at the time, I found I was left with nothing but more questions, desperate for the truth now that I was awake. Perhaps he could show me the way, but I clearly needed to tread this territory carefully. I wasn't the only one in danger of getting hurt anymore, and I needed to take my hold on him responsibly. Like planets, our orbit would only work with the right amount of space, too much, and we would drift apart, lost in space; too close, and we risk colliding, destroying each other completely. Desperate to navigate these treacherous waters without capsizing, I turned abruptly without waiting for an answer and headed toward the back deck to buy myself a few more minutes to organize my thoughts. I knew without a doubt he would follow me. I sat down on the oversized rocker looking out onto the pond, a muted dim green in the morning light, unsurprised as he dropped in the seat next to me, gingerly sipping the steaming mocha.

"This is delicious, another one on my list. I've had more cups than I can count, and I can genuinely say this is one of the best. You brew a good brew." He was staring forward as he sipped his coffee slowly. His shoulders were relaxed, he wanted to seem nonchalant, but there was a defensiveness in his eyes. He was being cautious, but he didn't want me to know it. Allowing him the space he needed to process, I took a sip of the drink. Warm liquid exploded on my tastebuds, overwhelming me with its complex aroma and flavor like I was drinking coffee for the first time ever.

I couldn't suppress the gasp that escaped my lips. "Wow. Now *that is* coffee. What the hell have I been drinking my whole life? I'm not sure that had much to do with my own skills, honestly." I scoffed at myself before gulping down another glorious sip.

His eyes melted as laughter broke the tension, his eyes already rolling at my obnoxious behavior. "Well, you're not totally wrong. That's one of the finest coffees this planet has to offer. Honestly, though, even for Kingdom coffee, you have a talent for the craft. Also, I'm sure your awakening has more to do with it than anything." His eyes had drifted back to me. Even when he didn't want to, he couldn't seem to keep his gaze away from me. That shouldn't make me as happy as it did, but I would deal with that later.

"So, I'm not going crazy? Everything seems so...*heightened.*" I chose the best word I could find to describe the feeling because no word really seemed to do it justice.

He nodded solemnly, shouldering the serious responsibility of welcoming me into my new state of being. "That's just the start of it. The awakening is a process, it unfolds over days and weeks, depending on the individual, it comes in waves of highs and lows, and it can take months to years to master the powers it reveals. There's no telling what you'll be capable of in the end, but if you put stock in prophecies, you're destined to be more powerful than the rest of the Riders combined. You're destined to be more powerful than anyone on this plane of existence, in fact, and after what I saw last night, I'd be the first to buy stock in that prophecy because you are extraordinary. I've never seen untapped potential like this on a bounded plane." The reverence had sparked in his eyes again, glowing with utter absolute devotion. It sent a chill down my spine that settled in my root, leaving me uneasy and biting my lip.

I tried to cool the burning flames inside that almost sent me flinging across the small coffee table separating us. Clearly, all my emotions were affected by this intense overdrive. I cleared my throat. "Do you think you could show me anything? After all, it's pretty treacherous times around here." I smiled alluringly, eager and ready to explore this new power.

He leaned in, matching my intensity with sparks in his eyes. "I thought you'd never ask." He grabbed my hand and swooped me off the deck in a flurry of movement, bounding excitedly into our uncertain future.

CHAPTER 6 – COGNITIVE DISSONANCE

The blast of blinding white light burnt into my skin, dissolving me away painfully piece by piece. I resisted the urge to scream, refusing to give him the pleasure as I shattered into a million pieces. My ashes drifted away, my consciousness desperately trying to maintain some awareness of who I was as it floated along in the breeze, trapped in the whirlwind of fate. Vivid images flashed across my mind's eyes, a little girl laughing as she ran through a field of flowers, lovers embracing as the sun set in an ethereal technicolor land, a great storm splitting the sky apart, fire burning where beauty once blossomed. Images flashed one after the next of a life I'd never lived in a world I'd never seen. They pulled at emotions that shouldn't exist, making me long for someone I wasn't even sure I knew. As I spiraled further into the void, it became harder to hold on to what was real as I drifted endlessly into the darkness.

In the distance, I began to hear the soft muffled sounds of the hounds, barking viciously as they tore across space and time, searching me out. Gathering my strength, I focused on what was left of my pure source. Moving in angles, I began to make progress in navigating the cosmic maze. I traveled in planes of existence and states of being, folding in and out of myself multiple times before finding the right combination of geometry to return to the original me. A mess of a girl, on my knees, retching out a vile substance, a sticky oil-like sludge that lingered in my mouth as black sweat poured out of every pore it could find. When my body finally quit heaving, I collapsed into a puddle of my own retched puke, gasping for air as I tried desperately to realign my consciousness with a dissonant vessel, altered to operate better on this plane but awfully ill-suited for my soul's essence.

Pushing myself to my feet, I looked down in disgust, irritated with my own arrogance. I should have seen that coming from a mile away, but I underestimated the Angel, and she was just so *distracting.* Such a plain girl had absolutely no right being so goddamn captivating when I had a mission to accomplish. Gathering my dreads into a messy heap on top of my head, I wrapped them up and attempted to brush myself off, to little effect. The black sludge just smudged further into the torn silk shreds of what was once a dress. Shrugging, I stalked off into the early morning light, ready to recalibrate and recalculate at the nearest Underpost. That was my best shot, and I couldn't believe I missed it. Cifer was going to have my head over this, just when I had gotten back on her good side again too.

I moved through the streets soundlessly, rapidly bleeding through the shadows, dawn approaching as I pressed onward toward my destination. The shadows couldn't regenerate like me, and it would take too long to find a portal—there was no time to wait. I couldn't even afford to reserve resources at this point. I pushed myself faster, all but blurring into thin air as I struggled to make up valuable lost time. Besides, I could get by; I had always been gifted when it came to the quality and quantity of my powers in this realm. Not to mention I had a few tricks up my sleeve that would help me get by in a pinch. That angel had another thing coming if he thought he would beat me that easily—it was time to pull out the big guns.

Stalking up to the nondescript house shoved between two run-down homes with faded paint and slopping steps, I paused at the doorstep, whispering softly as the markings on my hand lit up in response to the mantra. A soft click invited me to push the door open; the room ahead looked dark and damp, the sour smell of abandonment hitting hard as I hesitated on the porch momentarily. I pushed past the threshold, the room around me transforming from a desolate dump to a sleek modern room stocked like a hoarder's survival shack. Exposed shelves to the side at the entrance revealed a stash of canned and dry goods next to another shelf of medical supplies and camping gear. The final shelf was stacked with a variety of weapons, ranging from a collection of Japanese throwing knives to a small collection of guns and even a few hand grenades. While similar to the tools of this plane, they were carved with ancient markings and radiated with mystic energy.

I moved through the tiny safe house with purpose, stalking past the kitchen, through the bedroom, and straight into the bathroom. Ripping the frayed and stained white silk dress from my body, it fell to the ground in a sad pile of pieces. I examined my curved, muscular body in the mirror, taking stock of the damage. My dark skin did a good job at hiding it, but I was covered in bruises and gashes, my beautiful firestorm dreads were matted and covered in bile, and my normally glowing golden eyes were dim. My body was already working rapidly to seal the skin and soothe the bruises, my cells dividing tirelessly as they worked at a supernatural speed to return my vessel to its peak shape. That was costing me more ether, though, so I needed to stay focused.

Turning the hot water knob as far as it would go, I jumped in, letting the searing water pierce through my hard icy skin. I burned away the irritation of defeat, the anxiety of disappointing Cifer, and the image of *her* before I let the shadows descend up them. I took a series of deep breaths as I forced myself to let go of all the trivial distractions. I could do this. I knew I could do this. I *had* to do this.

We could discover so much if only we had free rein on this plane, and yet they would continue to just let this place fester as a hopeless breeding ground for a lesser species. It was downright disrespectful to a universe gracious enough to present us with so much raw potential and material to just squander our resources and limit our imagination as they had for millennia. They found comfort in the little box of ideas they called home. I had never been one for being in the box. It was high time I set them free of theirs. It would all be for the best in the end, Cifer had promised me that much, and I had to believe her. I mean, what could go wrong with a divine apocalypse, after all? I let out a sigh. Clearly, this water wasn't hot enough to burn away these intrusive thoughts, thoughts that had been plaguing me since I started this mission.

Thoughts I didn't have time for right now. I shoved them away as I twisted the shower off, grabbed a towel, and hurried off into the bedroom to raid the absurdly extravagant closet, slipping on a skintight pair of destroyed high-rise red jeans that let vast amounts of my rich skin peek through and a basic muted blue cropped tank in a clingy soft rayon that pulled out the blue streaks in my hair. I topped the outfit with a bright white leather jacket with a jagged, asymmetrical hemline. Using my towel to soak up as much water out of my dreads as possible, I finally tossed it aside and grabbed a thick pair of stark white combat boots, sturdy but just a bit too fashion-forward for standard issue. I laced them up and stomped into the other room, heading for the supply shelves to stock up for the mission ahead. I pulled on a double holster of fine white leather, buckling the straps in place before picking out two small revolvers cast in ivory and carved with intricate golden pentagonal geometry. Before stashing them into the holsters, I loaded them expertly with bullets bearing the same carvings. Grabbing a small crossbody backpack from the shelf, I shoved several boxes of ammunition, a set of carved throwing knives, a handful of small explosives, two full-sized grenades, and the entire stock of teriyaki beef jerky inside.

Kicking the back door open, I headed out into the crisp air of the dawning day. The door slammed shut behind me, and I crossed the yard in a few bounds, stopping at a run-down shed leaning heavily toward the left—an *Arc*, just what I needed. I set the bag down, stepping up to the door. I placed my hand there and began chanting softly, picturing the object of my desire, bending the geometry in and out of itself to create something new altogether. A soft glow radiated from the building, fading as my mantra came to a close, and I pulled the door open. Inside was a sleek black dirt bike covered in pentagonal geometry, equipped with tires that looked like they came off a monster truck. I stepped into the condemned building and up to the beast of a bike. Tossing my bag into the storage compartment, I threw my leg over the side, adjusted the gear, and revved the engine, grinning as the bike roared to life beneath me. I reached forward, pulled the throttle, and took off, tires screeching like hungry banshees.

My metallic steed quickly bridged the gap and won back the distance I had lost while transmuting back to this vessel. Before I knew it, the roads I'd traveled north through the morning and into the afternoon started to look familiar. This was the town I stayed in the night before we found *you*, which meant *you* couldn't be far off now, even if you guys had been moving as fast as possible. Besides, I doubted he would be reckless enough to waste his ether like that when protecting such precious cargo. Even with all the resources of the Kingdom behind him, it was a difficult journey, and guiding an unawakened Rider, who, let's face it, as a human, seemed pretty weak and worthless, couldn't be making it any easier. This was bound to give me an opportunity to make my move, but I needed to be ready to take it. So far, my best plan was to go in with everything I had all at once, guns blazing and grenades exploding; then, before the dust settled, I pulled a classic snatch-and-grab. Before they knew what hit them, I rode off into the sunset on my bike with my fair maiden hogtied to the back. Something told me it wasn't quite foolproof, but I had a solid track record of winging it successfully when plans went south, so this should be just fine. Turning off the deserted highway, I traveled down winding country roads, guided by a very faint tugging sensation in my chest. I let my intuition take the wheel, my dreads billowing in the wind behind me as the orange sun burned low in the sky ahead.

Pulling off the road as the deep glow of golden hour settled on the land, I followed a twisting dirt path through the wild woods, pulling my handlebars just right and revving the gas to overcome fallen trees, twisted roots, and rocky slopes that tried to reclaim my machine for the ancient forest. I tore my way through the woods as the final rays of the setting sun ignited the trees with their fiery red light. It became clear that my imagination wasn't running wild when roots began trying to wrap themselves around the tires of my dirt bike. I had heard of this; it was a defensive tactic for the Keeps. Well, I'll be damned if some walking trees stop me. Leaning low against the handlebars, I revved the engine and took off through the trees at high speed, tearing through the branches, weaving impossibly through the small gaps and openings as my odometer topped out. Try as they might, nothing could get a hold of me at this speed. As long as I stayed focused, nothing would stop me now —I could *feel* her, she must be so close.

The draw was almost too intense, and I found myself leaning forward inch by inch as I pushed the bike faster and faster, tearing through the undergrowth, desperate to reach my goal. Focused on nothing but the break in the trees ahead that looked like it opened to a sprawling flower-filled meadow, I failed to notice the rather large tree branch shooting directly toward me from my three o'clock. It forcefully shoved its way through my front wheel, crumpling my bike in a painfully loud metallic screech as it came to a halting stop, bucking me off its back. Flying through the air, I didn't know which way was up as the trees blurred past, still trying to lash out at me with their twisted branches. It dawned on me a moment too late that I should try to protect myself from the inevitable landing. As the mantra started to escape my lips, I was already crashing to the ground below. With a muted and wet thud, my head bounced off several rocks as my body followed in a mess of bones and flesh, tumbling like some macabre rag doll. Suddenly, everything went black.

I wasn't sure how much time had passed by when I finally opened my eyes, but everything hurt to move, and the forest floor had started slowly growing over me, trying to consume me and reclaim me for the earth. I sat up tenderly, letting out a low cry when my tattoos seared momentarily as fire plunged out toward the vines that had wrapped around me, eating them alive and spreading in a circle around me and consuming all the vegetation in a ten-foot radius as I tried to take stock of the damage. Whispering under my breath, the golden geometry scatted across my body came to life with light again, glowing brighter as I hummed out the mantra louder. I winced as the golden light seared through my body, resetting my broken leg, burning closed several massive gashes, and sealing up the worst of my injuries across this vessel. I stopped short of fully healing myself; I was down a vehicle and on my own, so it was essential I saved my resources. Standing up, I attempted to brush off what was left of my frayed and destroyed outfit. The leather jacket and boots were the only things that survived the crash.

Giving up, I began tracing my steps backward, locating my bike in a sad mess of black metal crushed into what could be mistaken for an abstract art piece. Rooting around for a moment awarded me with the torn bag that I was able to get out from under the contorted frame of the bike with a bit of effort, although half the contents had been lost in the wreck. Short my grenades, throwing knives, and motorcycle, it looked like a new plan was in order. I tossed the bag over my shoulder and took off sluggishly through the wild undergrowth, eyes set on the meadow, determined to get this done one way or another. Breaking through the forest, I finally felt like I could breathe as the pressure of whatever was possessing those trees released me from its clutches. The night sky was alive above me, twinkling with a plethora of stars, and the flowers seemed to be singing softly to me as I walked the field. I made sure to step on as many of them as I could.

Stopping at a small stream, I washed the caked dirt and blood off my hands before I pulled at the zipper of my bag and fished around for some clothes. I pulled out a dainty strappy golden yellow dress that flared out at the hips and quickly stripped away the shreds of my old outfit. After getting dressed, I pulled back on my rugged boots, a wonderfully stark contrast to my feminine dress, and shrugged my way back into my double holster. Topping it off with the white leather jacket, I grabbed my things and was off again determinedly into the night, following the golden glow of the house several football fields ahead. My beacon in the night, leading me to her, leading me toward a new future.

I could practically taste the victory in my mouth, and it was all I could do to keep from running, but the healing had stopped short, and my recently broken leg wasn't quite up to the task. Approaching from the south, I began to see the back of the house take shape, the twinkle of string lights becoming clearer on the back deck as I grew closer to the massive body of water separating me and my target. Kneeling next to the water, I gazed into the greenish-blue depths that glowed and were alive with a variety of fish swimming in synchronicity. There was something very familiar about the water; it reminded me of a forgotten memory, of the visions that haunted my time in between. Visions I had never told anyone about, not even Mother.

The loud creak of a door opening fractured the silence of the night air, breaking me away from my train of thought as my head jolted up. Crashing sideways onto the ground, I grabbed my bag and crawled on my knees and elbows to the nearest cropping of bushes, overgrown with fragrant white flowers large enough for me to stash myself inside. Watching from my vantage point in the bushes, I could see the two figures bounding down the stairs, stopping at the edge of the water directly opposite of me. With a soft whisper of a mantra, the bag in my hand began glowing softly before folding in on itself and disappearing completely. Some time passed as I watched them sit on the shore, I could just barely make them out, but I was downwind, and based on the smell, I could figure out what they were up to. After waiting patiently, my moment finally came. His idiotic laughter broke up the night, signaling their movement toward the water. As he dipped below the surface and she hesitated, distracted, at the precipice, I slinked my way along the edge of the lagoon, closing half the distance between my prey in one fluid movement.

Dropping under the cover of more bushes before I could be discovered, I was finally close enough to see her properly, shivering in the night air, exposed and beautiful in every way, which was absurd because she was awkward and lanky, her features were too sharp, her hair was greasy, even freshly washed, and she was pale and sickly. Yet despite all of those flaws, something about her was captivating. Her green eyes were alive with streaks of blue and gold, her aura was pulsating with an unbridled power that clearly was looking to run free, and when she stood ready to leap in the waters, you could see the true strength in her shoulders expanding out from her soul. She wasn't like any being I'd ever encountered, and sitting there watching her jump awkwardly into the pool below took my breath away.

As she bobbed back to the surface, I knew I should make my move, but I hesitated, frozen, absolutely fascinated. Trapped by the overwhelming force of her presence, I settled back down on the mossy ground below, convincing myself that further observation was essential before launching my attack. Like a cat, my eyes followed her relentlessly as she swam, ears perked as I caught bits and pieces of their hushed conversation, oddly hard to pick up at this distance despite my usually heightened hearing. I'm sure he was already trying to spin some divine prophecy on her, but would he be honest about the true consequences? The price that would have to be paid to reach their supposedly holy redemption. Something told me he would be less than forthcoming—after all, angels were masters at half-truths. Convinced that righteousness was the same thing as morality, it must be nice to be able to hide from your sins by pretending to be a saint. I might be far from perfect, but at least I was honest with myself about who and what I was. Perhaps I *was* facilitating the end of their pathetic society, but truth be told, that was a lot better than what *they* had in store.

Tension in the atmosphere captured my attention as the mood shifted drastically. Scanning the waters I had become distracted from while mulling over my thoughts, I quickly found the source of the obnoxious laughter as that angel closed the space between them swiftly. She froze in his arms; I could feel her reluctance from here, and I couldn't help but smile smugly. *Don't let his tricks work on you, love. You're better than that.* I subconsciously leaned forward, eyes locked on them, waiting for her reaction— irrationally invested, considering I didn't know her. Honestly, she was nothing more than a pawn to me, beautiful or not. Suddenly, she collapsed in his arms. Part of me wanted to laugh at his ridiculous failure, but another part of me was intensely concerned, pushing me to rush to her side and ensure she was okay. What the fuck was that? *Get it together, Mia. There's no time for some lamb and the lion bullshit. Cifer is counting on you. Are you going to deliver, or are you going to keep falling short of her expectations?*

Focusing on them again, I watched her touching him tenderly. A small flame of envy sparked inside, and it became increasingly frustrating that I couldn't hear their conversation properly. All of a sudden, her lips were on his, and the flame inside me erupted into a full fledge fireball. Angry and spitting, eating up everything inside me and turning my vision red with fury. I had been born with all the abilities and blessings any demon or woman could want, and I had very little trouble seeking out what I wanted in this world and the next, so jealousy was not an emotion I was altogether familiar with. It consumed me completely and nearly compelled me to flee my cover and attack the angel head-on despite my better senses. Fortunately, my composure kicked in just in time, and I released some of the rages in the form of a long low primal hiss as I dug my tense fingers into the soggy mossy ground.

Breathing through the waves of emotion gripping me, I clenched my teeth, muscles tensed, waiting out the brutally intimate moment I couldn't bring myself to look away from. When he finally took his hands off her, it was like someone taking a hundred-pound weight off my chest. The anxiety and anger subsided with the more space he put between them, and I felt an intense desire to keep him from touching her ever again, so intense I was delightfully envisioning removing his large hands. They were on the move now, drifting toward the shallow end of the lagoon. I stalked in the shadows after them silently.

I watched curiously as he began dipping her into the water. I was drawn in closer when, all of a sudden, the moment she went under, I was ripped from my body. Tumbling through the twists and turns of a dimension I'd never seen, I tried desperately to move in familiar patterns, but the folds were all wrong, and the shapes kept collapsing around me. I was being crushed by the eternity, bearing down closer with each failed attempt to collapse and expand, pentagons in peril, leaving me perplexed. It felt like the ether was swallowing me. The barking was echoing all around me; the walls were closing in. Eternal epiphanies gripped me, and my mind's eye opened fully as I fell backward, releasing myself, expanding naturally to the internal harmony hidden beneath the layers upon layers I hadn't been aware of, folding endlessly into infinity.

CHAPTER 7 – RIGHTEOUS RETRIBUTION

The morning dragged on; training had been far less exciting than expected. Amil had insisted on starting slow, and for the past hour and a half, we had been sitting on the mossy ground, warm from the rising sun, meditating to the soft mantra rising from the flowers. Drifting in the fuzzy current inside my mind's eye, hours passed as a slow, pleasant slideshow of colors, geometry, and kaleidoscopic visions played in a repetitive series that puzzled my mind yet seemed to make perfect sense to my body. When I opened my eyes, there was a deep peace in my previously buzzing bones, like someone had tucked me in with a soft, warm blanket. Laying back, staring at the clouds rolling peacefully by, I took in the moment, deep breath in, deep breath out.

It was a surreal feeling, so absolutely in sync with the world around me, as if I was it and it was me, we were one. I had spent most of my existence feeling like an outcast, out of place, a lost soul in a sea of mediocrity. Now everything made sense. I had a place, even if I didn't understand it, and I knew I could *trust* it. Never in my life had I felt so certain of something, and perhaps if I didn't feel so relaxed, I might be concerned by such blind faith. Routine was a friend of mine, though. I knew my path forward now, and all there was left to do was follow through, one step at a time. Pushing myself up with another deep breath, I finally looked over at Amil. He was perched perfectly still, staring at me, transfixed. When we caught eyes, he dropped his gaze quickly, trying to conceal the reverence in those pearly baby blues.

Pretending not to notice, I stretched exaggeratedly, basking in his affections with a smug smile, even if I knew I shouldn't indulge myself. A massive tension I had been carrying around on my shoulders my whole life had suddenly been lifted, and I couldn't help feeling giddy and light. Sure, the tethers of my ego remained, a lifetime of experiences is hard to forget, but I'd suddenly set down the deep despair I'd carried for so long. I released myself of the longing for there to be something more, to understand why the world was so broken, why *I* was so broken. That was the thing; there wasn't a reason. No wonder it had felt like so much struggling for nothing, because it was. At least the truth set me free from this disappointing reality, set me free from the traumas of my youth, and set me free of my expectations of my fellow humans. After all, you can't expect cattle to be anything but cattle, and I couldn't blame them for mindlessly consuming anything they could get their hands on. Humans were just a disease on this planet, a plague I could help cure. Holding the fate of the world in the palm of my hand was oddly liberating. It felt good to be in control for once, even if the tiny voice inside was trying to undercut me with apprehension and uncertainty. Silencing the spiraling negative thoughts, I bounded to my feet, eager again as I offered my hand to Amil with a playful smile. "Enough with this new age nonsense. I'm ready to do something spectacular."

Rolling his eyes, he took my hand, sparks exploding between us with the simplest touch. Overcome with a newfound sense of confidence, I smiled and held his gaze intensely, curious to explore this feeling. I vaguely recalled a series of rational reasons for resisting him last night, but since our encounter in the pool, the tugging sensation in my chest made it harder and harder to deny the flames crawling beneath my skin. He was gazing back at me, matching my intensity, holding his breath as he searched for some type of signal in my eyes. The tiny voice was back, trying to cheerlead for my silly, insecure, human mindset, chanting out the many reasons I would have held back in another lifetime as another girl.

She sounded desperate to me now, and awakening made these trivial things insignificant. I wanted to shed myself from my old fears and explore everything I had been holding back from, and I wanted to be alive in this body while I still could. Moving slowly, purposely, I watched his guarded eyes as I leaned forward, hands still locked, closing the gap between us. It felt like the very ground we stood on would explode at any moment under the pressure building between us. Holding that space, savoring the controlled burn between us, I placed my hand on his face and held him there, locked in that uncertain gaze. I hadn't noticed how tall he was before, not enough to stand out in a crowd, but enough to force me on my tippy toes to bridge that final gap.

Perfectly still, he met my soft kiss with a reserved tenderness, matching my parted lips with measure and control. He never took more than I offered yet responded willingly to what I wanted to give. Whether his reverse psychology was intentional or not, one thing was certain: it was effective as hell. Like some Chinese finger trap, the more he held back, the more I wanted to pull him closer. Out of control, I had never felt more liberated, and I gave myself over to that. Our tongues danced as our bodies imploded, rolling in the grass as the world whirled by. Had I been the one that pushed us over? He was pushing into me now, his mouth moving from mine to my ear, my neck, my exposed collarbone, planting soft kisses across my body that pulled a muted gasp of air from my lips, my eyes rolling back the further south he traveled.

It was all I could do not to scream his name, biting my lip as he consumed me, my body squirming as his lips hovered at my waistband, planting soft kisses along my navel as he pulled teasingly at the elastic of my leggings, sending shockwaves that shook my resolve with each light brush across my skin. Quivering under the pleasant weight of his body on mine, the world was fading away, and all I could see was him. I had never been so sure of someone in my life, all I wanted was him, and I could have him, all of him; all I had to do was pluck the apple from the tree. As the words formed on my tongue, the correct string of vowels and syllables that would bring him to me completely, a soft clearing of a throat brought me crashing back down from my little slice of heaven to my own personal hell. Jolting upwards, still panting and red in the face, I was suddenly scrambling to my feet as I comprehended what my eyes were seeing. Crouched and as feral as I'd last seen her, Mia stood before us with a wild look in her eyes.

Amil let out a primal roar, thick with frustration, as he jumped to his feet and planted himself firmly between us in a defensive position. "Damn you, demon. You have some timing." His brow was furrowed, the most irritated I had ever seen him, and I couldn't help but smile a little, knowing it probably had little to do with the danger at hand. Shaking my head and pulling myself back down from cloud nine, I took a deep breath as I puzzled over this mysterious creature before me, surprised she had revealed her position and passed up such a prime moment for an ambush. Amil clearly wasn't interested in figuring out her intentions because he was already stalking forward, ready for the fight, when her hands shot in the air in surrender.

"Listen, angel. I'm not here for a fight. For once in your life, I need you to stop following orders and just listen for a minute." Perhaps she thought a coy attitude would catch him off guard, a miscalculation. Her arrogance had the opposite effect; his electric blue eyes darkened as he leaned forward.

"Your tricks won't work on me, demon." With that, he was off in a bolt of blue lightning, leaving sparks in his wake as he descended upon her in an explosion of energy.

As his body slammed into hers, a flash of bright fiery light seared across the land, painting it completely white momentarily and leaving little fires scattered across the meadow, the burnt flowers screaming out in soft sopranos as the flames ate up their fragile petals. The shockwave that followed shook the earth and blasted through my body, knocking me off my feet as I flew several feet back before crashing to the ground.

What should have been a painful collision at high speeds with the unforgiving ground below was softened by an orb of glowing golden light surrounding me, pulsating rapidly with my runaway heartbeat. I stared at my hand in awe as another glowing hexagonal tattoo snaked its way up the same arm the flower of life had grown from, etching its way permanently into my skin in a painful sear of burning white light. Quietly reflecting on my new skill, I took a moment to tune in to my temple, realizing the protective barrier was emanating from my heart. Pushing and pulling at the boundaries of the golden encasement, I began to understand I could expand and contract my shield by focusing on the pool of energy radiating from my heart.

Momentarily, I was lost marveling in wonder at the magic I could have never imagined in a million years wielding as a powerless little girl crying herself to sleep in another desolate foster bed. Time was against us, though, and another loud collision ruptured my concentration as Mia returned Amil's surprise attack. No longer kneeled in submission, she was on the offense, attacking wildly at any opening she could find like a cornered cat. I watched in terror as she lashed out at him again and again, trying desperately to make contact with any part of him as he dove in and out of her reach. Occasionally their hard powerful bodies would collide, and another loud crash would rupture the air around them, ripping powerfully through the trees and shaking them nearly out of their roots as sparks of blue and red cascaded off them, like metal was being struck together.

They finally broke apart, seeming to both reevaluate their position in the fight, stalking around each other in circles as they calculated their next moves. Amil dropped, hitting his glowing palms on the ground as a string of mantras escaped his lips at breakneck speeds. The ground ruptured under his hands, the moss and flowers crumbling as the earth below rose in a giant wave, collapsing on Mia in a heap of fresh dirt, burying her in the wet spring mud. Amil whipped around and was already running for me, ready to make a break for it while she was preoccupied. Miscalculating her drive, she was already erupting from the ground the moment his back turned. Golden geometry across her entire body came to life in a surge of power that lifted her straight into the air, where she gravitated, raining down a hailstorm of flaming shards of ice at alarming speeds as Amil dodged in and out, narrowly avoiding her barrage.

Luck is a fickle lady, though. Amil took one wrong step, and a massive stalactite of ice shot through his torso, erupting in flames as it pinned him to the ground, the hungry flames devouring every inch of skin they could reach as an agonizing scream tore through his lips. Mia floated back down to the ground, stumbling as she touched down, her tattoos flickering as her powers seemed to falter after the intense display of force. Amil picked up on her fading ether and grabbed the icy spear, ripping it from his chest in one brutal cry, the gaping wound already sealing under the golden light radiating from his chest as his tattoos continued to sear brightly. She might have some impressive abilities, there was no denying that, but from where I was standing, it seemed there was no way he wouldn't outlast her. She was fading fast before my eyes, and his rage only seemed to make him stronger with each passing moment.

Rushing forward in a surge of sonic force, Amil seemed to

split the air around him as he moved with such speed, I almost couldn't comprehend it. Just as quickly, Mia dodged to the right, producing two tiny yet commanding ivory pistols from within the folds of her jacket, her lips moving as a mantra escaped them, the geometry carved on the outside of the guns coming to life as she aimed. Time slowed as my mind worked in overdrive to process what was unfolding before me, as six explosions tore through the air, back-to-back, one after the other. Bullets exploded from her guns in a shocking pulse of blinding light as the small pellets tore through the atmosphere, rupturing the space-time continuum, allowing them to move in impossible ways. One minute they were just barely escaping the barrels of the guns, the next they were rupturing through Amil's unsuspecting chest, riddling him with holes, halting him abruptly in his tracks as the force of the shots counteracted his intense speed with a boom that sent him flying backward into the lagoon where he rapidly sunk lifeless beneath the surface. A startled cry escaped my lips as I stood paralyzed, knowing I should run while I still could, yet desperate to dash to the water's edge to dive in and recover Amil before it was too late. Mia had turned her attention to me and seemed to be smiling, amused at my dilemma, as she perched herself intimidatingly between the water and me.

Surprisingly she straightened her posture, relaxing her shoulders into a less defensive position, and raised her hands once more as she twisted her smile into a more sincerely friendly gaze. "Seriously, you can relax. I really do just want to talk to you." I wasn't convinced. A shocked chuckle escaped my lips before I could stop myself.

"Yeah, clearly. Hence why you just destroyed my friend there." My voice came out grounded and strong despite the earthquakes threatening to shatter me internally, fear kicking my adrenaline into overdrive. I was abundantly aware that without

Amil, I was a sitting duck, but I'd be damned if I was going to give her the pleasure of knowing she had me shaken. "Has your angel been honest with you about this new society? It's a lot more Orwellian than they'd want you to believe." She was stalking in closer; her words were a distraction, and I wouldn't let it work.

I planted my feet as I desperately searched for any shred of power that might manifest itself and save me from this desperate situation. Her cackling laughter broke the tension in the air as she waved casually behind her to the pool of water Amil had disappeared into.

"You worry too much, love, and not enough at all. You'll give yourself wrinkles with all that frowning. Have a little faith. I'm sure your angel will be just fine, *eventually*." She curled her tongue on the last word, grinning wickedly as she stalked forward, rapidly closing the space between us as my heartbeat picked up the pace with each step she took. "You didn't answer my question, though. Do you really know what they are asking of you? Have you considered your alternatives?"

Without waiting for an answer, she was suddenly leaping through the air, hands out with a wild look of victory beaming on her face as she hurtled toward me, my breath frozen in my chest as I stared like a deer in headlights, trapped by her overwhelmingly cold presence. I knew I was in danger; I knew it was now or never. I knew I needed to do something, *anything*.

Just as her lanky fingers moved to clutch me in their eager grasp, a wall of water hit Mia from behind with bone-breaking force before taking a physics-defying ninety-degree turn upward to avoid colliding with me. It was surreal viewing the water from such an angle, still alive with colorful fish, swimming chaotically as their world whirled around them, one with my thoughts and feelings as it moved at my command willingly like a puppy desperate to please its new master.

Mia screamed a savage protest as the water rose her higher and higher into the air before driving her face first with the force of a catapult into the ground below. The force of the thousands of gallons of water that had once filled the pool followed, cascading down on her limp body, crushing her beneath its sheer force. As my thoughts rapidly shifted, Amil's limp body abruptly floated up from the deserted, dry crater of the once beautiful pool, back arched and head cocked backward in an unnatural, broken way, as intense white light emitted from every orifice of his body.

Like a doll coming to life, I watched his bones click back into place and the structure come back to his frame as he hit the ground running without missing a beat as the odd white glow subsided. The determined man I knew returned to those incredible blue eyes, eyes I realized I had thought I'd never see again as I fought back the burning tears I didn't have time for right now. As the last dregs of water crashed down on Mia, Amil was already on her, colliding from up high with the full force of the heavens behind him. He descended on her without holding back. Blow by blow, he beat her body further into the earth, the ground crackling with electricity with each hit. He seemed determined not to underestimate her again and set on finishing her then and there. Trembling, it was torture to watch him like this, to witness her demise, to experience such violence, and it had me questioning if I really had what it took to stand by and watch the whole world burn after all.

Just when I figured she couldn't be alive anymore, a whisper cracked through the air like a whip, sincere enough to bring Amil's blind rage to a momentary halt. "Have mercy, I beg of you."

She was a heap of blood, mud, and shattered bones, broken and pleading with those intense golden eyes, full of fear, searching for an ounce of pity, begging for a shred of his empathy. Humbly, she pushed her distorted body up, bowing down on her knees before him as she laid her head and hands on the ground like she was praying in some ancient way.

Amil's eyes turned dark again, disgust painted his face as he sneered down at her. "How *dare* you."

I hadn't realized the gravity of their exchange was so intense it had been subconsciously drawing me closer, inch by inch, until Amil lifted his hand angrily, glaring down at her dubiously as he made his final move to end her. Before I knew what was happening, my feet were carrying me forward, closing the gap between the three of us as I hurled my body between hers and his. A look of shock and pain twisted across Amil's confused face as he abruptly pulled his hit, stumbling back a few steps in his immense effort to stop the force of his punch. The anger in his eyes quickly transmuted to a soft look of empathy that concealed the hurt lurking in the deep blue depths.

"Don't fall for her tricks, my lady. *She's* not worth your time. Now move before you get hurt." I bristled at his authoritative tone, my inner rebellious foster kid triggered by the command, causing me to snap back sharper than I ever intended.

"I can decide for myself, thanks. You don't *own* me." He recoiled at my harsh tone, jarred by my antagonistic outburst, the hurt confusion in his eyes apparent now. Regret was already gripping me when he moved forward to grab my hand. Instinctually I stepped back, recoiling from his advances. It was a learned reflex and the last thing I ever intended. My heart broke just a bit as I watched the wave of rejection wash over him, dampening his eyes as his arm dropped limply to his side. Before I could reach out to comfort him, a harsh cackle broke my concentration as I whipped my head around to the disfigured shell of a girl on the ground next to me.

"Well, look at that. It actually worked." Mia reached out a twisted hand, wrapping it around my ankle in an unbreakable grasp as a malicious grin took over her gnarled face. Time seemed to slow down in a surreal way as she tossed one of the tiny explosives she had stashed away in her coat pocket at the ground, the mantra escaping in a tumble of words that opened the ground below them and swallowed the two of them up as Amil's screams faded away into the distance. As I fell endlessly through that dark, cold void, my voice lost in the nothingness, I couldn't get the image of Amil's terrified face as we slipped out of my mind. It haunted me relentlessly, regret and remorse gripping my chest to the point where I could barely breathe as I dropped further and further into the unknown, vaguely aware of a cold hard hand wrapped securely around my ankle, gripping me like a lifeline in the endless void.

CHAPTER 8 – DOWN THE RABBIT HOLE

Dissolving into the wormhole, I shattered into a million pieces, disintegrating into the void before rapidly materializing back together in an unfamiliar land, the quantum leap depositing me in a heap of heaving, spinning confusion as my cells tried desperately to right themselves in a fraction of a second. As the spins subsided, I pushed myself onto my knees and tried to get my bearings as I scanned the woods for my captor. Muted gasping alerted me to a limp, broken heap in the bushes a few yards away from me, blood pooling in the crushed grass. Her body convulsed softly every few moments as if her consciousness was physically fighting to cling to this shattered vessel. My heart commanded me forward, demanding action from my shaking hands, as my brain fought for any rational way to save this helpless creature dying on the ground before me. I shouldn't care. I should let her bleed out. I should run and find my way back to Amil—I should do literally anything except what I was about to do.

Dropping to my knees, I hesitantly placed my hands on her twisted chest, ignoring the sick feeling of her bones through her torn skin as I bowed my head, concentrating on pushing the tiny golden glow from my heart outward. From deep in my subconscious, I recalled the soft mantra Amil had once chanted over my unconscious body, allowing it to flow instinctually from my lips as the markings on my hand began to glow. Light spread from my fingertips, warm and all-consuming as it traversed across her broken frame, setting bones and healing gashes as Mia let out a searing primal scream, eyes rolling in the back of her head as her broken back arched into place. It became all I could do to contain the massive energy pouring forth from my body, searching out every corner of her vessel and restoring it to perfection, capturing us both in the current of blinding light that burned all the way to the heavens in a cylinder of golden glory.

Collapsing suddenly as the pillar of energy disappeared completely, imploding into itself in a flash, I sprawled across her heaving chest, matching her panting breath as I tried to regain control of my numb tingling limbs. Finally able to move my arms, I leveraged myself off her and rolled onto my back, staring up at the clouds, floating lazily in the sky, still struggling to fill my lungs with enough oxygen as I tried to reconcile with my choices. Any moment, she was bound to spring into action and carry me off to the Underworld against my will, and I had just used every ounce of my power to save her life for reasons that suddenly eluded me. What the hell had compelled me to do something so stupid?

Tension gripped my chest as my breath slowed, getting deeper with each inhale and exhale, dread and uncertainty creeping under my skin as the moments seemed to drag on while I waited in terror for her to break the silence. I wasn't bold enough to meet her eyes when she sat up, stretching her limber arms as she looked over her restored body in amazement before looking at me in confusion.

"Why would you do that?" She demanded answers from me with a furious look as her brows furrowed, obviously irritated.

Sitting up, I gazed at the ground as I mumbled under my breath. "I couldn't leave you like that." I was blushing like a moron as I messed absently with my shoe, afraid to look at her and expose the truth behind my dull green eyes.

She stood gracefully in one sweeping motion with a frustrated huff as she pulled at the shreds of her once bright yellow sundress. "I'm going to run out of outfits before the day's up at this rate. Now where the hell did that bag go?"

Mia stalked off, searching the nearby area high and low before finally producing a dark purple miniature backpack, dirty and somewhat torn yet with a slight iridescence shining through the filth. It had been cast aside in a cropping of rose bushes during the abrupt transition through space and time when Mia had transmuted it across the globe prior to her attack.

"Well, I would say that went mostly according to plan for something that risky. Head-to-head combat with an angel, especially one of *his* caliber, was almost certain death, but I just had to get close to you." The beaming glow of victory was back as she shuffled through the contents of the bag before pulling out a lacy white tea dress.

Ignoring my presence as I continued to sit on the ground watching her uncertainly, she stripped off the old torn dress, dropping it on the ground as she stretched, her bones popping as everything settled into place. Staring at her long, lean frame, I caught myself tracing the hard lines of her dark, muscular body, exploring the wild planes of her mostly exposed skin, caught off guard by her confidence in her natural form as she stalked around in the warm afternoon sunlight with no regard to my lingering eyes. She knew I was watching her, but it didn't seem to faze her in the slightest as she took her time dressing, pulling the folds of fabric over the curves of her body slowly in an exaggerated motion, basking in my attention as she pretended not to smile while still avoiding my gaze. I could see the corners of her cherry-red lips pull up ever so slightly, giving her away. She danced around me as she collected the scattered possessions that had flung themselves from the torn bag upon landing, preparing for the journey ahead.

Finally, she approached, her eyes playful but cautious, hiding something important. Holding out a tiny shred of black fabric, she addressed me curtly. "Put this on. They'll be able to track anything from the Keep." She crossed her arms menacingly as I stood, unsteady on my feet, a small tremble taking hold of my body as I stood uncertainly before this powerful and unpredictable creature. After an awkward moment where it became abundantly clear she had no intention of allowing me a private moment to change, I finally began ungracefully stripping away my outfit as I dropped my eyes to the ground, the familiar feeling of shame sprouting forth from the lost little girl inside, still fighting to take the wheel and steer with fear. Resolution dawned on her face as she read my body language, a sympathetic half-smile cutting her sharp features momentarily before she abruptly turned her back to me, rolling her eyes as her red and blue dreads whipped around in a tangle of oil-slick hair.

Placing one hand on her hips, she ran the other through her locks, pulling her dreads into order in a bored fashion as she tapped her foot impatiently, hurrying me along sharply as I mumbled an embarrassed thanks and fumbled with the delicate strappy slip of a dress. Finally working my way into the silky contraption, I looked down at the too-tight article that seemed to expose every small curve of my petite body that had been hiding for years under layers of sweaters and oversized overalls. It made me uncomfortable as I pulled at the short twirling hem that fell just shy of my knees, eventually giving up and settling on hugging my arms across my chest to cover the plunging neckline. It was by far the most ridiculous thing I'd ever worn in my life, especially in the cool breeze of a northwestern spring in the middle of the mountains, although it made me starkly aware of the subtle heat that seemed to radiate from my heart now that kept the chills at bay.

Lacing up the black combat boots Mia had handed me, I pulled my long lanky gray locks into a smooth bun on the crown of my head and turned, ready to face whatever destiny had in store for me with some sense of dignity. To my surprise, Mia was standing there staring at me reverently, a fierce glorious glow in her eyes as she stretched her hand out to me. Compelled by her intense presence, I couldn't resist the offer. Not like there was much point anyway; I didn't stand a chance against her at full strength. I firmly grasped her cold, smooth hand, interlocking my fingers with hers, ignoring the fiery sparks crackling between our skin despite the cold. Lightly she pranced forward, dragging me along in her wake, singing a familiar mantra before tossing another small geometrically encrypted explosive at the ground in front of us. The ground ripped apart in a force of wind and mud, revealing a swirling pool of dark energy, another wormhole identical to the one from earlier.

Mia turned with a mischievous grin pulling her face into a twisted hungry expression. "Ready?" Falling backward into the portal, she pulled me in after, a muffled scream escaping my lips as we dissolved together before reappearing in a tangled mess in the middle of a busy market square, heaving less this time as my body seemed to adjust to the quantum jump—however, much more publicly. Several passersby lingered rudely in a nosey, not-looking-to-help kind of way as I struggled to right myself and calm my uneasy stomach.

Mia was already on her feet, brushing away the dirt from her delicate ivory dress that matched the carved revolvers she wore openly in the leather holsters with little regard to what bystanders might think. Weak in the knees, I finally forced myself up, looking around the market for any clues as to where we might be as I straightened my dress, pulling desperately at the fabric in one last feeble attempt to cover my exposed pale skin that had my cheeks burning as I avoided catching the eyes of passing admirers.

Striding hurriedly down the block, Mia was already several

yards ahead of me as I raced after her, stumbling in my haste. As I settled into a brisk walk behind her, my eyes wandered around the colorful and lively market. It was like something out of a storybook. Vendors lined the streets selling everything from fresh fruits to colorful hand-cast pottery. Even a few musicians and artists performed live for delighted audiences that filled their guitar cases and overturned hats with spare change. The open-air stalls displayed an assortment of tapestry roofs that billowed in the breeze, providing some relief from the overbearing sun overhead. Mia moved like a local, dipping in and out of side streets without ever once seeming to question her route or check a street sign. Without warning, she veered into a shady-looking brick alley, unnaturally dark in the bright afternoon sun. An unreadable rusted sign hung askew on a half-broken post above an unnaturally large and old door, more at home on a castle than in the alley of a sprawling city. Mia paused momentarily, rapping out a complicated series of knocks on the door before pushing it open, a delightful mix of dreamy pop music and fruity smoke greeting us as we walked through the threshold.

Sprawled out across the dimly lit room was the most eclectic range of individuals, from a gaggle of gothic-looking teenagers who looked up at me with deep red hungry eyes to a horde of glistening girls, white flowing hair moving ethereally, defying gravity as the strands floating softly in the air around them as if they were submerged in water, their sparkling skin catching the soft lights. A hunched figure at the bar had familiar hexagonal geometry carved up his arms, but it seemed long faded, and he looked away quickly when our eyes met as he downed the rest of his drink and pushed himself away from the bar and out the door in a hurried pace. Mia's eyes flickered at his departure before carrying on toward the bar. She took a seat a few down from a sun-kissed shirtless man bent over the counter, hiding his face under thick layers of long straight dusty blonde hair, patchy hair scattered across his massive frame.

I took the seat on the other side of her, eager to put as much distance between myself and the furry muscular man as possible. She ordered two drinks I didn't catch the name of as I continued to peer around the room, trying to comprehend what I saw here, forcing my mind to accept the unacceptable. I was in a room of mythical creatures. Not only had I spent the night on the run with an angel and been captured by a psychopathic demon set on starting the apocalypse, but *now* I was sitting in a bar full of creatures from fairytales and nightmares. Grasping the bar to stop myself from falling over, I took a series of deep breaths to convince myself that this was real life and not some twisted nightmare brought on by some accident.

A nervous laugh escaped under my breath; I had come full circle to the coma theory again. I shook my head, trying to collect my thoughts and accept my situation as I turned back to the creature at the bar that was staring at me intensely, golden eyes glowing, the ring of purple around her irises prominent in the blue lighting of the bar. Casually she handed me a fruity cocktail, a grin spread across her face as she offered her glass and we cheers'd like we were old friends—it was bizarre. I didn't even bother to take a sip of the drink before setting it down.

An intense desire to have any sense of control overtook me as I rushed to speak before Mia could; she'd at least have to answer my question if she was going to have her way with me. "You seem like you know the city pretty well. Where are we?"

She grinned, raising an eyebrow, clearly aware of my pathetic attempt at dominating the conversation. Still, she played along. "I'm fairly local. It's irrelevant, though, just a stepping stone on the path to redemption."

I scoffed, bolder than I'd expected myself to be in my

current circumstances, as the words came out louder than intended. "Redemption?! That's a funny way of saying destruction and devastation to all of mankind." Mia looked down contemplatively at her drink, still grinning despite my outburst.

"Yeah, it does kind of look bad from the outside, doesn't it?" She looked up at me, eyes all aglow, piercing past my cold exterior as she seemed to search for the right words to compel me. "I hate to break it to you, sweetheart, but what the Kingdom has in store isn't what it seems either. You think you're saving the world, but the irony is you'll be the one who truly destroys it." A fire swelled in my chest. I expected her to attempt to manipulate me, yet I was caught off guard by her accusation regardless. My voice exploded out of me as I tried to ignore the small audience turning toward me as I garnished the attention of the other patrons.

"You don't know me, what I've seen already. I *trust* Amil, and the visions I've been gifted have shown me the way. I am the blessed one, the final Rider, and I *will* bring forth a new age of peace and prosperity for humans."

Passion had never been a thing in my life before, and I was honestly shocked by how strongly I already felt about my mission. Had this been imbued in me during the awakening? Was this part of blossoming into my potential as the Rider? It was strange to feel my blood boiling, my heart hammering, and my chest swelling with pride as I talked about the divine prophecy and the first title I had ever become attached to in this previously pointless existence. I had never been a daughter, a friend, or a lover, but I *was a Rider.*

More cackling laughter broke the tension in my body as Mia rolled her eyes and turned to the bar to take a long swig of her lime green beverage that glowed radioactively. "Figures they already brainwashed you. To tell the truth, I expected nothing less." My brow furrowed at her condescending tone, but as quickly as I had found my voice, I'd lost it again. "Guess there's nothing left to do now but to show you the way. Even I didn't really understand it before, but everything is *so* clear now."

She drained the rest of her drink as she turned to me once more, the reverent glow back, another wicked grin twisting her face. "I'm sure I can find a way to persuade you if you'd give me a chance." She winked at me casually, laughing at my confused expression as she gestured toward my untouched drink, dark pink bubbles still fizzling to the top of the luminescent purple beverage as the ice slowly melted, condensations dripping on the sides and pooling along the counter.

"Please, have a drink. You're making a scene." Reluctantly I pulled the beverage toward me. I didn't want to let my guard down around her, and I didn't trust she wouldn't take advantage of any crack in my foundation of resolve to plant seeds of doubt. I didn't want to admit that the little voice inside would spring at the opportunity to water those seeds with the sprinkled whispers of fear that remained from that small spark of ego that seemed no amount of enlightenment could completely extinguish. Lifting the drink to my lips, I intended to take just a small sip. However, the fruity mix hit me with an explosive force of flavor, strawberry, mango, and pineapple mixed with more exotic fruits like dragon fruit, lilikoi, papaya, and something else I couldn't quite place in a perfectly balanced blend that tasted like a tropical island liquified. I found myself gulping the drink down in massive chugs as if it were the first sip of cold water after weeks lost in a desert.

I ignored the chuckle from my left as I set the glass down, completely empty, as she was already ordering another round from a dainty little girl with pale blonde hair and a light blue teacup dress. She was covered in tattoos and wore bright red lipstick that contrasted intensely against her porcelain skin. A battered name tag read Alice, and I figured it must be a coincidence. Subverting Mia's cryptic nature, I addressed the bartender directly, grasping for any small piece of the puzzle.

"What is this place?" A smile spread across her ruby-red lips as she opened her arms proudly, beaming as she looked over her bar.

"Welcome to Wonderland, baby. Home to freaks and fallouts, misfits and murderers. Everyone is welcome within these walls as long as they all play along nicely. Otherwise, the clock runs out, and they go down the rabbit hole." She spoke so matter-of-factly, as if every word out of her mouth wasn't absolute insanity. I stared for a moment too long with my mouth open, and she dismissed herself awkwardly before I even got a word in. Mia was laughing again, an incessant sound that was becoming rather irritating.

"Wow, super smooth. You really aren't the social type, are you?" My cheeks were burning again.

"It's hard to make sense of words when everything around me makes no sense at all." I was mumbling, my defense was weak, but I'd stand by it regardless.

Grabbing the new drink, I forced myself to sip the sensational beverage slower this time, a soft buzz settling over me, calming my heart as I tried to gather my racing thoughts. Staring at the intricately carved bar, a soft hand on my shoulder startled me, derailing my train of thought. Mia didn't retract her hand as our eyes met. The look of devotion was back, I suppose it was pride for her mission, and it made me wonder momentarily what drove her soul; the softness of her voice surprised me even more.

"You think too much. You'll wrinkle that pretty face of yours." Slowly, purposefully, she moved her hand to my face, brushing her cold fingers across my cheek, sending currents of electricity up and down my spine as she captured a loose hair and swept it tenderly behind my ear. It all became too much, and I couldn't suppress the shudder that rippled through my body as she brushed my ear. My cheeks flushed again as I cursed this vessel for betraying me, another series of pleased chuckles bursting forth from her wild red and gold lips as she pulled back from me. Every part of me wanted to pull her back into my orbit. She already had too much power over me, and I needed to get a grip. I shook my head, trying to break her spell.

"Don't do that. It's not fair."

Smiling innocently, she shrugged. "Do what? You're the one in control. I've been trying to tell you that. Not me, not even them, it's you. You have all the power here. You just have to wake up and see it." Now I was the one laughing. Sure, I'd come a long way from the pathetic girl I was, somehow, just two short nights ago, but I was nothing compared to the sheer force of strength I saw on that battlefield between her and Amil.

"If that was true, I wouldn't be here right now." She shrugged again as she finished off her second drink.

"Maybe, maybe not. I didn't think I'd be here yesterday, either. Sometimes destiny just has a way of intervening. If things had gone according to plan, we'd already be knocking at the gates of the Underworld right now. As fate would have it, it seems we have to take a bit of a detour first." She pushed herself up from the bar abruptly. "She's here."

In a twirl of dreads, she was off toward the darkest corner of the bar where a very hard-to-miss figure had taken residence, transforming the entire booth into a makeshift fortune stand, equipped with everything from rich pink and orange drapery to a crystal ball. I stared at her, perplexed, certain I would have noticed this obnoxious setup when we walked in and positive I hadn't seen anyone come or go through the door since that odd man.

Rushing after Mia, I clutched the half-drunk juice as I followed, battling the fierce devotion to the cause coursing through my veins while the curious little voice inside craved more answers from this delightfully dangerous creature who threatened to consume me.

Sliding into the booth after her, I looked at the woman before us—intricate braids of black and gold piled loosely on the crown of her head, wrapped with a silky piece of ivory fabric, golden bangles jingled on her wrist, an array of gold and ivory fabrics hung loosely over her lithe frame. Vivid lilac eyes contrasted fiercely against her jet-black skin. She stared into my eyes with eternal wisdom, seeing into the depths of my soul. I couldn't look away; it was as if I was trapped in her gaze. I could do nothing but give her my secrets, falling helplessly under her spell as the room faded to black.

CHAPTER 9 – FORTUNES AND FAVORS

Abruptly she released me, my consciousness tumbling back into my body haphazardly. She turned her gaze to her crystal ball, and her voice came out in a soft monotone. "Two paths lay before you. Two beacons will guide you. It all ends where it all begins." She grew silent as she continued to gaze into the orb, chanting softly in tongues. The crystal responded to her voice, glowing softly at first before building into a burning beacon of light. I strained my eyes to see past the blinding light, watching her expertly manipulate the ball of energy that seemed to have shifted from a solid orb to molten liquid. She twisted it, pulling and stretching the liquid, ripping it into pieces, and wrapping it into small shapes.

As the glow faded and the dim light of the bar settled my eyes, I was able to look at the assortment of platonic solids the fortune teller had crafted from the orb, solid once more, crystal as the ball had once been. Gathering them up, she placed them in a small silk bag before producing a deck of cards from a fold in her dress as a coy smile spread across her face. "Pick a card. Let Ora read you the signs." She carefully shuffled the cards before fanning them out, holding them toward me. I couldn't resist the urge as I grabbed the card with the strongest pull.

Mia huffed as she crossed her arms, defiantly leaning back in her seat. "We don't have time for these trite carnival tricks." Ora ignored her completely as she had for all the encounters thus far, eyes still fixed on me as she took the card I pulled.

Closing her eyes, she slowly turned the card in meditative

circles in her hands, chanting softly in tongues again. I was shocked when she finally laid the card on the table face up. I had assumed I would pull death—I mean, it only made sense, right? Instead, staring back at me was the chariot card, an intricate card with a glowing goddess at the helm of a black and white steed pulling in opposite directions, their unbridled power harnessed by the pale-haired rider, commanding the intricate geometry-covered chariot she rode in with a look of fierce determination. Perplexed, I stared down at the card while she fixated on me, seemingly reading my thoughts.

"Not the card you were expecting, I see, but just the one you needed. Light and dark are destined to come together, and only one has the power to harness their conflicting energies. Two choices lie before you, but both paths are perilous. Look where you least expect, and answers you will find."

Exactly what I needed, more cryptic riddles—I guess I wasn't sure why I thought a fortune teller of all people would give it to me straight. Leaning forward, Mia's humor returned as she laughed at my frustrated expression.

"See what I mean? Oracles might be all-knowing, but they only leave you with more questions. I only come for the cookies." My frustration turned to confusion. Had I just misheard her? What did she mean by cookies? I turned to her, bewildered as I stumbled to phrase my question.

"Cookies? What does that have to do with *anything?*" She cackled again, tossing her dreads to the side as she leaned against the table, closing the distance between her and the Oracle.

"So, Ora, what's it gonna take for you to give one up?" She raised her fierce red and blue eyebrows in question as she bore into those unnerving eyes with her equally intense golden ones. Ora held her gaze with a confident indifference as a lifetime passed between them, some unspoken argument dragging out for decades in just a matter of moments before suddenly releasing in the next. Mia's shoulders relaxed as her posture loosened, and she began digging through the small bag she had retrieved from her stash in the woods, pulling out a handful of engraved worldly weapons that included a collection of gold-tipped bullets and even more small explosives she had used to jump through the wormhole that had delivered us first to the wooded mountains and next to this crowded market square. Reluctantly she held her stock out to Ora, anxiety painting her smooth features despite her best efforts to hide her hesitations.

"You can have one, only one. I'm working with a limited stock, you know." Ora's face lit up as she leaned in, expressing emotion and passion for the first time since I'd entered her mystical booth.

"It's hard to take *me* by surprise, demon. I don't see something *new* very often. Where did you procure such a creation?" Ora had picked up one of the small explosives and was twirling it in her hands as she gazed at it in absolute wonder, those bright purple eyes twinkling with curiosity.

Excitement and pride seemed to get the best of Mia as she began enthusiastically explaining her curated goods. "I *made* them. It took decades of research, and it's far from perfect, but I finally figured out how to encode our geometrics into the weapons of this world. It allows me to embed just a fraction of my power into these tools that channel that energy, marrying it into the explosive powers they are already capable of, expanding the destructive force a hundred-fold while barely draining my limited resources. This breakthrough levels the playing field, bridging the gap between the powers the angels hold on this plane compared to the rest of us." She paused for a moment, weighing her words carefully before she continued.

"Full disclosure, these are just prototypes. I'm still working out the exact geometry necessary to mass-produce these so that the average demon or mythical creature could utilize this technology. Something is off in my calculations, and I just can't figure out what I'm missing." Mia collapsed in her seat, clearly irritated at herself for being so transparent in her defeats. It surprised me that she would be so forthcoming with this strange woman.

Mia caught me staring at her and smiled while shrugging slightly. "It's pointless to lie to an Oracle anyway. They'll see right through you—might as well be honest about what I'm offering." She turned back to the curious woman, still gazing at the small explosive in absolute wonder. "So what do you say?" Ora looked up, her eyes blazing with untethered excitement.

"Give this to me, and perhaps I can find the missing puzzle piece. In exchange, I will give you not one but two cookies. One for now, one for later. Do we have a deal?"

Mia cackled again as she looked at the Oracle curiously. "Not adept at bargaining, I see. Why offer more than I ask?"

Ora smiled, sacred wisdom in her eyes as she crossed her arms in contemplation. "Equal exchange is important in this realm, and a creation is worth what it's worth. Who am I to question that?" Smiling coyly, she tilted her head in such a matter-of-fact way that Mia was silent, left with no room to argue. Producing two perfectly baked golden-brown real-life fortune cookies from the folds of her sleeves, I had to admit I half expected something marvelous and otherworldly, but they were as common as the ones I had received in the takeout orders I'd devoured in the few good foster homes along the way in the system. Reaching out eagerly, Mia snatched them up with hunger, already pulling at the plastic of the first cookie with unfettered enthusiasm.

The cookie cracked in two with a snap, a small piece of paper popping out of the center. Mia popped the first piece of cookie into her mouth before tentatively offering me the second.

"For good luck, you know." She pushed it toward me, and I couldn't hide the amused grin that spread across my face.

"I thought you didn't believe in trite tricks and all?" She rolled her eyes, blushing as she pushed the cookie closer toward me.

"Just eat the damn cookie."

I chuckled before tossing the cookie into my mouth, crunching into a literal party of flavor in my mouth, mixing and mingling in a way I never even thought possible, cinnamon and nutmeg swirling with vanilla as an undercurrent of orange carried the whole pallet. The delightful array of flavors was gone in a flash, and every cell in my body craved another taste. In fact, I was suddenly certain I could spend the rest of my life eating nothing but fortune cookies and be completely content, and I was also certain I would do absolutely anything for another. I shook my head, trying to clear my thoughts. I was acting like some kind of drug addict, and a soft chuckle broke my spiraling stream of thoughts.

"Amazing, huh?" Mia's fierce golden eyes were burrowing into mine, and I wanted to look away, but in that moment, it was as if the cookie had left me clouded, and I wanted nothing more but to close the distance between us, to throw myself at this strange and compelling creature before me and forget everything else. I shook my head again. What in the actual fuck was wrong with me? More laughter grounded me again.

"Take a deep breath. It's an intense high, but it ends quickly." I noticed Mia's hands clenching the table as if holding herself back from something. I wanted to ask her what, but the buzz was fading fast and taking my courage with it. The danger was settling back in, and I knew sooner or later, I was going to have to find a way out of her grasp before I became trapped permanently in her gravity. Doubt clouded my previous high as my thoughts started to spiral. I began to question all the choices that had led me to this dark, damp bar that suddenly reminded me all too much of the small dark rooms of my childhood nightmares. The walls were closing in on me, and it was getting hard to breathe. I began to panic as I looked around at the calm faces of the two women before me at the table. I was on the verge of screaming when Mia flung herself toward me, pressing her lips to mine without warning.

Parting my lips fiercely, she welcomed herself without a moment's hesitation, her surprisingly hot tongue pushing against mine unapologetically as her cold hard skin pressed into me. Losing myself in her overwhelming presence, my hands were suddenly tangled in her thick, soft dreads, pulling her closer as I began matching the ferocity of her kiss, a fire swelling in my body that threatened to implode at any moment. Abruptly, she pulled away, flushed and eyes glowing as she tried to collect herself and regain her composure. She looked at me, grinning wickedly.

"Calm down there, cowgirl. I was just trying to do you a favor. The fortune cookie has to flesh out your fears and desires to sort out the past and future. It can be intense the first time, and you didn't look like you were handling the comedown well." Mia began adjusting the beads in her ruffled dreads as my eyes dropped to the ground, tears stinging at the corners of my eyes as the cold wave of rejection hit me. I was able to fight back the tears, but I couldn't hide the burning red of my cheeks as I looked back at Mia. She was staring at me in an uncomfortable way, searching for answers in my wounded eyes. Desperate to move past this moment and put it as far behind me as possible, I turned my attention to the piece of paper in her hand.

"Well? What does it say?" I felt like an idiot; at least I could still get some answers and then get the hell out of there.

Mia turned reluctantly to the scrap of paper in her hand, taking a deep breath before unfolding it. A small, neat blueprint occupied the limited space of white paper, as normal as any fortune cookie, but the message was anything but. Her voice was like liquid as she recited the words like some sort of poet. I found myself leaning in, drawn in by the pleasant rhythm and my burning curiosity, something I'd felt more in the past forty-eight hours than in my entire lifetime.

"You all share a common affiliation rooted in another situation. The path to repentance is in the den of serpents. The keeper of the keys can show the way with ease."

Mia's brow began to furrow as she came to a close on the short prose. She turned to the fortune teller, and her eyes clouded with accusation. "The last time I got one of these, the message was a hell of a lot clearer. What gives?"

Ora simply shrugged, a coy smile spreading across her face. "What can I say? You get what you get." Mia was obviously irritated at her nonchalance and picked up her other cookie.

"When can I open this?" Ora shrugged again just as casually.

"You'll know." Mia fumed as she crashed back against the seat, sulking as she read the statement again and again, whispering the riddle to herself under her breath. I turned back to Ora, who had redirected her piercing gaze on me, sending chills down my spine as goosebumps raised across my entire body at her unnerving energy. She reached out for my hand, and without a moment's hesitation, I obliged, holding out my palm to her.

Expecting the most epic, and for that matter, only palm reading of my life, I was surprised when she began tracing geometric lines in my unmarked palm, golden light searing into my skin following her delicate dark finger as it shaped a perfect pentagonal star encased in a boundary of glowing golden lines. I held my breath this time, recognizing the pain from my first engraving as I clutched my other hand, which held the white flower of life bestowed upon me by Amil that had slowly grown its way up my arm with each use of my powers, blossoming into more versions of hexagonal geometry wrapped in an ancient language. When she finished, she looked up at me with that all-knowing smile, her eyes wells of wisdom.

"You're going to need that. You're also going to need these." She grabbed the small silk bag, iridescent and sparkly, that she had filled with the small geometric crystals earlier. "The other Riders are waiting for you to lead the way. These will help you guide them and harness their potential." I looked deep into her eyes. I had so many questions that I was at a loss for words. I was trying desperately to form the questions to understand the conflict I felt inside, the burning devotion pushing against the curious void that had once consumed me but now compelled me forward in search of the truth.

Was humanity really destined to be nothing but a failed experiment, a prerequisite to a purer existence? Couldn't she show me a path that didn't just lead to utter destruction? After all, I already knew I had two paths, but they both had the same ending, really, didn't they? Was she simply telling me that I should just accept this and pursue forward? It seemed a bit redundant considering that was already the plan—not much of a fortune, really. I guess I hadn't even considered that I would need to find these other Riders. I had never been much of a team player, and the idea of being a leader was even less appealing to me, to be honest. I had assumed they would just do their thing, and I would do mine; at least, that's how Amil had made it seem. I couldn't fathom what they could learn from me, considering I was the last to wake. I took a deep breath, calming my racing mind as I started to piece together the words that would unravel her riddles when she held her hand up to silence me.

"It's been a pleasure. However, I must be going. Be ever

blessed." Just like that, she snapped her fingers, and her entire setup, the drapes and pillows, the tapestries and string lights, the incense, and candles, all disappeared in a flash right along with her. As she disappeared, the door to the bar slammed open as an eclectic group of burly young men pushed their way into the room, decorated in the same kind of golden pentagonal geometry and tribal markings that covered Mia's skin. My heart sank as my brain caught up with what my body already knew. I had already instinctually clutched the booth, terror grasping my entire vessel. *Backup*, they must be more demons from the Underworld here to help Mia escort me to Cifer. Looking at them, I even recognized a few faces from the crowd of shadows in the woods.

I started to shake as the gravity of the situation was all but smothering me. Amil was never going to find me, and it was too late. I should have never hesitated. I should have left her crumpled and dying in the woods and fled the first chance I had. I couldn't stop the tears that started to spill silently out of my eyes. I thought I could be brave in the face of danger with these newfound powers, small and unpredictable as they may be, but here I was again, nothing but a victim of my circumstances. They moved toward us at a hurried pace, patrons of the bar clearing their path without hesitation. Surprisingly, Mia stood, positioning herself defensively between myself and the arriving company.

"Hello, *boys*. Nice of you to finally join me." Her voice was dry as she continued. "Fortunately, I've already got the situation handled, so your services won't be necessary." She was casual, almost professional, despite the thick layer of sarcasm underscoring her tone, but she held her position between us firmly, keeping me just out of their reach as I backed further into the corner booth like a frightened animal. The lead figure was a tall, pale, muscular guy who appeared to be in his early twenties with long, perfect ocean-blue ringlets of hair falling past his shoulders, his golden eyes smoldering as he leaned past Mia, trying to get a better glance at me. His deep voice was like liquid honey, designed to lure prey in and trap it in his deadly grasp, no doubt.

"The more, the merrier, right, Mia? Cifer sent us to ensure there were no mistakes. Just because you're her *daughter* doesn't mean your *special*. I follow her orders, after all, not yours." Mia's posture was growing tenser by the moment as she stiffened against his advancing approaches, putting more effort into holding him back while clearly trying to maintain her composure and calm. I noticed she seemed to be eyeing the exit. Was she calculating a plan? I couldn't fathom why. After all, this should be everything she wanted. Why not accept the help and complete her mission while she had the chance? I was so captivated trying to figure out her motivation that my tears had dried, and I found myself leaning forward again. The empowering effect she had on me was bizarre, the ability to quell my desperate mind with fascination and reverence. Perhaps I would find it somewhat unnerving if she wasn't so damn alluring, posed, and powerful, standing between me and my certain doom.

"Levi, listen, let's be diplomatic." Relaxing her defensive posture, she placed both hands softly on his chest, sinking into his body, looking up at him with those deep hypnotic eyes. His tough guy facade seemed to evaporate as he leaned into her, captured in her clutches. I guess even demon guys were still just guys, after all. "We both know what you really want, all of the glory and none of the work. Let me handle this. You have my word that we can present her to Cifer together. You guys have been shadowing my work for centuries. You thought that nickname was cute once, didn't you? What's one more time?"

She was leaning in further with each word, pushing up on her tiptoes to close the distance between their faces. There seemed to be chemistry there, like this wasn't a first-time experience. He was fixed on her, searching her eyes for something I couldn't place. He was leaning in now, too, succumbing to her little seductress act. Who could blame him? The fear in my chest had turned to an envious fire. What I wouldn't give to trade places with him, to have her look at me like that. I wanted to look away, yet I couldn't tear my eyes off them, trapped watching this slow-moving train wreck as my heart beat sporadically against my chest with each moment of palpable tension. Just when I thought he would crumble and my heart would explode into a million pieces over a girl I shouldn't care about, a sharp cackle fractured the small space between their lips.

Firmly, he placed his broad hands on her shoulders, pulling her back with a cold look in his eyes as a coy, calculating smile spread across his face. "You might've had your way with me for centuries, Mia, but now I'm the one holding the cards."

In a flash, the scene changed in a million ways. Mia was flying through the air, shock and betrayal already giving way to a calculated look as she twisted herself in his grasp and launched a full-body counter kick directly toward Levi.

That was the last thing I saw before the previously silent horde of demons in the shadows were on top of me, closing in on me from every angle in a single heartbeat. Their bulky cold bodies were pressing in on me, suffocating me under their deep growls and cackling laughter as several strong hands grabbed me anywhere they could. I faintly heard a primal screech as they began shuffling away from the tangled bodies in the corner still locked in battle—this had obviously been their plan all along, and Mia had played right into it.

I guess this was what I got for following a demon. I tried desperately to reach deep inside, calling out to the little spark that fueled my powers, but the cold fear pressing down on me was too much to overcome.

One of the men pushed a warm rag against my mouth, and I began hyperventilating, gasping rapidly until I could hardly breathe at all. Panic gripped my chest, and I went limp, just barely conscious, as they pushed their way out of the door of the bar and into the blinding sunlight of the busy market square.

CHAPTER 10 – EVE EVERLASTING

A single gunshot cut through the room with the explosive power of a rocket launcher, crunching sickeningly as the bullet met the cold, hard flesh of the blue-haired demon still grasping tightly to me as we struggled on the floor of the dingy bar. It exploded into a massive ball of powerful light that lit up the entire room, decimating everything in its vicinity and shattering several nearby windows. With slow brutality, Levi ripped apart into a million pieces before my very eyes, loathing and hatred twisting his beautiful features as he dissipated into the air. I turned, trying to hide the single tear that escaped, pushing down the pain and regret that tried to surface. This was no time to reminisce on something that could never be—*she* was in danger.

Returning the ivory pistol to its holster, I pushed myself to my feet, brushing off my lacy white dress as I looked up at the audience of curious and shocked patrons. Alice stood behind the bar, looking particularly annoyed. "Add it to my tab?" I grinned sheepishly, hesitant to offend Alice and cut off my ties with the Under-Wonderland and its convenient connections.

Rolling her eyes, she gestured toward the door in an irritated manner for me to carry on, snapping dryly. "Isn't there a damsel in distress?" Nodding, I turned back to the destroyed booth, fishing around in the rubble of wood for my small bag, throwing it over my shoulder as I turned for the door. A small glint caught my eye before I could leave. Kneeling back down, I found a delicate gold necklace with an intricate ivory-carved octopus wrapped in gold markings. I recognized it well. Pocketing the totem, I pushed myself to my feet and swiftly toward the door.

Bursting into the sunlight, I momentarily lifted my hand to cover my eyes to give them some reprieve as they adjusted to the harsh afternoon light. Immediately I spotted a small fire escape and dashed up the ladder in a few powerful bounds, using my newfound vantage point poised on the side of the building to scan the crowds vigilantly. Desperation was creeping in as the streets revealed nothing but laughing children, chatting patrons haggling over the price of bread, and lovers by the fountain making out in a wet, disgusting way that these ears could pick up all too well from here. I was pushing my senses to their limits, searching for her, for any sign that might point toward her.

A startled gasp pierced through my brain with explosive ferocity, and I was already on the move. My feet pushed off the old brick wall as my body flung gracefully through the air, flipping with ease a handful of times before sticking the landing for a stunned crowd. I couldn't resist the pull to bow arrogantly as the crowd around me cheered nervously before I was already off through the streets, chasing after the fading sound that had caught my attention. Weaving and ducking through the crowds, everything around me became a blur as I pushed my vessel to its limits, feet pushing against the ground faster and faster to close the distance between us. Bursting through the crowd and into the fountain square, I immediately caught sight of the small group of men clustered around her lifeless body, confused as they looked around for some unseen signal. I suppose Levi had assumed he would get the best of me—*bold* of him. Stalking forward across the square, I closed in on my prey in a heartbeat, a primal snarl erupting from the beast that lives deep inside me as I lunged.

They didn't stand a chance; it was almost pathetic how quickly I picked them off. The first crushed and popped under the weight of my jump like bubble wrap, the second two I beheaded together, symmetrically beautiful in a morbid sort of way. The fourth tried to flee screaming, and I took his heart for being a coward and abandoning his fellows. Ironically, three of his chaps tried to save him, but I moved through them effortlessly like a dancer with a snapped neck, a severed brain stem, and a broken back.

I stood in a pile of broken bodies, breathing heavily as the shocked crowd around me began giving way to shrill screams and scattered sobs. Slowly the gruesome scene began to dissolve as their vessels began breaking apart, scattering into the wind, causing the terrified crowd to stampede, trampling over one another in a desperate attempt to avoid the ash. Scrambling forward, I dropped to the ground, shaking Nato desperately.

"Come on. You need to wake up!" Nothing, she was cold as ice and limp in my hands, barely even breathing at this point, and her pulse was all but nonexistent. Hesitating momentarily, I leaned forward and kissed her softly, her tender lips warm and inviting but completely unresponsive. Still *nothing*. What a shame—that always worked in the fairytales. *It looks like we have to do this the hard way, love.*

Standing up, I gently collected her rag doll body in my arms, pulling her close to my chest as I surveyed the chaos before us. Moving swiftly through the crowds of callous humans, pushing aggressively against each other with only their own safety in mind, I found a back alley that seemed strangely familiar and followed my intuition call to venture down it. Several turns later, I was certain I recognized the area, despite clearly remembering it never being in this town before. I turned once more to find myself in a luscious little walkway, surrounded by a wild assortment of fragrant plants and trees in their prime spring bloom, sprouting forth from as many pots as the small brick alley could hold. A vintage-style post lantern lit up a small golden yellow door arched in a charming sort of way, decorated with an ornate floral knocker. White geometry ranging through all the shapes was painted intricately in a shimmering pearly white paint that seemed alive, moving and swirling in its own liquid current.

Despite the dire situation, I couldn't suppress the small smile that spread across my face. Now this *was* a treat. Confidently I walked toward the door, shifting Nato slightly to free my hand to reach out and grab hold of the intricate old-school knocker. Rapping out a soft and pleasant rhythm that went on for several minutes, I could hear the harmony playing in my heart, a sound embedded in me that I would never forget in a hundred lifetimes. Immediately the door flung open in response, and a radiant, glowing woman filled the space where the door had once been, beaming from ear to ear. Rich green curls cascaded down either side of her soft, dark freckled face, and her twinkling green and gold eyes were filled with deep kindness—one look, and you were home. I couldn't even remember the last time I had seen Eve, but I knew in this second it had been far too long, and my heart had been aching for this moment, even if I would never admit it.

"I need your help." Perhaps I should be more tactful after all this time, but I didn't have time to waste.

"I know, Mia, that's why I'm here." She smiled with all-knowing wisdom as she stepped aside, gesturing for me to come inside. Of course she knew; she always knew when I needed her most, even if it had been lifetimes. Walking into the room, I was overwhelmed with the fragrant aroma that greeted me, the olfactory system of this vessel operating on overdrive from the fragrance emanating from the surreal number of flowers and plants packed into every corner of the room, shoved into bookshelves, sitting on counters, covering every windowsill, and even spilling out of the kitchen sink. Heading for the oversized mustard yellow couch in the corner of the room by the window, warmed by the late afternoon sun peeking through the sheer drapes, I dropped to my knees and gently set her lifeless body down, worry seeping through the cracks of my frozen heart against my will.

Furrowing my brow, I set my hand softly on her face, trying to will her back to me before it was too late. I told myself I was just worried about waiting through another cycle, but the truth was much more difficult to deal with. Dishes clashed together before Eve began fussing with her vintage stove, clicking several times before finally catching a small flame coming to life on the burner. She set an overly large and ornate silver tea kettle on the burner and began pulling a wide assortment of cakes, snacks, and fresh fruit from her refrigerator. She expertly started finely dicing a couple of perfectly red apples, tender and juicy as the knife cut through their soft skins. She tossed them into a bowl and reached into her cupboards for an assortment of glass jars filled with a variety of homegrown spices and dried herbs, and she began sprinkling them into the bowl with seemingly no recipes or measurements. When the kettle began to whistle, Eve tossed the ingredients in and started setting out the snacks on the coffee table while the mixture brewed, humming a soft and pleasant tune to herself as she worked.

Finally, she joined me on the couch, placing two iridescent shimmering teacups down along with the steaming tea kettle before settling into an oversized floral armchair. Pouring the piping hot, fragrant tea, she added a lemon slice to each cup before picking up a bundle of sage and a small box of matches. Striking the match on the box, it erupted into a bright flame, flickering at first before finding its strength. She lit the sage on fire momentarily before blowing it out. Billows of smoke coiled into the air forming shapes on their own accord. Eve placed the sage on a beautifully hand-painted plate where it puffed away, filling the space with tiny smoke

shapes before turning to me and offering the cup of tea. "Drink."
Silently we sipped the tea; it was spicy, rich with cinnamon and
vanilla, balanced by the sour lemon. The aftertaste was sweet,
heavy with apple, and something I couldn't place. Time ticked by
slowly, my mind easing with each sip as I pensively watched the
smoke show, occasionally snacking on one of the delectable
homemade treats, each a little slice of heaven.

At some point, Eve started humming something foreign yet
familiar. Some small part of my brain knew I should be worried
about Nato, but the haze settling over me was drowning out that
voice fast. A lightness was overcoming me. I hadn't realized how
heavy I had become over the centuries, lifetimes of burdens
building a boundary I didn't even know existed. As I popped
several large green grapes into my mouth, exploding in a
delightfully sour way, Eve refilled my empty cup with another
round of hot apple tea, and I realized I wasn't quite sure when I
had finished the first cup. In fact, I wasn't even sure how much
time had passed since I walked through the threshold, but I was
aware that the full plates had emptied around me. Had I eaten all
that food? Such delightful treats; they must have gone down quickly
without me noticing. Taking another long sip of the drink, it
started to become hard to keep my eyes open, the soft melody was
pulling me under, and I couldn't fight it. Distantly I heard my cup
crash to the floor as I drifted off.

Jolting awake, on my feet instantly, everything around me
was dark as I fumbled around blindly for a light. Finding the
switch, I clicked it on to discover the entire apartment completely
empty except for the golden couch, a soft indent in the worn fabric
where her body had once been. Panic tried to work its way under
my skin as I moved hastily between the rooms flicking all the lights
on, desperate for any sign of her. I quickly ran out of rooms to
search in the tiny home. Pushing aside my fears, I was already

formulating a plan when a jarringly bright light caught my attention from the previously pitch-black window at the front of the house. Rushing to the door, I swung it open, fully expecting to find myself in the dark brick alleyway. Yet instead, before me was a wild and isolated beach, untouched by man, a million stars twinkling in the clear evening skies above. I was hit with a wave of fresh salty air that compelled me forward to the lapping waves, brushing against the shore in a soft lullaby.

A fire was burning down by the far end of the beach, gold, green, purple, and blue; it was a sign that I intended to follow. It took me some time to get across the coastline. My feet seemed to drag in the sand, and it felt like I was shedding something with each step. I didn't know what, but I was certain I no longer needed it. After what felt like a lifetime, I finally reached the other side of the shore, where the fire was cackling, creating a beautiful little harmony with the waves. Hidden by the flames previously, Eve sat perched peacefully on a smooth rock by the edge of the fire, legs crossed and eyes closed in meditation. As I approached, her wide green and gold eyes shot open, looking up at me with delight as a smile spread across her face, deep wrinkles momentarily pulling at her ageless face from lifetimes of smiles and laughter.

"I'm glad you found me. I never know if someone is going to open the right door." She gestured for me to take a seat next to her on another large smooth rock. "Please, join me." Obviously, I obliged.

"Welcome to Eve Everlasting. It's my own little twilight realm between the worlds. It was the only place I could be sure we could talk alone, without any flies on the wall, if you know what I mean." I nodded solemnly, looking into the enchanting fire, swirling in an array of colors as the salty driftwood burned vivid and surreal. "Literal flies, though, not metaphorical ones. I swear they send them to spy on me." I turned to her brow furrowed in confusion; sometimes Eve said really profound things, but sometimes Eve said really crazy things too. She dazed into space for a moment before shaking her head, seeming to brush off whatever train of thought had momentarily distracted her as she casually tossed her long green curls back and turned to me with an intensely serious look.

"You've gotten in over your head this time, haven't you? You should have listened to me when I warned you years ago." The depths of my confusion only grew. What was she even talking about? She had never warned me of anything. She was the one furrowing her green brows now. "I guess that was before. Oh well, it doesn't matter. We still have time if we act now."

It was always a struggle to keep up with Eve once she did start talking, but the years seemed to have degraded her—she was rambling a lot more than usual. "Hey! It's not that bad." My head whipped upward. Had she heard my thoughts? I never remembered that being a skill of hers previously. She giggled like a small child at my surprise as she shrugged. "Just here, perhaps because I created the space. They can tell it's here, but I've hidden it well. This form is difficult to function in, though. They don't want me to have it. They corrupted it to keep me away from it."

I was trying to keep up with her. Who was she talking about, Cifer, perhaps? More laughter in response to my conclusion. Talk about rude. "Cifer *wishes*. It's much bigger than her. It doesn't matter now, though. What matters is your next move." Could it really be Hova trying to stop her? Why would Hova even care? Everything here must seem so insignificant. Cifer had always told me that's why Hova couldn't understand her vision for the future. Eve snapped abruptly at me. "You're not *listening!* This isn't about me, or even Cifer or Hova, for that matter. It's about *you.*"

Rolling my eyes heavily, I looked her square in the face as I followed flatly. "I'm just a cog in the machine, Eve. My *mother* has always made that clear. I don't know if it was you that sent that vision the other day, but it doesn't matter. I have to do what I have to do." Her intense green eyebrows shot up so high they nearly got lost in her thick blunt bangs.

"Vision?! What vision? You must tell me more." I stumbled for a moment, trying to find the words to explain the experience the other evening on the edge of the lagoon.

"There are no words for it. Perhaps I could show you?" Eve nodded eagerly as I took a deep breath and relaxed my mind, letting myself fall back into the hallucination, momentarily lost in the folds as my body acted on instinct, yet this time I was able to quickly find the right forms of geometry to move through the space, gracefully stepping through the angles as I allowed Eve to explore every corner of my waking dream.

Bell-like giggles broke the boundaries of the other realm as Eve, always one step ahead, brought me crashing back down to this reality, the fire still crackling beneath a sparkling sky. Her green and gold eyes were alive, streaks of electric blue surging to the surface as her eyes flicked back and forth like she was reading something in thin air. As her body lifted into the air, floating ever so slightly, a faint glow began emitting from her heart and wrapping around her in a sparkling golden torus. The energy fed into itself for several cycles before collapsing into a ball of condensed light above her heart. The little orb, pulsing and alive, weaved its way down her arm before resting in her palm. Eve reached her hand out to me, beseeching me to join her with those all-knowing tricolor eyes. My intuition was screaming at me to follow her lead even if my logical mind was pulling at me to stick to the plan—to follow *Mother's* orders. Passion and curiosity won the debate, and I reached my hand out to her. The spark moved between us in a flash, explosive and charged as it raced up my arm and burst into my heart.

Wild screams filled the still twilight air. Was that me? The intense rush of energy was overwhelming as it rocketed into my heart and back out of my body in a blinding surge of light, knowledge, and mystery. Suddenly it was as if every door to the universe was thrown open, and I was walking down every path simultaneously. Answers to questions I would have never known to ask were before me in a wave of enlightenment, crashing over me, consuming my whole identity, tossing me around like a rag doll while my physical body remained paralyzed in the toroidal sea of gold. I was trapped outside of myself, tumbling and crumbling, struggling to hold on to any sense of who I once was. My brain was working overtime, firing off synapses like it was the Fourth of July in an attempt to keep up with the sudden assimilation of data. Downloads came in further surges bringing a massive comprehension of numbers, language, physics, geometry, and math in a way that I had only scratched the surface of previously. My body began to convulse as the knowledge became too much, pulling my vessel apart at the seams. Just as it felt like I would combust, the light suddenly released me, my physical and spiritual being colliding and collapsing into one another before dropping, exhausted and overwhelmed, into the soft, cool sand of the beach as I gasped, shallow breathes wheezing in and out of my constricted lungs.

Eve's voice was soft and soothing when she finally broke the silence. "There's something inside you that even I can't explain, something I've never seen. The vision showed you the language. Your soul could even instinctually process it, but it's as if you'd been banished from understanding it. I could not remove all the blocks, but I processed as many as I could to help show you the way. The rest is up to you." I was still crumpled in the sand, trying to catch my breath, but I forced myself up on my hands and knees to look her in the eye.

"Even with *all this*, I don't know where to go from here.

Everything used to make sense, and now nothing does." Eve nodded solemnly, placing a comforting hand on my shoulder as she kneeled next to me.

"Waking up can be a lot like that. It's worth it to seek out the truth, I promise. I can't see your future, but I *can* see the next step. Take her to the first Rider, find Pestilence, and you will be on the path to finding your truth."

I stared at her, desperate for more answers. What was happening to me? How could I understand so much yet only feel like I had many more questions? I missed the comfort of my own arrogance, of the shelter of lies I had called home for so long. What had Cifer been hiding from me all this time?

Eve just smiled as she nodded consolingly once more at my racing thoughts. "Trust the process. In time it will all make sense. Till then, it was nice to see you, my old friend. I hope our paths cross again soon." Frantically, unexpectedly, I reached out to embrace her before she was gone, but it was too late. She slipped through my fingertips as I jolted awake alone in a stranger's bed. I could still hear the echo of the waves lapping against my eardrums.

CHAPTER 11 – CHILDREN OF EDEN

Soft music drifted in from the other room, light, intricate dreamy piano accompanied by a single sweet, sultry, sorrowful violin, dancing together in a perfectly contrasting harmony. The smell of fresh bread baking made my stomach grumble, but I was still fighting the urge to open my eyes, savoring these few peaceful moments curled up in the warm puddle of sun drifting in from the open window. My mind pushed back at the building anxiety as my last conscious moments started creeping back. Large hands grabbed me as terror froze me in their grip. One had covered my mouth in a strange-smelling cloth, and everything began slipping away. Shooting up in the once-comforting bed, I began scanning my surroundings; where could they have taken me? My brain was still foggy, but perhaps I was still dreaming. The paintings on the walls, the books on the shelves, the plants spilling off the windowsill, and the odd little geometric knickknacks in gold and silver all once lived in my tragically destroyed home.

Jumping suddenly as a soft snore startled me, I jerked my head to the side to find Mia sprawled across the bed, blue and red oil-slick dreads cascading across her peaceful face, her short dress riding even higher to expose her dark, muscular thighs, covered in interwoven golden geometric tattoos, spiraling down from her hips to just above her knees, falling just short of the ones spiraling up from her feet. I couldn't help but stare at her, watching her chest rise softly with each slow breath she took. Her eyes moved rapidly back and forth behind her eyelids. Was she dreaming? I wondered what it would be like in her dreams, what a girl like her would find in that realm, curious if she ever saw me there.

I shook my head viciously; there was something seriously wrong with me. I must crave punishment and pain. What was I doing fawning over someone like her? Amil was waiting for me, and I needed to get out of here. Even if this place smelled like my favorite bread, played my favorite music, and had all of my long-lost belongings, I was no fool; this had all the makings of a classic setup for a trap, after all.

Pushing myself off the bed, I stumbled toward the door, my legs exploding into a numb buzzing sensation that made my feet feel like balloons. How long had I been asleep? Gingerly I stepped one foot in front of the other as the tingling slowly subsided, my legs awakening as I crossed the room and reached the threshold. I flung open the door, ready to fight tooth and nail if that's what it took to make my escape. I wouldn't be trapped by fear this time. I wouldn't succumb to the scared little girl who always took the wheel when I needed my resolve.

Yet for all my conviction, nothing could prepare me for what I saw on the other side of the door; it, in fact, took several moments for my brain to process the scene in front of me, a large smile erupting across my face as my anxiety melted away into sheer pure joy. Wrinkly and soft, Eden stood at the counter, eyes crinkled as the biggest smile spread across her worn face to match mine. She set down the knife she was cutting apples with and reached her arms out to me as we embraced warmly.

Tears began flooding my eyes uncontrollably, and I incoherently tried to piece together the words to explain what had happened to her cabin, the animals, and all of her belongings, how I was powerless to stop it all, how I would have traded my life for theirs in a heartbeat, how I didn't mean to let her down when she was counting on me. Sobbing like I had never sobbed in my life,

Eden's embrace just became stronger as all of the emotions, the fear, the anger, the loss, came tumbling out all at once, cascading out of me like a dam broken till nothing remained, and I was just an empty shell of a girl, held up only by her surprisingly sturdy grasp for an old broad—her words, not mine.

Softly she chuckled, surprising me enough to knock me out of my self-pity spiral. I pulled back, scowling at her. *What a low blow to laugh at me while I'm at my weakest.* She pushed her wrinkly fingers against my forehead, trying to literally smooth out my scowl.

"You worry too much, child! You always have, my dear. Look around, why don't you!?"

Wiping tears from my cheeks as I snorted loudly in a rude way, I began to take in my surroundings, sniffling quieter this time as realization slowly dawned on me. The oversized and over-loved mustard yellow armchair, the giant storybook window, and the shelves upon shelves of books, musty, old, and some even charred from the fires that stole their original homes, or perhaps mine. This *was* my cabin! Stunned, I pushed past Eden to approach the window. It looked out on a different view, tucked away in a field of wildflowers with an unfamiliar collection of old colorful homes scattered in the distant hills, yet my animals were there, roaming free and delightfully sampling the wild foliage.

"How?! How is this possible?" A wave of emotion overwhelmed me, consuming me as the heavy weight of loss that had been silently pulling me down for the past few days lifted, freeing me in a way that left me giddy and light after the intense emptiness I had just experienced. Turning to her, I bounded across the room and grabbed her hands, spinning her around in a delightful dance as we giggled like small children. Her old wise green eyes were sparkling with excitement, and mine were still streaming freely with tears of joy or sorrow—I wasn't quite sure anymore.

"Sit, sit, my dear! Well, first, take this. We have so much we need to speak of."

Nodding, I accepted the tray of cakes she forced upon me as she turned back to the stove, fiddling with the teapot that was still steaming from before I woke up and interrupted her morning routine. Heading to the living room, I deposited the tray of tiny, layered cakes, a wide array of strawberries, chocolate, vanilla, carrot, and spice, before collapsing into my familiar yellow chair, rubbing my hands softly on the worn fabric. *Oh, how I missed you, old friend.* A few moments later, Eden followed after me, balancing two trays with ease in her small, tanned, wrinkled hands, one full of tiny fruit pies and fresh bread with a large side of sweet cinnamon butter and one with an ornate vintage tea kettle, two piping hot cups of tea, an empty third cup upside down, and a bowl of fresh sliced apples with a side of caramel for dipping. Eden did always know how to go over the top both when hosting or visiting, which, to be honest, I wasn't sure if she was the guest right now or if I was.

Settling into the large couch next to the chair, she placed the trays down before offering me the cup of tea. Gratefully I sipped the warm fruity tea, buzzing with fresh honey, as I chowed down a few cakes, forgetting my manners as hunger overtook me and a few cakes rapidly became more than a handful in a rather gluttonous fashion. Eden giggled quietly as she started sipping her tea, pushing the tray of fruit pies and bread closer to me. She didn't have to ask me twice. I grabbed a large slice of bread, fresh and warm from the oven still, and began smearing a generous portion of the honey butter on top before shoving it into my mouth whole, unintentionally moaning in delight as I chewed the soft sweet bread. I followed with two more pieces of buttered bread, several apple slices dipped into the decadent homemade caramel, and a whole miniature apple pie before I settled back into my seat and took several more long sips of tea, finally feeling somewhat satiated.

Loud creaking from the other room caused me to snap my head to the side, catching eyes with Mia as she stepped forth from the threshold. She froze momentarily, crouching slightly, caught like a deer in the headlights. She seemed to be torn between running away and diving toward me. Unfazed by her arrival, Eden finished her long sip of tea before clearing her throat calmly.

"Mia, it's nice of you to join us. Why don't you come to take a seat." She seemed startled as her posture snapped straight, yet she stalked confidently into the room, looking at Eden curiously as she smiled politely, gesturing for her to take the seat next to her on the couch, the seat closest to me. I curled into myself as Mia sat down casually, stretching out and taking up far more space than necessary, putting her too close for comfort, even with the barrier of my favorite chair to protect me. Eden grabbed the empty teacup and filled it before handing it to Mia, who leaned forward in a rather aggressive posture to drink. She was clearly uncomfortable that she was outnumbered in a strange environment, not that this little old lady was much of a threat, and my track record so far wasn't looking great either.

Sipping her tea pensively, Mia was still staring at Eden intensely with those piercing golden eyes, the ring of purple seeming to pulsate as she interrogated her with her gaze. Eden turned to her happily, green eyes sparkly again as she set down her tea and picked up the tray of fruit pies, pushing it toward her. Reluctantly Mia took one and popped it in her mouth, her vivid red and blue-tinged brows furrowing as she chewed the sweet cherry pie. Upon swallowing, Mia took another long swig of tea while keeping a suspicious eye on Eden before setting the empty cup down. She suddenly leaned in close, grabbing Eden's old, wrinkled chin and lifting her face close to hers, nearly touching nose to nose. Her voice was cold and coy.

"You remind me of someone I know. Explain yourself." I was tense. Instinctually I had leaned forward in my chair, clutching my teacup as I readied myself to protect Eden, if necessary; even if I had no idea how I'd do anything against Mia, I knew I'd have to do *something*. Shattering the tension with her soft bell-like chuckle, Eden grabbed Mia's hand in her own and squeezed it gently, her natural maternal energy calming the whole room instantly.

"I imagine you're speaking of Eve, yes?" Mia's eyes narrowed further as she pulled her hand back aggressively, raising her brow as she impatiently gestured for Eden to explain further. Still chuckling softly, she poured us all more tea as we all settled back into our seats, attention fixed on Eden as she launched into her story.

"Long, long ago, in the land before time and space as we know it here, there was a young angel who went down a dark path, far from all that was light and pure. She was led astray by a temptress with a silver tongue, preaching of a world full of many freedoms but little consequence, yet plotting only ways to expand her ego, growing her powers at the cost of those in her charge. Several angels broke away from her gravity and found their way back to the light, returning in shame to the Kingdom and their creator, Hova. Ever graceful, a path to redemption was offered to them, a secret mission for each one to atone for their sins. However, it drove them all apart, off on different paths that would never again cross as part of their punishment. Eve was paired with an angel named Adam, a mysterious angel who had been banished long before the Fall. Together they were gifted eternal life on this plane and tasked with starting a new population to be culled here on Earth of their very own flesh and body, children created in the image of their own ribs yet diluted with each generation, slipping further away from their godliness as time passed.

"Over the lifetimes, Eve passed the time, distracting herself from the cruel fate of her children with her studies, becoming proficient with the geometry that made up this world, learning to bend it and fold it in magical ways that created a life where nothing existed before. Eve had grown close with several of her children, more pure versions of humans whose lives far outstretched the lives of her distant children of today, though still paling in comparison to Eve's eternal life. She began sharing with her children the ways of this world, weaving her knowledge into their bloodlines as the years passed on, creating what would become known as the Children of Eden, a secret order of gifted individuals that would eventually branch out and give birth to all modern forms of the Occult, Paganism, and other worshippers of nature, the elements, and the cosmos, all the way to today's third mass awakening of witches."

Eden took a dramatic pause, taking a long sip from her still-steaming tea. Mia and I were both perched on the edge of our seats, waiting for her to continue.

"Eve had many children, daughters and sons that spanned across centuries. I was the last of her direct children, born so many lifetimes after her first that I was able to long outlive the rest. For many years now, I have been carrying on Eve's work, spreading her messages and sharing her knowledge of the frequencies, shapes, and patterns. So much time has passed that even I don't remember all of the teachings or what her true mission was, yet I've carried as much as I could for as long as I could. Now all I can do is pass the mantle on to you and hope for the best."

She grew silent, pensively staring off into space while sipping what remained of her tea, absently nibbling on the corner of a tiny cake, lost in her thoughts and memories. Staring at her in wonder, I was still just trying to see this little old woman I had known for so long, worn and wrinkled skin, tanned from years of sun and densely freckled, wispy white hair, streaked with a single vivid green strand, with those eyes that did always seem to know a little too much, as some ethereal daughter of Eve herself, like *the* Eve, mother to all mankind and whatnot, when Mia let out a rude and rambunctious laugh.

"You can't possibly expect us to believe that, can you?" Mia had crossed her arms defiantly across her chest. I guess trust wasn't something that came naturally to her. I supposed she was boring into Eden with her intense golden eyes, trying to intimidate her, or perhaps she could sense people's feelings like Amil could? Eden just chuckled again, more bell-like sounds trilling through the room.

"Eve warned me you were a skeptic—no matter." Eden pushed herself off the couch slowly, shifted over to the cabinet in the corner, and began opening one drawer after another, searching noisily through the messy contents of the drawers. "I know it was around here somewhere." She was muttering under her breath as she searched for several more minutes, digging through drawer after drawer before suddenly holding something high in the air triumphantly. "Hah! Exactly where I thought it was." She began shuffling back to the couch, dragging her fuzzy pink slippers across the dark wood floor as she adjusted her worn floral robe.

Sitting down, she pushed back the few strands of white hair that had fallen forward, escaping the bounds of her loose braid that cascaded down her back almost to the floor. Leaning forward excitedly, she reached out her palm to Mia with a sparkle in her eyes. "The next piece to the puzzle. You're searching for Pestilence, aren't you, my dear? This will show you the way."

Stunned, Mia opened her hand silently. I didn't understand who Eden was talking about; I was trying to remember what Amil had told me in the woods, what felt like a lifetime ago. Everything from that night felt like a dream, but a small part of my brain recalled that being the name of another Rider. Either way, it seemed like a good enough answer to convince Mia. Eden dropped a small trinket in her open palm. Mia held up an ornate gold locket the size of a pocket watch, intricately carved in white hexagonal geometry. She popped the small lock holding the contraption closed, and it shot open, revealing a five-pointed compass with five smaller points embedded between those. A metallic gold line connected the five major points, while a shiny silver line intersected it to connect the five smaller points, creating a decagram within the compass. The points moved fluidly around a long metallic green needle, which shifted itself rapidly, trying to chase after one specific spoke of the compass marked with a swirling symbol.

Unconsciously leaning in further, I was able to see that all of the major five points had a symbol carved within them, like the one point the hand seemed to be pursuing. "This belonged to my mother. It can find many things, including the other Riders *if* you can figure out how to use it." Eden turned back to her tea trays, pouring a final cup for herself as she popped a whole mini apple pie into her mouth, clearly as dignified as I was. I suppose that was why we'd always gotten along so well.

Mia's stunned silence evaporated as quickly as it arrived as she was scoffing again, demanding more answers. "What do you mean if? Doesn't this thing come with some instructions? You must know *something*." Eden just shrugged nonchalantly as she shoved a few cakes in after the pie and chewed almost purposefully slowly as Mia waited impatiently, her foot tapping the floor in an irritated way.

Finally, Eden spoke, soft and soothing. "Sorry, dear, but you're on your own for this one. Maybe if you'd come sooner, but at this point, I just don't recall. Best of luck though figuring it out." She turned to her and smiled the sweetest and most genuine smile, but it seemed like there was a glint in her eyes, something she was trying to hide. I knew her well enough to know when she had a secret on her mind; I also knew well enough not to push it.

Mia fumed momentarily before dropping her shoulders in defeat. She stood up and began pacing around the room as she muttered under her breath and held the compass close to her face, turning it in her hands to examine it from every angle. Eden giggled once more before pushing herself up as well, much slower, as she clutched the armrest and let her old bones unkink.

"You should both stay for lunch in the garden. Tomorrow is the Light of the Earth festival in the local village, and you wouldn't want to miss that now, would you? Gatherings this large are hard to come by these days." Matter-of-factly, she waltzed out of the room and off to the kitchen to prepare lunch without waiting for an answer to her invitation. Still absorbing the new information she had presented, I sat frozen in my chair, lost, gazing into the half-empty cup of tea in my hand that had grown cold during her tale. A small click from an ancient television in the corner broke the spell on me, and my head jolted up, captivated by the bright lights and loud sounds echoing out of the box. I couldn't remember the last time I had actually watched a TV; the object seemed foreign and alien to me. Mia clicked the old knob a few times before settling on a fuzzy news channel with a serious, somber-looking anchor.

"Just today, the CDC has reported 12,000 new cases as our death toll rises from the hundreds to the thousands here in the States. As our statewide quarantines fail to cull the Mevid-20 virus, we began to turn to the reality of an unprecedented nationwide lockdown as we follow the same deadly curve as previous countries already completely shut down by this pandemic." Caught up in my own little whirlwind of chaos, I had let go of my troubles concerning this realm, already writing them off as something below me, I suppose, as I accepted my higher calling as the final Rider, but I came crashing back down to reality in one five-minute news segment.

For weeks prior to Amil's arrival, the radios and bits of news I inadvertently was exposed to revealed chaos and panic as a deadly and contagious respiratory virus that violently targeted the lungs had been sweeping the world. Hospitals had become overrun, short on supplies, staff burning out and falling sick themselves as they worked overtime to try and keep up with the high volume. Five patients were waiting on every one bed in some of the worst-hit nations as world leaders scrambled to catch up with this fast-spreading, slow-growing, ruthless killer that crept through the air, lived on surfaces for days, and hid in the healthy and sick alike spreading for weeks before even showing the slightest systems. When you did show symptoms, though, it was only a matter of hours before the virus rapidly spread, devouring your body, ravaging the sick and the healthy without discrimination.

The panic, the fear, the confusion—it was unreal watching the news stories flash one after another, whole cities closed down, millions of people hiding in their homes, grocery stores cleared out as folks rushed to secure enough food to feed their families. Parents separated from their children as they tried to cross closed borders to catch the last flights home, people singing in the streets and from their balconies, separated yet still joined as one. Some folks fought over toilet paper and hoarding supplies, while others still worked around the clock to keep hospitals and food banks open as the community showed its best and worst colors all at once. My heart broke as the full weight of my choices began to settle in, pulling me down in its gravity. I was going to be a part of this. I was going to cause this fear and panic. Was I really okay with that? It was all too much as I shoved myself off the couch, crossing the room in a couple of irate strides as I shut the television off. Mia looked at me with one eyebrow raised.

"You okay?" Teeth clenched, I couldn't help but roll my

eyes, irritated and completely overwhelmed by the situation. I wanted to go back to when things were simple, when I was just a girl on a mission, into a cute guy and awakening to a divine purpose—back to before I let an old friend confuse me into thinking maybe I should be going after some other Rider with a girl I could trust about as far as I could throw. Pushing past her, I stormed off into the other room, desperate to put as much space between us as possible so I could think. She seemed to know better than to follow me.

CHAPTER 12 – LIGHT OF THE EARTH

Following Eden into the kitchen, I crumpled into the chair at the table as she started busying herself with the preparation of lunch, sighing heavily as the weight of the world came crashing down on me. Dropping my head to the table, I crossed my arms, hiding behind them as the tears streamed silently down my face, my mind racing. I thought I had left this girl behind, but I just kept coming back to her. Awakening in that pool of radiant water felt like a lifetime ago; the magical remnants seemed to have faded away, and I felt more human than ever, uncertain and afraid just like I had always been. Exposed and vulnerable, I sat at that table silently sobbing for at least an hour as Eden hummed quietly in the background, her knife thudding a soft rhythm against the wood-cutting board, never once interrupting my quiet collapse. As morning light gave way to afternoon sun, pouring in from the window at its new angle to warm the crown of my bowed head, self-pity released me from its sorrowful grasp as I raised my head once more, sniffling as I wiped away my tears.

It felt as if every ounce of water in my body had drained out of me and left me hollow and empty for the second time today, a shell of bones and skin, nothing but lost thoughts echoing in an empty chamber. Why was I like this? Why was it that I just couldn't be satisfied even when I thought I had finally found my purpose, the reason behind all these lonely nights drifting in a world I never belonged to? Why did I always have to look for more behind the curtain, to crave control in a way I simply could never have? Was something fundamentally flawed about me? Inherently broken in a way that just couldn't be repaired, a crossed wire somewhere sparked the need to fix the unfixable. I needed to heed the warnings of my visions and not let my earthly tethers keep me grounded in this realm. I needed to let go of the worldly desire to save this species, even if there were good bits here and there, like Eden and the only home I'd ever known that she'd somehow managed to salvage.

My eyes shot open at that thought. Eden was silently sitting across from me, two piping cups of tea resting between us, and I couldn't recall when the soft melody of her humming and chopping had stopped. Hoarse and raw, my voice cracked out of my dry, broken lips. "How? You never told me how you saved the cabin." Eden giggled softly, sipping her tea pensively for a moment before answering.

"Such a puzzle you are, child. Always concerned with the little details, for better or worse." She smiled kindly, clearly complimenting me more than insulting me. "My mother created a network of secret gardens, modified from Hova's designs for her Kingdom Keeps. After all, it *was* my mother who was the original architect of that particular marvel, so she was equipped with more than enough insight to expand upon the original concept in such a way that she could hide them in this plane from even Hova herself. Your cabin was but a small piece of my favorite garden, extracted to conceal you while we still could." She ended her tale abruptly, offering no further explanation for her involvement in my life until now as she began sipping her tea silently once more.

I just couldn't help myself—I retorted explosively. "That's it? What do you mean to conceal me? Conceal me from what? Whose side are you on? What is it you think I can even do for this world? I watched my cabin blow up. Was any of it real? Was what we had even real?" Everything came tumbling out all at once, and by the end of my tirade of questions, I had tears biting at the corners of my eyes, irritated at myself for hovering near the emotional edge again. *Get a fucking grip, Nato. Aren't you sick and tired of always being the victim?*

Eden's expression melted into a mixture of sympathy and regret, and she reached out, laying a soft wrinkled hand on my cheek adoringly as she cut straight to the core of what had me so upset. "My dear, of course what we had was real! You have been nothing less than a daughter to me. My *only* regret is that I didn't find you sooner. I searched relentlessly from the moment the spirits of nature told me you were back on this plane, yet someone powerful kept you from me despite my best efforts. We almost *didn't* find you. Eve used the last of her strength to connect us, and if it hadn't been for her sacrifice, I fear we would have lost you forever. I wish I could tell you what we were keeping you from. If I had answers to give, I would gladly do so. All I know is you needed time, and Eve said you needed as much time as I could give you, so I did what I could while I could." She dropped her eyes, staring into her steaming tea as tears pooled at the crinkled corners of her aging green eyes.

Devastated by her broken features, I flung myself across the table, nearly spilling our tea in the process as I wrapped my lanky, too-pale arms around her slightly hunched back. Dissolving into a blubbering mess, we both struggled to gush out unintelligible sentiments for each other over tears and soggy noses. It was honestly impressive to me that I even had anything left to cry, yet somehow more and more tears just kept coming as I released everything I had been holding on to for this entire miserable existence. All the fears, rejection, and lonely nights bubbled to the surface all at once and spilled out onto the floor at our feet, releasing me from its stifling grasp that had trapped me, barely able to breathe, for most of my life. The deluge of tears finally began to relent as we came to our senses, a massive smile spreading across my face as I felt genuine fullness for the first time in my life. Cradled in her feeble arms, I was finally home. Clearing her throat softly, Eden returned my smile as she stroked my hair, brushing a loose strand back into place.

"The cabin blowing up was a trick, a safety feature triggered by the attack that set off a well-played illusion so neither side would know of our involvement, theoretically giving us time to find you again. Believe me when I say I'm sorry for the pain I put you through. I hope you can understand now everything I did was to protect you the only way I knew how." Nodding my head compassionately, I collapsed into her embrace again, basking in her warmth. There was nothing she could do that I wouldn't forgive. I imagined that was what it must be like to love a mother. A spiteful chuckle interrupted our intimate moment from the doorway as a mocking voice caused me to jump to my feet, cheeks burning red, embarrassed to be caught in such a vulnerable position.

"Well, isn't this sweet? You finally found yourself a *mommy.*" Self-consciousness shifted rapidly to rage. What was her *problem?* Why did she always have to be so condescending?! Glaring at each other, Mia leaned casually against the doorway, adjusting her dreads piled on top of the crown of her head in a loose messy bun. She opened her mouth, most likely to harass me, but Eden abruptly cut her off.

"Lunch is ready! It's the perfect day for a picnic in the garden, don't you agree, ladies?"

With no room to argue, Eden quickly loaded us full of carved wooden trays of food, snacks, and drinks before leading our little caravan of colorful plates and delicious scents through the house and out the back door. Stepping onto the back stoop, I was greeted with a surreal sight, hundreds of plants sprawled across a sunken brick patio, every kind you could think of, from spiky cactus to bold blooming rose bushes, ivy crawling up the side of the house and even a cluster of small palm trees in the corner next to a large trellis covered in wisteria in full bloom, its bright, fragrant lavender-colored flowers shading an eclectic array of outdoor couches and loveseats around a large table draped in an extravagant geometric tapestry. Setting the collection of trays down on the table, I sat on one of the love seats as Eden sat across from me. Mia took the seat next to me again, annoyingly enough, especially considering all the empty seats available. She was smiling—*of course* she knew it was irritating me.

Eden began spreading the feast across the table, a collection of all my favorites. Baked brown sugar spiral ham smothered in gravy, chicken dumpling soup with the little homemade dumplings that I was obsessed with, steaming hot cabbage soup, bright red with the fresh tomato sauce sourced from the garden, roasted brussels sprouts covered in flakey parmesan cheese, potatoes cooked in any way you could imagine, fried, mashed, and roasted with the skins still on, transformed into a salad and even sliced into crispy chips, dips of every kind spread out next to chopped veggies, cheeses, and fruits, warm cookies, fresh from the oven, with even more of the tiny cakes and pies from earlier piled high next to a piping hot kettle of tea and a few pitchers of fruity colored wine. We passed away the afternoon lazily, gorging on the feast before us as we chased down the food with cup after cup of bright, fresh wine. The tension eased away as Mia and Eden chatted easily like old friends, laughing as they shared wild stories of their various adventures in this world. I couldn't help being enchanted, getting caught up in their cheer as the tales they spun got less and less feasible yet all the more wonderful.

As the plates cleared and the bottles emptied, Eden leaned back with an excited smile spreading across her content face, a twinkle in her green eyes. "Tonight is the Eve of Ostara. A time to reflect on new beginnings, light and dark come into balance once more as the seasons change and spring blooms eternal." Leaning forward, Eden began rummaging below the table, pulling out another carved wooden tray covered in ornate containers and an oddly familiar intricate clear rainbow glass pipe decorated in translucent crystals that sparkled in the late afternoon sun. It dawned on me that it reminded me of the cups from the Kingdom Keep.

"The Keep wasn't the only thing my mother mimicked. She took seeds from Hova's original garden to sow some of the rarest fruits and finest flowers in her secret gardens for generations to come." Eden opened up one of the ornate containers, iridescent, sparkling, and covered in shiny golden spirals. It revealed a stash of fluffy bright green buds covered in rich blue, purple, and pink hairs that shimmered slightly in the light trickling through the trellis. My eyes widened. I had done a lot of things with Eden over the years, but never something like this. It was hard to imagine the sweet little old lady I knew to always be busy baking away in the kitchen, getting high with me.

I couldn't suppress the shocked smile that erupted across my face as she leaned forward, handing me a large nugget to inspect. I took the bud in a daze as a small chuckle escaped my lips at the surreal situation I found myself in. Lifting the flower to my face, I inhaled the delicate sweet scent; the overwhelming fragrance made me feel high all by itself. Otherworldly notes filled my nose with an intoxicating mix of citrus, vanilla, and pine with a floral undercurrent I couldn't place. As I twisted the stem in my hand, the crystals on the herb sparkled, lighting my pale green eyes up with wonder, captivated by the kaleidoscope of colors. Eden loaded a small pearl-colored grinder with a couple of buds and began twisting the top before expertly packing the extravagant crystal bong. Lifting the pipe to her wise old face, she set the bowl on fire with an old-fashioned silver lighter carved with golden geometry, the fire lighting up her eyes as she ripped the entire hit in one deep breath. Mia and I both stared, mouths agape in utter amazement.

Billowing like a dragon, she released a massive cloud of iridescent smoke after holding her breath for several minutes without so much as a cough. A wrinkled grin spreading from ear to ear, she loaded the bong again before passing it to me. I accepted the crystal chalice with a small bow of my head, too stunned to speak as I tried to figure out if it was a trick of the light or if the smoke lingering in the air above her was actually shifting surreally through the spectrum. Sparking the lighter, the familiar bubbly draw of the bong was oddly soothing to me as I pulled the pillar of smoke up the tall pipe, exploding into my lungs, intensely sweet and relentlessly reaching for every small corner of my chest cavity as I took the deepest breath I could, determined to clear the bowl as effectively as Eden—my ego obviously still loved a challenge. Mia was watching me intensely, and it took everything in me to ignore her as I held the hit, the intense burning spreading rapidly through my chest, the sweet smoke slowly drowning me as my lungs demanded oxygen.

Falling short of Eden's impressive lung capacity, I gave in and released an, at the very least, equally large cloud, just as colorful as hers, shifting between blues, purples, pinks, yellows, and reds like a rainbow pool of watercolor paint. I stared transfixed by the display, certain now it was no trick of the light. It was like nothing I'd ever seen, even when smoking the high-quality herb Amil had offered. The little smoke show was nothing compared to the wave of intense euphoria already cascading over me, pushing me back into my seat as pure bliss spread over me in a thick blanket of warm golden light. Once again, my mind was heightened, processing all the small things around me, the wind blowing through the leaves of the wisteria trees as crickets chirped softly, a small army of ants marching a soft rhythm on the moist earth, and a nest of chicks chirping from a distant tree for a mother who didn't return their calls. However, my body was trapped, weighed down by the intense calm spreading through my limbs and slowing my heartbeat. Vaguely I was aware of Mia and Eden chuckling softly in the background as Eden handed her the chalice.

After several disorienting moments, I pushed myself up enough to catch the tail end of Mia's hit. She arched her shoulders as she tilted her head upward, parted her bright red and gold lips, and puffed out a series of perfect little smoke rings before blowing a stream of smoke directly through the rings. She turned to see my impressed expression and winked at me in a playful sort of way before rolling her eyes and turning back to Eden to hand her the pipe back, a small smile pulling at the corner of her mouth. She was such a perplexing creature but also painfully perfect, her back arching as she stretched her arms upwards, clearly relishing in the ripple of pleasure washing over her. Closing her eyes as she moaned softly, pushing her stretch to its full extent, the bones in her back snapped softly back into place. It reminded me of that gruesome scene in the woods when her bones were forced back together at my own hands, and the thought made me sick to the stomach.

Shaking my head to chase away the dark thoughts, I was instantly distracted by the weird trails in my vision. Light streams lingered behind everything as I moved my head. I blinked several times, trying to clear my vision. "Woah... What's happening?" Eden was giggling again as she leaned forward in her seat.

"Did I forget to mention fungi were another favorite of my mother's? She spent lifetimes perfecting strands, cross-breeding, and cultivating a flower that was one of a kind. Psychedelic in nature, potent and prophetic, this little plant packs a powerful punch while assuring a smooth ride. She considered it her masterpiece." Eden was smiling proudly, a sparkle of admiration in her wise old eyes as she reflected on the past. "Either way, it was the *only* way to celebrate our first Ostara." She looked at me with reverence. Was that pride in her eyes? "Come, child, follow me into the garden. Bring your little friend with you." She was already on her feet and twirling away toward an old iron gate on the side of the brick patio.

Mia immediately frolicked after her, locs bouncing behind her in a mesmerizing way as the light trails streamed after her in a blaze of red, blue, purple, and gold. Scoffing, I pushed myself up. I might be infatuated with this wild temptress, but a friend is the last thing I would call her. I knew better than to fall down the slippery slope of Stockholm syndrome, especially given the current circumstances. Not that I wasn't as down as the next girl for a mind-altering adventure, but it sure would have been nice for Eden to warn me she planned on dosing me; Mia was the last person I would have chosen to have this experience with, yet somehow here we were. Dragging my feet, I followed reluctantly in their path, stopping every few feet as I grew distracted by one delicate flower after the next. They all seemed to be singing little songs to me as fragrant clouds of pollen drew me closer, lingering just a bit longer with each flower I smelled.

Losing track of time, I wandered into a patch of rose bushes, yellow, red, and pink roses calling out to me in little bell voices as their fragrance wrapped its way around me, luring me into their grasp as thorny vines began creeping up my legs, twisting their way around my ankles, slowly engulfing me into the ground as more vines and roots began tugging at me, I was so captivated by the crescendo of their chorus I didn't even notice.

A mocking voice brought the symphony crashing to a halt. "Five minutes in, and we already nearly lost you. That doesn't bode well." Mia was hovering over me, a snide smirk twisting her beautiful features as she reached her hand out to me. Was she trying to help me? Odd. Noticing my predicament for the first time as I sunk another few inches into the ground, I decided to set my pride aside and accept her offer. Grasping her cool dark hand, she wrapped her long delicate fingers around mine in a surprisingly firm grip as she pulled, effortlessly lifting me from the earth in one try as the vines and roots ripped away from my feet, leaving me breathless as I landed on the solid ground next to her while the tattered roots screamed out angrily.

Expecting her to pull away, I gasped when she laced her fingers in mine, solidifying her grip on me with a small squeeze of her hand. "Wouldn't want you to wander off again now, would we?" With a grin, she dashed forward, dragging me along in her trail, utterly speechless. The colorful light trails coming off her dreads were overwhelming this close, and it was getting hard to keep my thoughts straight. Up close like this, I could see all the tiny golden beads intricately carved and twisted around her thick, soft dreads. Small white crystals were wrapped with wire around other strands, catching the light of the afternoon sun and shimmering softly; so many tiny objects scattered in her hair that it was like a small treasure trove, I couldn't help but wonder where they had come from. Had she collected them all by hand?

Tilting my head as I looked at this cat-like creature dragging me along, prowling even now as she chased after Eden, it was hard to imagine someone like her hunting for such trivial prey with all that power in those lean muscles poorly concealed by the silky golden sundress billowing behind her as she pushed ahead faster with those powerful legs. Surprisingly it was easy for me to keep pace with her despite the fact that I had never been much of an athlete prior, not that I couldn't hold my own if I needed. After all, it was no easy job taking care of a small farm, but you certainly wouldn't ever catch me running a mile just for the sake of it.

Pushing myself with each step, I gleefully explored the newfound strength in my legs. Was this an effect of the hallucinogens or a delayed effect of the awakening finally kicking in? Marveling over the mystery, I didn't notice Mia coming to an abrupt halt until I was already crashing into her, catapulting us both toward the ground in a tangle of tense laughter as the world whirled by in a frenzied blur.

CHAPTER 13 – NEVER KNOWS BEST

The afternoon passed in a haze as the clouds drifted slowly overhead. We had been finding all sorts of shapes and characters in the fluffy white clouds, piecing together stories that erupted into fits of giggles as one moment slipped into another. Eden had been with us for some time, and we had followed her deep into the maze of a garden, twisting and turning, the plants humming softly to us as we descended into their kingdom until we came upon a little grotto of blooming trees, plumerias of every color, white, pink, yellow and purple abundant on the branches. A few loose flowers drifted in the breeze, falling across the mossy ground next to the flowing stream in a breathtaking display. We had all collapsed among the flowers, listening to the symphony of the current and birds that had joined the soft serenades of the flowers, passing the hours by enjoying the warm sun and cool breeze. At some point, Eden had stood and insisted we stay and wait for her while she went to procure some drinks; however, some time had passed, and she still hadn't returned. I was beginning to suspect she had abandoned us to find our own way from here.

The dark rich hues of sunset were overtaking the previously pearly blue skies, vivid orange and pink clouds swirling among the twinkling stars that had started lighting up in the twilight sky. Fireflies came to life around us, sparkling like fallen stars from the heavens above. Pushing myself up from the warm mossy bed that had imprinted my shape over the hours, I looked on in wonder as the creek came alive with the setting sun, a bright luminescent glow radiating out of the turquoise waters as even more clusters of fireflies danced in time to nature's song above the flowing stream of liquid light.

Mesmerized, I couldn't resist the pull, the water was calling to me, and I had to answer; standing, I began pulling at the straps of my dress. A soft gasp pulled my attention momentarily back to the petite little girl curled up in the grass at my feet, all long gray strands of tangled hair and doe eyes that had a little too much sadness in them. She was nothing more than skin and bones, looking fragile, weak, and nothing like what I expected from the final Rider. Yet there was something to the curve of her cheeks, the arch of her back, at least when she wasn't slouching, and the spark of intelligence in those dead eyes, so hopeless but so curious, nonetheless. She was *fascinating*, an enigma of a girl, a puzzle calling my name.

"What are you doing?" Her thin gray eyebrows were raised as she looked at my hand, still lingering on the strap.

I grinned coyly as I shrugged. "What does it look like? Going for a swim, of course." In one smooth motion, I released the straps on both sides, and my dress dropped away, the soft silky fabric crumbling at my feet, leaving my chest bare and exposed, firm, supple breasts perked in the chill of the impending night, golden nipples and sprawling silver tattoos of an ancient scribe scrawled across my chest and shoulders. Bare-chested, you could see the full icosahedron carved in gold across my upper right breast, matching the various golden pentagonal geometric tattoos that cascaded down both my arms and down the sides of my rib cage, sprawling across my hips and down my legs, a lacy pair of golden yellow undies providing my only attempt at modesty. This time, her much more audible gasp sparked a fire in me, the coy grin erupting into a genuine smile at the burning blush bringing her deathly pale cheeks to life for the first time since I'd met her.

Resting my hands on my hips, I arched my back proudly, flaunting my toned figure unabashedly.

"Care to join me?" She stared at me for several minutes before stumbling over her words.

"How do you do that? How are you so sure of yourself?" Her numb green eyes searched mine desperately, looking for answers to questions I didn't quite understand.

"I am who I am." Shrugging softly, I continued flatly. "My place has always been clear to me. Mother drilled it into me from day one, after all." I turned, silently observing the stream before carrying on. "Things honestly actually haven't been so clear lately. It will work out, though. It always does. My instincts have yet to let me down."

Determination painted my features with a look of confidence and conviction as I turned back and reached out my hand. "You didn't answer my question, though. Join me, pretty please?" Her brows furrowed as she shook her head, the curtains of gray hair whisking in the wind, leaving trails of silvery light in their wake.

"Must be nice being so sure of yourself. I wouldn't know the feeling." Rolling her eyes, she grabbed my hand with an exasperated look as I lifted her easily to her feet in a single motion.

Awkwardly, Nato unclipped the straps and pulled the baggy legs of her destroyed overalls—something she had been rather confused yet overly delighted to find in Eden's closet earlier today —off one at a time. Stumbling slightly on the second leg, I caught her as her cheeks erupted bright red once more, mumbling apologies as she steadied herself. Stripping off her muted yellow tank, she stood in the moonlight in a basic matching olive set in soft cotton, wrapping her arms around her exposed body as she hunched slightly in on herself. She wasn't much of a presence at all, diminishing herself in every way, thin and boney, and those *eyes,* there was something off there, yet there was no denying that she was absolutely beautiful. She was like a porcelain doll with soft, symmetrical features and silky, flowing hair, even if it was always a bit of a mess. Reaching out, I placed my hand slowly on her cheek, just barely brushing it.

"You're one-of-a-kind, love. Stand up and be proud of who you are."

Unfolding, she arched her back as I pulled her chin up, closing the distance between us. Her eyes were burning with a ferocity I had never witnessed before, and a weight seemed to fall off her as a smile spread across her face.

"Shall we?" Pulling away from me, she suddenly skipped ahead, diving fearlessly into the waters headfirst, surfacing a few yards down where the stream pooled into slow-moving deep water at the edge of the grove. As I waded in slowly to join her, she moved with surprising grace through the water, slowly wading through the fields of lost plumerias and sparkling fireflies, waves of silvery hair swirling behind her, catching the moonlight, the soft glowing reflection of the water bouncing across her porcelain skin like an aurora borealis.

Mesmerized, I couldn't resist the pull anymore. I had been thinking about her lips on mine since the bar. I knew that no good would come of going down this path, but at this point, I didn't care what the consequences were. Maybe it was the psychedelics, but I knew what I wanted, and I knew before the night was over, I was going to have it. Once I had my prey in sight, there was no escape. Prowling forward, I dove into the bright waters, closing the distance between us in just a few strong strides before bursting to the surface, splashing her with a wave of water, sweet laughter tumbling out of those lips like church bells ringing; it made me want to worship at her temple.

Swimming in circles around her, I floated backward, letting

myself drift in the soft swirling current in the little pool. The weightlessness was a surreal feeling, and my skin crawled as I felt every drop of water touching it simultaneously. My dreads caught in the vortex pulled at my scalp, tickling my brain as the roots pulled beneath the surface, introspection overwhelming me as my senses became almost too much to bear. I drifted there for an immeasurable amount of time, aware that she joined me at some point, her soft, warm hand wrapped in mine so we could float, just barely connected as the tide carried us downstream ever so slowly. The waves of hallucinations seemed to be peaking as the stars and clouds morphed into elaborate displays above, folding and bending into each other to reveal an array of geometries I hadn't quite been able to decipher in my studies. As quickly as the answers formed, they slipped away again, my brain trying to store whatever bits and pieces it could cling to in my haze.

Time was passing in a strange series of sensations, the symphonies surrounding us reaching a crescendo as the river slowed to a crawl as we floated into another small lagoon, deeper and full of colorful fish and shiny iridescent rocks of every shape and size. Treading water again, we dove below the surface several times, chasing fish and trying to collect the coolest rock of the bunch before we ran out of breath and were laughing too hard to continue, the peaks of the trip spreading from my toes to my fingertips as an overwhelming sense of euphoria settled deep within me.

Instinctually, I closed the distance between us before I even had time to think about what I was doing. Suddenly, she was in my arms, my full fiery lips parting hers fiercely as my tongue searched hers out, pulling it out of its reluctant shell. One hand wrapping around her waist, one hand grasping her wet, tangled hair, I clutched her tight, pressing her soft body into mine as I kissed her harder, desperately searching for something she was holding back from me as her body became limp in my firm grasp.

Nato's eyes dropped as I pulled away, frustration furrowing my thick brows as I grabbed her face more intensely than I intended and forced her to look at me. "Spit it out. What's wrong?" Rolling her eyes for what must be the billionth time in the very short time we'd had together, her cheeks burned bright red as she defended herself stubbornly.

"I just don't want you to get the wrong idea, ya know." Laughing cruelly despite the echo of an ache in my heart at the pain in her eyes, I let go of her as I swam back a few feet, the tension between us palpable.

"You don't have to take everything so seriously, love. You *can* just have some fun, you know. I can *show* you how to have some fun." More laughter erupted out of me as she fumed, clearly unamused by my sense of humor as she furthered the distance between us. "Of course, if it's that important to you—if this is a matter of *virtue* or something—I could always get down on one knee right now."

My eyes were smoldering as I savored the words, casting them out like a lure as I taunted her with my offer, watching a series of strange emotions play across her green eyes before they turned dead and hostile again.

"*Very* funny, Mia. Absolutely hilarious." Swimming off in the opposite direction, I grinned as I chased after her; a single rejection was far from enough to stop me once I was in pursuit. *Consider the challenge accepted, love.*

Dripping, Nato walked slowly, dragging her feet in the sand as she made her way up the sloping beach and onto the sprawling field of wildflowers, ringing the water out of her hair as she followed a small stony path to a large patchwork quilt spread out beneath a massive apple tree, covered in fresh fruit ripe for the picking. Following her, I spotted a large picnic basket next to the base of the tree, filled with fresh clothes, food, and more pitchers of the fruity wine we had enjoyed with Eden that afternoon at the lunch party that now felt like a lifetime ago. I pulled on the soft, flowing white dress, a simple rayon gown, intricate straps crossing into a pentagon on the exposed chest, the soft fabric draping all the way to the ground. Depositing the only wet garment that had survived the trip with me, the dainty golden panties, back into the basket, I replaced my soaked undergarments with the matching white cotton panties I had found in the basket before I turned and offered Nato the other outfit from the bag, bowing as I averted my eyes to allow her to shred her soaking undergarments in privacy before she slipped into the flowing black dress identical to mine. Reaching out for her discarded clothes, she dropped her eyes as she handed me the garments. Stuffing them into the basket, I pulled out a container of cakes and a bottle of wine and began pouring two wooden cups to the brim as we settled into the plush quilt.

Slowly, I got her to open up to me. The tiny things came out one by one, like her favorite color, a rich golden yellow that reminded her of the sun right before it set, what she had wanted to be growing up, anything that got her out of the system, she said, but after further probing, she wanted to write children's books—she insisted it seemed pretty stupid now. She told me where she had always dreamed of living, visions of Hawaii life inspired by commercials as a small child; it seemed as far away as you could be from the rest of the world. From there, she spoke of darker things, like the horrors of growing up in the system, a series of abusive and negligent foster parents in what seemed almost surreally unlucky, searching unsuccessfully for her parents for years, how she met Eden by chance at a rainy bus stop in Portland, her beloved farm and its unlikely fall and rise, thanks to magical intervention. She even shared a bit about Amil, though she appeared to move on from that topic as quickly as possible, stuttering over her words momentarily.

It was oddly interesting dissecting this insignificant little creature who somehow held the future of the entire planet in her hands. I was amazed by how forthcoming she was, most likely compelled to share a bit too much, thanks to Eden. I honestly couldn't have asked for better luck, and I wouldn't get another opportunity like this. There was something there, though, that she was holding back. I could see it in the way she hesitated when she reached certain parts of her stories, eyes cold and hard only for a moment before she would carry on with the slightest pitch difference in her voice. It would be hard to catch if you weren't listening close, but it was there, nonetheless. After a long time, she finally ran out of stories; a silence settled upon us as her eyes locked on the cup in her hand, nearly empty. She stared pensively into the small pool of red liquid, moonlight shining bright on her silvery hair, casting a glowing aura around her head.

Leaning forward, I grabbed her face again, softer this time as I lifted her eyes to mine, crushing her under the full weight of my smoldering golden eyes, the purple ring around my iris pulsating again as I called forth the powers of persuasion I had been holding back from her. An oozing aura radiated off of me and wrapped its way around her with its invisible arms. I could see she was crumbling already, cheeks burning as she bit her lip hesitantly. I poured my words on her like honey, heavy and sweet.

"I want to kiss you." She swallowed hard, afraid to look away. She was trapped, and I already knew I had her. "May I?"

With the smallest nod of her head, I was already on top of her, pressing my lips into hers as they parted with ease this time, inviting me in as her tongue fought against mine, matching my force, hungry and searching for more as I pushed her harder into the ground. My hands caressed her body, exploring the curves of her breasts under the soft layers of fabric, brushing the soft, warm, pale skin of her exposed arms, twisting my cold fingers in the silky folds of her hair as I pulled her even closer, consumed by her completely.

The warmth of her skin on my cold hard body was electrifying, sparking through my bones and igniting a fire in me as her dress rode up and more of her flesh pressed against me, passion pushing me over the edge as my tongue thrashed relentlessly against hers. Clutching the edge of the long black gown, I pulled it up slowly, brushing her leg as I lifted the fabric up her ghostly white thighs, shivering in the cool night air. A soft gasp escaped her as I bit her lip, pulling away ever so slightly to savor her eyes rolling back as my hand lightly brushed the exposed skin of her inner thigh. Tracing the curves from her shallow stomach to her small, firm breasts with my thin fingers, she didn't seem to notice that I had her dress nearly off before I was suddenly pulling her up to lift it past the final threshold of her still-damp head of hair. Gasping loudly, she crashed back to the blanket, an intense shudder rippling through her body, exposed and glowing in the bright full moon. Carnal instincts overcame me as I pounced, planting sweet kisses across her skin, hands tracing patterns across her bare skin as she arched into me, putty in my more than capable hands.

Running my fingers along the elastic of the simple black underwear that stood as the only barrier between us now, she shot up suddenly, startling me as I nearly fell backward in my rush to push off of her to give her enough space to sit up, confusion already furrowing my red brows. "What's wrong *now*, love?" My voice was thick with irritation. I was sure I was reading all the signals right. I had yet to let a lover down; why was she denying herself this experience when I knew it was what she wanted? She didn't owe that angel anything. Would she really hold back at a time like this for his sake? They barely even knew each other; from what I'd seen, that kiss had nothing on ours. Nato's face dropped, eyes dark with shame as her cheeks burned brighter than they had all night. Was that a tear? Was she really crying right now? Tilting her chin back up softly, I looked at her, compassion melting my hard features as my irritation instantly gave way to worry and concern. "Seriously. You can tell me anything."

Tears swelled over her doe eyes as she burst into a sobbing mess, stumbling over her words as she gushed out gargled apologies. "Sorry, it's not you. It's me. I just… It's just, I've never been with someone like that, not willingly anyway." Pulling her chin back, her twinkling eyes dulled as a cloud of guilt shadowed her previously glowing aura. A swell of emotions consumed me, cascading across me in waves of anger more intense than I had ever expected, hands clenching as I envisioned crushing the person responsible for her pain. Heart breaking at the sad sight of this lost little girl, shaking softly as she wrapped her arms around herself, my anger melted away instantly into a sea of sympathy. Reaching out, petting her hair softly, I tamed several stray strands back into place before wiping away the stream of tears from her eyes. They flickered up at me, uncertain and full of caution, clearly uncomfortable being exposed and vulnerable as she bared her deepest darkest secrets to someone who should be her enemy.

"You deserved better, Nato." I wiped away more tears before grabbing her hands in mine, pulling them up to my lips as I planted soft kisses along her arms, pulling the twinkle back into her eyes that I had seen spark to life for the first time tonight. I didn't want to admit to myself how important it already was to me that those eyes never dim again.

"I can't change the past, and neither can you. The future is yours to take, though. He doesn't control that anymore. I can show you how if you want. I can show you what that night should have been like." Her eyes were locked on mine, processing my offer sluggishly as a million emotions danced across those sparkling green eyes. "It's your choice. I'm all yours if you want, but *only* if you want me."

Locked in a silent debate, I held my breath feeling exposed myself, something I was not used to, honestly, as I sat on the edge, awaiting her next move. After what felt like a lifetime, she unfroze, slowly lifting her porcelain hand to my face, barely touching the skin of my cheek as her hand brushed past my eyes, catching a loc of my dreads and tucking it behind my ear. Her eyes fixed on mine, unblinking as she moved forward with intention and purpose, closing the gap between us as I continued to hold my breath, the anticipation making my skin crawl.

Her hesitation evaporated instantly as her lips pressed into mine, lighting an all-consuming fire between us. She pushed forward, slamming me into the ground with a surprising amount of force as she parted my lips and released her inhibitions. Relenting to her controlling posture, my hands rode up her thighs, grabbing her hips and pulling her closer to me, moving with her body in submissive synchronicity as her hands and mouth explored my temple freely. Struggling with the tangled folds of my gown, clearly not as well-versed in the expert removal of a girl's dress as I was, I stifled a giggle as I lifted her unexpectedly off of me, dropping her back down on the quilt as I tore off the garment in one flick of the wrist.

Closing in on my prey, the buzz of victory hummed through my bones as I planted kisses across her torso, inching my way closer to her panty line as I began tugging off the last barrier to the final frontier as soft moans ushered me onward. My chest was nearly exploding as my heart thudded erratically. Tossing her underwear aside, I paused, gasping softly at her breathtaking beauty in the moonlight, stretched out and looking at me with an expression I had never seen before, smoldering green eyes that I wanted to dive into and never resurface from, lost in their sea for all of eternity. More than anything, I wanted to make her scream, I wanted my name coming out of those perfect pink lips, and before the night was over, she wasn't just screaming my name. I was screaming hers.

CHAPTER 14 – FAIRYTALES & FESTIVALS

Birds chirping in the distance, I opened my eyes slowly, squinting in the cool gray light of the predawn morning. A handful of fireflies lingered, still sparkling across the field of flowers, making the most of the last moments before the sun broke the horizon and flooded the land with her glorious light. Her chest moved softly beneath my hand, steady with still-sleeping deep breaths. I studied her features in the muted light, tracing the round lines along her face, usually so tense, relaxed in her slumber. Her smooth mocha skin gave way to deeply contrasting gold features scattering across her body, decorated like a work of art from head to toe, her soft red and blue dreads sprawled around her head in a halo of driftwood flames, red and gold lips moving ever so slightly as she mumbled in her sleep. Conflicted, I gingerly moved the arm she had wrapped around me and pushed myself up slowly, scooting away from her and searching the semi-darkness for my discarded gown.

Upon finding it, I slipped it on and rushed silently down to the water's edge, collapsing in a heap as I stared down at the girl looking back at me in the bioluminescent glow of the dawn-drenched water. Obviously, true to my inherent nature, I went off and did the exact thing I set out not to do. It was like I wanted to suffer; I wanted to ruin everything every chance I got. Clearly, it was not just some terrible course of events happening to me in life but rather a series of seriously questionable behavior that led to most of my misfortune. What had I been thinking last night? I mean, it was amazing, more than amazing in fact, it was magical in every way possible and more than I could have ever expected, and that was exactly the problem. I was in too deep; I was absolutely in over my head. How did I let this happen? Why did I let this happen? Shaking my head, a few tears bit at the corners of my eyes, confusion overwhelming me as I scooped a handful of cold water and splashed it on my face several times over, washing away the regrets and remorse.

A soft voice behind me nearly sent me tumbling into the water, save for her grabbing me just in time, twirling me around effortlessly in her powerful grasp as she pulled me in close to her still naked body, sleepy golden eyes smoldering me as a coy smile crept across her face.

"After a night like that, you'd think I'd at least deserve a good morning. Rude to run off like that." She pouted her lip out, exaggerating a look of hurt as she batted her eyes at me playfully. Even knowing it was a ruse, it was irresistible. Standing on my tiptoes, I kissed her once, soft and sweet, before pulling away, my cheeks burning fiercely as my eyes bore into hers intensely.

"Last night was everything you promised and then some, it was a gift I'll always cherish, and for that, I thank you." Bowing my head, she exploded into a fit of laughter before answering.

"Oddly formal, but sure. It was my pleasure."

Still chuckling slightly, she held my gaze a moment longer, hand still lingering on my waist before she turned, lumbering back to the informal campsite to, I could only hope, find her clothes and cover-up that terribly tempting temple. Turning back to the water, I took a few deep breaths, in and out, in and out, releasing the troubles of the past and clearing my mind so I could see the path forward. I became aware of a series of small vortexes of energy that I could suddenly sense within me, pooling along the endocrine system of my body, moving at will as I focused on them with each breath I took, directing the energy to flow freely from one synod to the next in a spectrum of energetic colors playing within my mind's eye. Minutes or hours could have passed as I shifted the internal spheres of energy, tuning my body into the harmony of nature, synchronizing with the symphony the flowers still sang as the sun rose on a new day and the final effects of the psychedelic herb faded away.

Opening my eyes, I saw the sun had fully risen, blanketing the land in her warmth, greeting the creatures of the earth with a new day of life. I took one last exaggerated breath, holding it as long as I could before I let go of everything that had transpired and cleared myself of what had been blocking my path forward. Standing silently behind me, I could feel Mia's eyes on me, watching me with those intense golden orbs that always seemed to be calculating the answer to a problem I couldn't even see. Pushing away the feeling of self-consciousness I felt in her presence after revealing myself in every way possible to her in the heat of the night, I walked past her without making eye contact as I headed back to the apple tree. Mia had already collected the remnants from our night shared here under the stars, folded and packed neatly in the basket, much like my feelings after the mediation by the river. Two freshly picked apples sat on top, perfectly ripe and oozing with a temptingly sweet smell. I presumed she intended to share them, and I smiled despite myself. Picking up the basket, I turned to find her directly behind me. Damn, how did she move so silently? It was unnerving, to say the least. I was seriously considering getting her a little cat collar with a bell at this point. She fit the bill, after all; a pair of cat ears, and I'd be convinced she was a genuine feline.

Reaching out, I handed her one of the bright yellow apples dotted with blotches of red. She accepted it with a toothy grin as she bit into the crisp, fleshy fruit, and it exploded with fragrant juice as she tore a massive chunk off, chomping down a quarter of the apple in one powerful bite. Eyes wide in shock at the ferocious display, I began nibbling on my own apple in tiny bites as she stomped ahead of me, gleefully swallowing the apple up in just a few more oversized bites as I followed behind, savoring the surreal little apple, popping with a delightfully sweet array of exciting flavors that changed with each bite. As I reached the end of what was hands down the best apple of my life, perhaps the best piece of fruit, really, I noticed Mia slowing her pace. Lifting my head to investigate, I spotted a large wooden yellow door, arched and ornate with one of those large vintage knockers in the center and a series of carved geometric shapes highlighted with silvery white paint flowing like liquid. The door stood completely alone and appeared to go nowhere.

Fearlessly, Mia stepped forward, knocking an intricate song into the door using the vintage knocker before pushing it open. I expected to see the other side of the path, but as the door swung open, it began pulling at the very fabric of reality, twisting and turning it into a bright electric blue glow as it spiraled into itself, creating a portal before us. Bold as ever, she reached back, grabbing hold of my hand before putting one foot in front of the other as she ventured into the unknown, towing me hesitantly in her wake. The swirling liquid lava was cool and porous, like jello against my skin, pressing and pulling against me as it tore me apart into a million pieces before building me back together again on the other side, square in the middle of Eden's elaborate kitchen—a different one than the tiny replica in my humble house that had been swallowed up by her sprawling eclectic mansion, wafting with the smells of freshly baked bread, bacon, and a menagerie of breakfast delights. I was relieved to find I was growing accustomed to this form of travel and could keep my uneasy stomach at bay now with some effort.

Turning toward us with a tray full of freshly baked cinnamon rolls, a massive smile erupted across the wrinkled features of Eden's face, reaching all the way to her twinkling green and gold eyes. "Good morning, ladies. Welcome home!" She brushed past us in a flurry as she stepped out onto the open patio, basked in the glowing morning sun, placing the tray of food down before bustling back inside. "Sorry we had to part ways last night. I had a feeling you were better off without me." An all-knowing grin crept across her face as my eyes dropped to the ground, my cheeks burning again.

Mia placed her hands on her hips, a proud smile shining on her face. She seemed to be beaming, a great sense of accomplishment oozing off of her. "Can I help you, Eden?" Dropping her victory stance, she stepped forward, grabbing several trays of fresh fruit, bread, bacon, and eggs, balancing them expertly as she followed Eden back outside. I followed after with a few pitchers of fresh squeezed orange juice, dragging my feet along the way, regret creeping its way back under my skin. It was an ugly feeling that left me suddenly intensely aware of how much I needed a shower.

Stepping out onto this new garden, I was greeted with an Asian-inspired oasis, equipped with everything from pagodas to happy little Buddha statues, arching bridges over rippling creeks, pounding a soft rhythm out on the large moss-covered river rocks, and even a sprawling Zen Garden in the corner, perfectly raked and in pristine order. Cherry blossom trees in full bloom painted the sky with bright pinks, a slow flow of flowers cascaded to the garden floor with each passing breeze, the songs of birds native only to China filling the air despite me being fairly certain we were somewhere in Europe. Turning around, I was able to grasp the full scale of the house for the first time, a massive collection of sprawling eclectic windows stacked haphazardly one on top of the next all the way up the side of the crumbling Victorian-style architecture of the east-facing wall. Commanding towers of faded brick framed all four corners of the house, wrapped in ivy all the way to their peaks so high up that just looking at them from this angle made my stomach queasy.

Wandering away from the idle chat of Mia and Eden, I found myself taking a small stone path around the west end of the remarkably high patchwork mansion. It was there I found a small piece of familiar landscape as my stone cottage came into view, a minuscule microcosm attached to the macrocosm that was Eden's home, with the sunken plant-filled brick patio that had never been a part of my small home before. Tiny white trimmed windows and a round yellow door, the patchwork of animals sprawling across the open pastures, unfamiliar sprawling mountains, and a sprawling city of ancient architecture, still sparkling in the morning light with a thousand string lights and colored festival flags waving in the morning breeze, mere flecks of color in the sky at this distance—it was all so familiar yet so different at the same time. Oddly enough, I found the background somehow completed the picture in a way I would have never expected yet always imagined, somewhere in forgotten dreams. Following the trail back to the Asian garden gathering, I paused, staring at the women before me, a mother I never thought I'd have and a girl I never truly could have, paired with a fate I still didn't quite understand; I was finding it to be a really weird time to be alive.

Reluctantly I joined them at the table; natural as ever, they chatted away, Mia often making obnoxious innuendos as she glanced at me, a smug grin crawling across her face each time, sometimes winking, sometimes sticking her tongue out in a playful manner. Intent on resisting the urge to rise to her taunts, I spent the morning rolling my eyes and, at times, straight up ignoring her as intentionally as possible as I snacked on the various breakfast delights before me and engaged in delightful conversations with Eden about her incredible garden. I drilled her about her knowledge of every plant, herb, fungi, and tree I could remember from my incredible journey the night before, at least before Mia had distracted me, trying to dissect millennia of botanical information in a matter of hours as the sun passed idly in the sky. Eden indulged me for some time before pausing with a very serious look, her eyes darkening as she leaned forward in her ornamental chair, satin and covered in embroidered flowers. Following her gaze, I noticed a massive boa constrictor, iridescent scales shifting through the spectrum of the rainbow as it crawled slowly toward us, creeping its way inch by inch up Eden's chair, its muscles moving surreally under its smooth, silky skin as it wrapped its way casually around Eden. It rested its head on Eden's shoulder before looking directly at me and flickering its tongue several times over.

"You're right, Lilith. It is time. We must prepare for the festival. Ostara is a sacred time when the light and the dark come together to birth new life. Today we gather and repent for our shadows and rejoice for our souls. There is an ancient tale that the light and dark will meet upon the spectrum, igniting a new dimension of understanding and opening the path of redemption for us all. We come together every year to remember this prophecy and to open the collective consciousness so we may be ready to receive such a blessing, aligning ourselves for the new age of awakening.

"My mother devoted her whole existence to teaching as many of her children this as possible with the hope that one day we would find you and we may stand by your side as you bring forth the new world. Come with me and dance the night away. Let us give our minds, bodies, and souls to the spirits above and rejoice in her vision finally coming to life, even if she isn't here to see it." She spoke with such certainty in her voice, tainted with the smallest amount of sadness at the end.

Rising with all-knowing confidence and authority, there was no option but to follow, even for Mia, whom I hadn't seen obey so quickly the entire time I'd known her. Leaving behind a scattered table of half-eaten dishes, I noticed from the corner of my eyes that several of my animals, and even a few I didn't know, were creeping up to the table to have their way with the leftovers as we followed Eden back inside and into the bedrooms at her direction, leading me to my familiar room before guiding Mia off to the main part of the house.

Finding myself alone in another strange, expansive closet, deceptively larger than I could have ever guessed from the outside door in my room and nothing like I remember it being when I used to live here, I was surrounded by an obnoxious number of elaborate gowns made of silks, satins, cashmere, and lace. Dresses that stretched on for miles, and ones that sparkled with a million diamonds, layers of lace cascading one upon the next, creating elaborate bell shape skirts contrasted with laced corset bodices. If a girl could dream it, she could find it here—if you were that type of girl, which I just was not. Never being one to dress up in more than baggy jeans and chucks, I was overwhelmed by the alarmingly large collection of clothes, unsure where to even start, and already considering curling back up in my comfortable overalls and avoiding this whole adventure together. I had never been one for crowds and had never been to many festivals growing up; I just didn't see their appeal at this point in my life, all things considered. Paired with the current atmosphere globally, I couldn't even imagine it was worth it; you would have thought they would cancel such a large gathering, yet I could only assume Eden must be behind it somehow.

Bleakly staring at my surroundings, a soft cough caused me to jump several feet in the air, a burst of laughter turning my cheeks a bright red as I whipped around to see Mia leaning casually against the doorframe of the closet.

My words came out harsher than I really intended. "Don't you have your *own* closet? I'm fairly certain Eden showed you off for a reason. Last night didn't mean anything, so I'd appreciate a bit of space if you don't mind." My own anxieties were making me snappy, and I instantly regretted my harsh words as a dark look crossed Mia's eyes momentarily before a tight smile spread across her face as she pushed forward, unabashed.

Her voice was soft and coy, throwing her hands up in defeat. "Hey, I get it. I just figured you could use a hand getting dressed, no offense, but you don't seem like the most fashion-forward person to me, and I didn't want you going to the festival looking a hot mess."

My cheeks burned even brighter as my eyes dropped, and I gestured for her to proceed, tongue-tied and unable to come up with a good defense to her rather true accusation.

Filtering through the clothes with ease and expertise, she pulled out several gowns—a long draping silvery gown sparkling in the dim closet light, a short frilly, pale blue gossamer teacup dress, a slim-fitting pink number covered in a million embroidered flowers and trails of silk. Each item she held up toward me, looking at me with one eye closed like an artist trying to compose the perfect canvas with each dress.

After a moment of debate, she shook her head excitedly. "No, not this one either!" She joyfully put each dress back as she searched for a new one, like a kid in a candy store.

I had never seen her having quite so much fun over such a trivial activity. I couldn't quite piece together this strange creature in front of me and what really motivated her, what inspired her, and what brought her soul to life. Every time I thought I understood, I found myself questioning everything I knew about her, which, to be fair, I guess was very little after all. As she pranced around, pulling out what felt like a million and one gowns, unsatisfied with every single one, it began to take a small hit on my confidence. Maybe the problem wasn't the dresses; maybe the problem was me. There was a reason I hid in overalls and oversized sweaters my whole life; I knew this body was nothing worth showing off, and I honestly had little desire for anyone to look at me anyway. After all, I got enough strange looks thanks to my standout nearly white hair and these dead green eyes.

Spiraling suddenly again, I couldn't help but wonder, had my emotions always been this out of control? I was never one for much composure, but lately, it felt like all I did was cry as if all this negative energy was trying to purge itself out of my body, but I had a never-ending well of defeat and depression that seemed like it would never stop gushing. Suddenly Mia popped up in front of me, catching me off guard as she yanked me out of my dismal thoughts, her eyes sparkling as she clutched a sheer forest green floor-length gown glimmering with embroidered gold geometry swirling in and out of the shimmering dark green folds of fabric that billowed out at the waist, a ribbon of gold laced up the tight-fitting pale green satin corset covered in tiny gold and silver embroidered flowers giving way to billowing sheer sleeves that sparkled like the night sky on a moonless night. It was the single most beautiful piece of clothing I'd ever seen, and I couldn't even *begin* to picture myself in it.

"This is the one!" She was beaming with sheer unabashed joy as she held it up against my body, already pulling my hair up with her spare hand, her eyes calculating as she seemed to be envisioning all the ways she could pull and prod me apart and put me back together again into someone I wouldn't recognize, someone I could only pretend to be.

Suddenly setting down the dress, she was pulling my face

up to hers again. These goddamn mood readers were really inconvenient sometimes. "Listen, love, you're not a fraud. You're a flower, closed up so tight that no one can see you as anything more than a weed waiting to be plucked. With a little water, though, you can blossom, and when you do, you'll be the most beautiful girl in the room. I can keep telling you how spectacular you are, but you have to believe it before it will ever actually be true."

She held my gaze for several seconds; it felt like lifetimes, my cheeks were burning, and my skin was crawling. I didn't like the calculating look in her eyes. It made my insides squirm as I anxiously waited for her to finish whatever internal debate was going on behind those intimidating eyes. With a soft sigh, she suddenly released me, turning her back to me as she strolled across the closet and to the small bag I hadn't noticed she'd brought in with her. Silently she shuffled through the sack for several minutes before finally producing a small glint of ivory that she twirled in her hands thoughtfully as she turned back toward me, closing the distance between us in a few committed strides.

"I made this a long time ago. I thought it was for someone else, and I was clearly wrong. I think I actually made it for you…" Her usually fierce eyes had dropped to the ground, something soft was hiding there, and she didn't want me to see it. "I don't want it to be weird or anything. I don't expect it to mean anything. It just is what it is. I've never questioned my intuition before, so I surely shouldn't start now."

She took another step forward. Unconsciously I held my breath as she reached out to me, holding a small, intricately carved ivory octopus covered in swirling gold geometry. She hesitated, her voice softer than I had ever heard it. Was that a tinge of nervousness I detected? "May I?"

Stunned into speechlessness, I bobbed my head softly like an idiot and turned, nearly tripping over my own feet in my haste. I could see her in the full-length mirror as she draped the necklace over my head and around my neck, expertly fastening the small intricate clasp in one easy snap as she avoided making eye contact in the mirror.

I opened my mouth to thank her, yet only screams came pouring out as searing pain erupted, blinding light whiting out the small room as a new tattoo erupted, burning white hot against my flesh as an octopus sprawled its way to life across my back, settling into a new tattoo.

CHAPTER 15 – PANDORA'S BOX

After a bunch of fussing and fidgeting, Mia had forced me into the confines of the elaborate dress, pushing me toward a sprawling vanity covered in more makeup, perfumes, and odd-looking hair tools than I'd ever seen in my life. As I struggled not to trip over all the layers of sheer sparkling fabric, she pushed me onto an oversized mustard yellow stool in front of a massive Victorian-style mirror surrounded by oversized white lights. She began pulling the silk ribbons harshly, one at a time, a small gasp of air escaping my lips with each tug as she tightened the old-fashioned boned corset, the top pressing against the raw skin of my shoulder blades where my new tattoo was shiny and tender.

I caught her grinning in the mirror and couldn't help but be irritated. She was treating me like some kind of Barbie doll—this was all a game to her, and she enjoyed making me hurt, probably a lot more than she enjoyed pleasing me. Memories from the night before came rushing back to me as my cheeks flushed. It didn't escape Mia's attention, yet she was silent, a weird look crossing her face as my eyes dropped. Barely touching me, Mia gathered my hair at the base of my neck, sending a shockwave of shivers down my spine that I knew must be noticeable. I kept staring at the ground as she began pulling a brush through the tangled mess so softly that I could barely feel the knots falling apart.

Without a word, she smoothed my matted strands, running her fingers through my hair to fish out any final tangles before she began rubbing my head, moving her fingers in soft circles that finally pulled my gaze up as I unconsciously leaned into her, mesmerized by her whisper-soft touch, clearly much to her amusement as a soft chuckle broke the tension between us. "It loosens your roots, so your hair goes up easier, but I'll keep in mind that you're a fan in the future."

Winking, she moved to brush my hair once more as I rolled my eyes before she began expertly pulling and twisting my silver strands a million different ways. Twirling and tying for what felt like a lifetime, pin after pin plucked into my head at every angle before she finally relented and turned to raid the endless stash of makeup in the vanity, Mia grabbed just a small handful of items as she playfully collapsed into my lap, leaning in close. "You're a natural beauty, so pulling that out won't take much." Blushing even harder than ever before at her compliment, I felt like my cheeks must be on fire. "Plus, you certainly don't need to apply any blush with me around, apparently." I rolled my eyes again.

She just couldn't help herself. Chuckling, she began painting a few splashes of eyeliner, a dash of mascara, a bit of muted dark red lipstick, and a sheer gold sparkling eyeshadow that shimmered as brilliantly as the dress. After what felt like an hour, she finally hopped off my lap, her eyes gleaming as she held her hands out, presenting her masterpiece to me with the pride of a true artist.

Leaning forward, I barely recognized the girl staring back at me there. My usually lank, tangled strands were twisted into the most elaborate set of braids I had ever seen, twirling in and out of each other on top of my head in impossible ways, just the right number of loose strands falling in my face to frame my too shallow cheeks. My dead eyes had come to life with a few well-placed dark lines and a million sparkling golden galaxies on my eyelids, shining life into my green eyes in a way I'd never seen before. Was it all just the makeup that had my eyes twinkling? Full parted lips pulled up at the corners as I smiled at myself in an unfamiliar way, a weird burning sensation spreading in my chest. Was this pride? Overcome with wonder, I spent several moments admiring myself and the new shiny white and gold geometric tattoos lacing up my arms and now sprawling across my back. Finally, I stood, taking several steps back from the stool to twirl like a little girl playing dress up, giggling as the folds of fabric swirled around me. Mia broke my concentration with a soft hand placed on my shoulder. Looking down at me with those smoldering golden eyes, she placed a hand on my face, pulling it up toward her.

"Now you see what I see." I don't know what overcame me, and I don't know what I was thinking. I knew this needed to be over; I knew I shouldn't be doing this. I was definitely not doing this. I was *not* doing this. Goddamn it. I *was* doing this. My lips were suddenly on hers, hard and fast, craving so much more from her, an encore of a night that should have never been, and she matched me in every way possible, pushing me against the wall as her lips parted mine and her tongue twisting wildly, hungry and pushing for more. Pulling her closer, I wanted it all. I wanted everything I shouldn't have; I wanted *her*, which was a fucking problem.

Breaking away from me, it felt like my soul was shattering as she pulled away suddenly, a cruel smile spreading across her face. "So last night meant nothing, yeah?" Abruptly she turned away, marching out of the closet and off to her own room, leaving me panting, breathless, confused, and frustrated.

I walked out to the kitchen, and Eden had, as always, put out an elaborate spread. How she was endlessly baking so much food honestly seemed to defy physics. Having picked at my breakfast, I waited for my odd companions to join me, fortunate for Mia's foresight on my oblivious nature with an unbelievably waterproof lipstick.

As I stared idly out the window, gazing at the garden, a shadow caught my eye, rippling in the air like a mirage before scattering across the small creek, creating a series of ripples as it shimmered across the surface. Pushing myself up from the table, I grabbed handfuls of my elaborate dress and dashed out the door as quickly as possible, yards of sparkling fabric billowing after me in my haste. Reaching the water's edge, I began picking my way through a tightly knit group of flowering bushes, blooming in all the colors of the rainbow and rich with a delicious fragrance, yet dreadfully hard to navigate as the folds of my dress caught on every stray branch. It was no wonder women couldn't get anything done back in the day; these outfits were the furthest thing from functional.

Pushing and pulling, a loud rhythmic thudding ahead of me, like the hoofs of a racing horse, was calling out to me from the waters rippling just past the thicket. With a final desperate tug, I stumbled out of the brush, my dress somehow unscathed, searching desperately for the source of the sound. A small waterfall up ahead was pouring into the pool of water feeding the stream that led to the arching oriental bridge I had left behind, trickling over the rocks with a soft roar as it fed the land with rich, vibrant life. Noticing a small worn pathway leading behind the waterfall, I rushed forward, the call growing louder the closer I got to the waterfall. I gathered my dress up again as I crept along the small pathway behind the splashing raging waters, basically ruining any efforts to keep my dress dry as I dropped the layers in defeat and used my hands to better balance. I hurried forward on the narrow path to the source of the sound. The thudding was growing so loud I could feel it in my heart, beating out a familiar rhythm, pushing me onward, faster across the rocky slopes, when suddenly my foot twisted in a fold of the billowing fabric. I attempted desperately to recover on the slick rocks when gravity overtook me, and I slipped, cascading into the full force of the waterfall.

Crashing into the torrent of gushing water below, my body slammed into a cropping of rocks, stars exploding across my blurred eyes as the darkness tried to overtake me. I fought against it, invigorated by the unbearably loud thudding emanating from a small glowing box at the center of the cove. If I had been smart, if I was thinking clearly and hadn't just smashed my head into a pile of rocks, perhaps I would have thought to go to the surface and get air first, but my body was already propelling me forward, desperate to find out what was calling out to me. Dragging along in the water, weighed down by the layers and layers of fabric, a clear indication that I would be avoiding clothing like this ever again in my life, it felt like it took me a lifetime to reach my goal—a small pearl-colored elaborate geometric box with no clear opening. The thudding was deafening the closer I got, and it shook my entire body as I reached out my trembling hand to pull it free from its rocky grave.

As I touched it, the noise suddenly stopped completely, and an eerie quiet settled over the deep pool, the distorted underwater roar of the waterfall nearly silent comparatively. Mesmerized and possibly suffering from a mild concussion, I spent several valuable moments puzzling over the perplexing, odd-shaped box before realizing I should be well on my way toward the surface as my lungs began seizing, demanding air suddenly and fiercely. Kicking off from the ground for an extra start, I began desperately flailing my arms and legs as fast as I could as I pushed against the weight of my dress and the darkness trying to crawl into the edges of my eyes as the oxygen in my body depleted. It didn't seem this deep from the surface, and I didn't really think I had swum that far down. Why was it taking so long to get to the top? Why didn't I start swimming right away? What was I... What was I... The blackness was overcoming me; I wasn't going to make it—all this way, and I was going to drown because of a stupid dress. Oh, the irony. Darkness swallowed me whole as I drifted to the depth below.

Drifting. I was drifting in a white light, surrounded by reassuring warmth and peaceful in a way I'd never experienced before, as if nothing could ever go wrong again. Which I guess it couldn't. This was it, so much for fate, I always had been nothing, and now I always would be nothing, and that was okay, honestly. In fact, it was better this way. Letting go of all the pain, suffering, emptiness, and expectations, I drifted further and further into the light, folding in on me one layer at a time. Images flickering behind my eyes, not a collection of moments from a pathetic existence but secret truths revealing themselves to me one angle at a time. The numbers were trying to show me something different than the visions in the pool at the Keep, yet the knowledge was just out of my reach, hiding behind the veil. It all seemed pretty pointless now, anyway. What had it all been for, a tragic end to a tragic beginning, full of tragic days every step in between? I didn't expect to be bitter at the end, and this is what I had always secretly wanted, right? Still, it felt like a rip-off as I drifted further into the light, my mind finally drifting, too, and sweet silence filling my brain.

Jolting my body, an electric shock tore through me rapidly, spreading across my veins and breaking into my bones. *Again*, cascading through my body in an intensely painful wave of burning heat as the sparks searched out every cell in my body. Dying shouldn't be this painful, that was the drowning part—this part should be easy. I just let go, right? Why can't I let go? Another jolt rocked me, tearing me apart from the inside out as I collided back into my physical form, bolting upright as a torrent of water gushed out of my mouth in waves of burning regret. Gallons of water poured out of me as I coughed and hacked, my head a pounding echo of the stampeding beat that had been calling out to me and my vision still starry as the night sky as I gasped for air. Fire tore across my ravaged throat with a relentlessness as this painful existence latched itself back onto me with a vengeance, the fire spreading through my eyes and into my very bones. I didn't know everything could hurt so bad all at once. I was still gasping as the blackness began fading slowly from my still-burning eyes to reveal the blurred figure of my savior.

Collected and calm as ever, Mia was already wringing out her drenched dreads as she took stock of her soaked dress, a classically cut Victorian dress billowing out in layers upon layers of ivory lace, small white buttons going all the way up the high collar, the lace along her collar and running down the tight-fitting see-through sleeves, contrasting against her dark skin and stunning on her even drenched from her rescue attempt.

Glaring down at me, I couldn't help but notice the intense worry underlying the fury in her voice. "What were you *doing?!* You could have died!"

Searching frantically for my little treasure at the mention of it, I ruffled through the wet layers of sparkling green fabric to locate the secret pocket I had stashed the box away in, gratefully pulling it forth and presenting it to her. "Never mind that. Look what I found!"

Mia's eyes widened as she took the box from me cautiously, mouth open in a look of pure amazement. "A Pandora's Box! Now that *is* something." She was twisting it in her hands with a puzzled look, her anger melting away as her eyes sparkled. I could literally see the cogs working in that complex brain of hers. "These are said to hold mythical beasts, one-of-a-kind creatures that can only be tamed by the person who solves the puzzle."

A small spark of anxiety flared inside me as she continued to marvel at the iridescent pearl icosahedron, twirling it in her hands with a hungry look in her eyes. "Give it back to me." I reached my hand out as I demanded my hard-earned prize back flatly.

Surprisingly, her eyes shot up full of pain before quickly turning cold as ice. "I save your life, and that's what you think of me? Good to know."

Ashamed, I dropped my eyes as she willingly deposited the object back into my outstretched hand. "Sorry, I didn't mean it like that."

Pushing herself up, she shrugged nonchalantly as she answered coldly. "It doesn't matter, we need to go, but first, we need to do something about these dresses." Reluctantly she held her hand out to me and pulled me to my unstable feet in one quick swoop. My legs were shaking, and my lungs were raw as I clutched the small Pandora's box in my hand.

"There's no time like the present to learn a new trick, I suppose. I can teach you a little fire trick with that symbol the fortune teller gave you." She held up the hand she hadn't relinquished yet, turning the shiny gold pentagram tattoo in the sun. Letting go of my hand, she stepped back and put her palms together. "I want you to envision the spark that burns within your heart. I want you to put all your intentions on that spark, harness that power, and push it outwards. Then there's a small chant that goes a little something like this."

Closing her eyes and bowing her head, she began speaking softly in tongues, an ancient language that I didn't understand at all, but it seemed so familiar. I recognized words from the chant Amil had used on me and I had instinctually replicated on Mia. A warm rush of air burst forth from her in an aura of golden light as her dress and dreads billowed around her in the forceful blast of wind radiating from within her.

Eager to show off, I collapsed my hands together and mimicked her chant, the words forming easily on my tongue on the first try as if it remembered the language from some other lifetime.

Faintly, I could sense the little spark she spoke of, but it seemed so small and didn't want to respond to me at all.

Frustrated, I pushed and pulled at it as I chanted louder and louder, fighting against the heat burning my cheeks and the tears biting at my eyes. I had always had the embarrassing habit of crying when I was angry, especially with myself, and that incredibly irritating trait was awful in any situation, but especially this one. Just short of full-out bursting into tears, I dropped my hands with a loud huff, giving up as I dropped my eyes and shoulders. I really was worthless. I don't know why everyone had such high expectations for me; I was only going to let them down.

A soft hand lifted my chin as Mia released that overwhelming look on me again, trapping me in her gaze. "You're a water element, love. Obviously, fire would be the hardest for you to master, but I know you can do it if you focus. I believe in you. You're powerful. You just need to realize it and stop doubting yourself." Lost in her glowing eyes for several moments, the ring of intense purple surrounding her iris beginning to pulse harder and harder the longer I looked, I could feel the confidence swelling in me like she was literally pouring from her cup to mine.

Releasing me from her gaze, she gestured for me to try again. Nodding my head with a newfound sense of determination, I clapped my hands together and bowed my head, the chant falling off my tongue with ease once more. This time I could feel the fire fiercely burning inside, calling out to me to tame it, to wrap it in my hands and twist it into a condensed dodecahedron of warmth and light. The fire pulsed eagerly against the confines of its new container, pushing with all its might to escape and explode. Holding onto the energy as long as possible as it kept building and building, I finally was forced to let go, releasing a massive wave of heat rippling all around me, swirling through the layers of my dress and drying me completely, warming me all the way down to the bones—even my lungs felt dryer as I stood in total awe at the force of power that had come from within me.

Grinning, Mia began clapping softly, clearly impressed. "Now that's my girl! Most folks could only dabble in an element outside their own. You, my dear, are a full-on prodigy."

I was blushing intensely but also beaming; for once, I didn't feel like the compliment was undeserved. Pride was swelling in my chest, feeding that little spark even more.

"Let's hurry up. We're going to be late. We don't want to keep Eden waiting." Grabbing my hand again, she twirled around, all layers of lace and red and blue dreads, as she skipped off toward the house, dragging me along in her wake.

Gleefully I trailed behind her, giddy with the rush of power and the sudden feeling of control I'd never experienced before, or perhaps it was just a leftover high from the lack of oxygen and total adrenaline rush of yet another near-death experience. Either way, for once, I felt like my body was my own, and it was one worth owning. I felt good, I felt powerful, I felt… happy? Yeah, I guess that was what this was—happiness, and there was more to it than the little parlor trick I'd just learned or even evading death's door again.

Staring at the girl in front of me, I couldn't deny how much she had to do with it, my heart beating faster as I dared to let my thoughts wrap themselves around the abstract concept of caring about someone on such an intimate level. It was never something I had imagined in this lifetime; maybe as a little girl, I had thought of falling in love with some white knight who saved me from my sad, miserable life, but time took away that fantasy, and each night that grew darker took with it a little more hope. How did I find myself hand in hand with a demon, of all people, who, for *some* reason, I had shared everything with without hesitation? My chaotic heart was beating out a truth I didn't even want to begin to acknowledge with each skipping step we took.

Wrapped up in my thoughts, we arrived at the house in what felt like moments. Eden came rushing up, pushing Mia aside rudely as she grabbed my face, lifting it as she examined me for any damage, raising my arms one by one and even spinning me around to make sure I was in full working order. Her worry seemed to melt a little as a warm smile spread across her face.

"Don't scare me like that, dear! You're lucky I know everything that happens in this garden, or else I wouldn't have sent Mia in time. Although I didn't realize that *gem* was hidden there all this time, so I guess I don't know *everything*." Her eyes were sparkling as she reached her hand out. "Can I see?"

Without hesitation, I handed the box over to her eager hand as she twirled it expertly in her hand before tossing it into the air several times, her eyes following the way it moved with intense precision.

"Interesting, and to find it on Ostara, synchronistic indeed." With a final twirl, she deposited the pearl-colored treasure back in my hands before turning back to Mia, shock twisting her usually cool features as Eden collapsed around her, hugging her with all her might. The hug went on for several moments, and surprisingly Mia's shock eventually gave way to a small smile that she was struggling to hide as she finally melted a few degrees into Eden's warm grasp. Eventually pulling away, she kept her wrinkled hands on her shoulders as she gazed deep into those golden orbs.

"Thank you, Mia. I owe you a debt of gratitude. Anything you ever need, it's yours."

Uncomfortably Mia mumbled something about not mentioning it but seemed to know better than to explicitly turn down such a valuable offer. Turning to us both, she spread her arms in a grand gesture.

"It is time. Follow me, ladies. Adventure awaits." Her layers of red silk swirled effortlessly behind her as she skirted off, surprisingly agile for her age.

Mia and I exchanged a humored look before skipping after her, excitement shining on both our faces despite ourselves.

CHAPTER 16 – OSTARA

We stood at the massive old wooden gateway, painted with faded yellow paint and covered in a rainbow archway of flowers and pastel streamers blowing in the late afternoon spring breeze. A stream of colorful people flocked through the gates dressed in elaborate gowns, dapper suits, and costumes of every kind, massive hats, detailed masks, surreal wigs, and intricate hairdos, all celebrating and welcoming back the long-awaited spring, face masks cleverly designed into several of the costumes. Most seemed unconcerned, as if something greater was at work to protect them from this outbreak that had the rest of the world outside this little bubble at a standstill. Pondering on it, I began to wonder if, perhaps, considering the knowledge Eve had taught her children, there was something more protecting these people and this place in general. Turning back to my companions, I had to catch my breath as the sun caught her silver strands, shining on her pale skin, bringing it to life as a million sparkles erupted across her green dress as it swirled around her in the sunlight, the carefully picked color livening her normally dull eyes.

She really was a vision. It was such a shame she didn't see it, that her confidence had been stripped away one layer at a time. The small protective fire flared up inside of my heart again, thinking about the men who tried to dim her shine. I really needed to step back, she wasn't mine to protect, but she was making it hard to keep my priorities straight, especially after last night. I needed to focus now, though. I had to find the other Riders if I was going to have any chance of convincing my *mother* of this new plan. It was already going to be hard enough to tell her about my vision. She never had much faith in me, and at this point, she was going to think I was absolutely nuts, but I knew now that I had to try, and I needed every advantage I could get. Now if I could just catch a break and get a lead on this slippery little fellow Pestilence. He was doing so much damage in the world right now, yet no one seemed to know where he was, and that fortune had been much less helpful than I had hoped.

Deep down, I knew I was on the right path; my intuition had never let me down before, and Eve had told me to trust the process, so that's exactly what I was doing. This festival had the answers, and I just had to find them. Determined to go with the flow and see where the fates took me, I turned to Nato, a massive smile spread across my face as I bowed, asking for her hand to escort her through the gateway per the legends Eden had shared on the short ride to town in an elegant horse-drawn carriage straight out of a fairytale. Stories of the light and dark joining as they passed the threshold to bring forth the new tide of life that comes with the masculine and the feminine coming together in celebration of the spring equinox. I don't know if we exactly fit the bill, but we seemed close enough, and either way, I was superstitious enough that I wasn't going to be the one to break the local custom. Curtsying as she blushed, she dropped the twinkling folds of her gown to take my hand, wrapping her arm in mine as we walked through the gate. I couldn't help but stare at her as she determinedly looked dead ahead. Behind us, I caught sight of an old man approaching Eden and asking for her hand. Giggling like a small schoolgirl, she took his wrinkled hand in hers and followed behind us under the festive archway and into the palpable vibe of excitement and joy that filled the crowded decorated streets.

Strings of flags hung between colorful old stone buildings,

pieced together in a time when homes were fashioned by hand, and each stone was personally picked and placed with care. Layers of paint told stories of the centuries that had passed away in this timeless town. The old meeting the new as ancient flame-lit lanterns lined the brick streets, while modern food trucks filled the sidewalks, offering delights of every kind, from savory and sweetmeats sizzling on open grills to deep-fried anything you could imagine, even an extravagantly dressed man offering cotton candy folded and shaped into oversized flowers. Colorful stands displaying trinkets and treasures scattered between the food trucks, a vast collection of gifts from the Goddess Spring and Mother Earth. Floral crowns and naturally dyed clothes, fabric, and wools, handmade wands, crystals, crowns, and dry herbs for casting spells, incense of every kind, and even a booth full of an assortment of specimens preserved in jars.

It was every Wiccan's wonderland. If you were looking for a hard-to-find spell book, to expand your crystal collection with a rare specimen, to collect herbs that you wouldn't find at your normal corner store, or even just dabble in the food, culture, and myths of paganism, this would be the place to go. Honestly, I had never seen anything quite like it among humans, and I considered myself pretty well-versed in their culture. I suppose I had heard of this festival, yet something always kept me away; somehow never found myself near this fabled town at the right time to take advantage of seeing it with my own eyes all these years. Only now did I realize how much I had been missing out on. I couldn't help but wonder if more had been at work than I had thought to keep me away from here. Reminiscent of the Keeps and their BioWare to keep intruders at bay, perhaps there were boundaries here that made it harder for my kind to cross. Odd they hadn't stood in my way today.

Overcome with curiosity, I pushed my thoughts aside and

frolicked from one stand to the next, dragging Nato behind me, who, despite her much lower levels of enthusiasm, secretly seemed just as fascinated by all the little odds and ends we found among the eccentric vendors, each dressed stranger than the last and full of unbelievable tales and fantastic stories. Eden had found a wonderfully worn bench near a trickling fountain full of lotus flowers and massive lily pads, and we had wandered off while she rested, making a game of finding the most bizarre and curious object the festival had to offer. After a fierce debate over a single purple glass eyeball that kept moving on its own accord, said to have belonged to a fabled wizard and to contain magical properties, a two-headed cat fetus preserved in a jar, and a grotesquely mounted raccoon in a rather suggestive position with a possum, I finally had to succeed the game when Nato came bounding up, a twinkle in her eye, as she produced a rather old-looking and worn vintage doll.

It was clearly up-cycled by hand with a variety of materials that seemed to include sparkly paint, bloodstained baby clothes, actual human hair, and cavity-filled rotted teeth glued into the smiling mouth, void-less empty eye sockets somehow stared directly into my soul in an extremely unnerving way, even by my standards. Giggling uncontrollably, we haggled with the ancient little lady, covered in handmade jewelry fashioned of old ornaments and a discarded doll head nearly as creepy as the one we were trying to purchase. Perhaps she was the original artist, an impressively large turban wrapped around her head a hundred times over. We eventually settled on what I considered a pretty premium price for a prize piece of junk before wandering back to Eden to present her with her new gift.

We found several more stalls that captured our attention, a handmade dress that caught my eye, an old musty book about some ancient dead civilization that Nato spent several minutes searching through before reluctantly returning it to the shelf, a display of trained rats that performed a little circus act, much to our shared amusement. The day passed easily with her like we were just two normal girls enjoying a festival and all its trivial joys without the weight of the entire world on our shoulders. I could have abandoned my mission entirely and stashed her away, spending the rest of my days passing easily away like this, but deep down, a little voice was already listing out all the impossibilities. The obvious—that a girl like her would never stay long with a girl like me, not to mention we would be spending the rest of her days running from demons and angels alike. Her days—that was just it, in a blink of an eye, she would age before me, and next thing you know, I'd have fallen for a simple girl who turned into a wrinkly old lady. I couldn't imagine it really being worth it, even if she did happen to be the most stunning creature I'd ever seen walk this earth.

Much to our surprise, when we finally found Eden, she was overly delighted with her bizarre gift, shrieking with sheer joy and excitement, igniting several more fits of laughter from both of us. "This is exactly what I wanted!! She will go perfectly with my doll collection."

My laughter gave way to curiosity. I needed to see this doll collection someday; I couldn't imagine it was anything short of extraordinary if she considered this an acceptable addition to it. Ready to finally move along again, Eden, ever hungry, suggested we find something to eat and shuffled off toward the nearest cluster of food trucks as we followed at a slow pace. Feeling emboldened by the day's events, I reached out casually, grabbing her warm hand in mine and lacing our fingers together. She didn't look at me, but she didn't pull away either. A plethora of mouth-water scents greeted us as we reached the group of trucks, getting in line for several different plates from all the food trucks that caught our eye. While waiting in line for some pineapple jerk chicken with rice and sweet and spicy beef empanadas from the food truck Nato seemed most impatiently excited about, standing on her tiptoes as she tried desperately to see over the gentlemen in front of us behind a tall, shaggy-looking guy who was indecisively holding up the line, I could overhear the group ahead of us talking in hushed voices.

"Did you hear about those crazy locusts?" A Middle Eastern-looking guy with a Hawaiian floral button down on and his dark curly hair pulled back into a low ponytail was leaning in toward his companion, a fiery-haired guy, tall with soft brown eyes and a splash of freckles on his oddly tan skin who was nodding solemnly.

"Yeah, man. They are devastating the crops in Africa, and between that and the pandemic, they're seeing major food shortages now. I can't even believe they pulled off this festival. They say this is one of the only places in the world that hasn't seen any cases—it's some biblical shit, bro."

I couldn't help but snicker slightly under my breath; if only he knew how right he was. They both turned to me, looking indignant as they debated engaging with me. Fortunately, for their sake, the lady at the counter called impatiently for them to move forward and order as I grinned delightfully, waving at them coyly as they turned away.

Immediately my attention shifted as the oversized man who had been holding up the line lumbered past, all strands of sleek gold, rust, and gunmetal grey hair twisted into a long tricolor braid, patches of dense hair sneaking out of his shirt and shorts every chance it got, white nearly transparent scars covering his body, a vast collection of barely visible geometry. His eyes, one bright green and the other a rich amber, were brooding and soft as he stared at his dark tan bare feet, lost in his own thoughts.

His aura was so intense it was calling to me, and before I could stop myself, I reached out and grabbed his arm, bluntly demanding his name. "Who are you?"

Nato's silver eyebrows shot up in total shock, and the stranger froze, towering over me by several feet as he slowly leaned in, sniffing the air in an exaggerated matter before a toothy grin spread across his face. "Hello, demon. I guess it's a pleasure? My name is Maicoh. Would you say friend or foe?" He raised his thick eyebrows in honest curiosity, seeming unconcerned with my answer as if he had asked me about sugar in my tea. I suppose his overwhelming height had given him an inherent sense of confidence in life, not to mention he clearly was *something.*

"Friend. For now, at least. My name is Mia, not demon, for starters, if we are going to be friends, though."

He grinned again as he leaned in, eyeing Nato with far too much interest as far as I was concerned. "And your beautiful friend here?" Irrationally I reached for her hand again. Sometimes I could be a real moron like that, and she saved me the embarrassment of revealing my unfounded claim when she didn't pull away.

She spoke up for herself softly. "Nato, how do you do?" She bowed ever so slightly, eyes dropped to the ground and cheeks burning bright red as she clenched my hand. She seemed intimidated; perhaps it was his height.

No wonder she hadn't pulled away. Looking back at him, I couldn't say I blamed her. He must be a good seven feet tall *at least.* He barely registered as a threat to me, though. Regardless of *what* he was, I was more than equipped to protect us both from anything short of a full-on angel invasion, which, unfortunately, I knew wasn't completely out of the question, although fortunately unlikely with the current celestial projections. Time was short, though, and we had a lot to do. If he had answers, and I had a feeling he did, I needed them now.

"I suppose the proper question was, *what* are you?"

He hesitated, staring deep into my eyes for several moments, his aura wrapping around me, coursing in my veins, and pounding through my pulse. Abruptly the screeching voice of the shrill short-tempered cashier caused the moment to collapse, my arm dropping as he released me from his gaze.

"Meet me by the clock tower when the fireworks start. I have a lot to tell you." Slipping away, he strode back to the counter in a few oversized steps and grabbed the massive tray of food, looking as if he had ordered one of everything off the menu, before stalking off into the distance, disappearing into the crowds. Absently I let Nato drag me forward as she started ordering for both of us as I stared after the mysterious man.

He seemed oddly familiar to me, but I couldn't place why I felt that way. I was certain I had never seen him in my life. There was something about him, though, the hair, the height, the appetite, the overwhelming aura. I had heard of tales of natives to the land with the spirit of wolf coursing through their blood, strengthened by the moon and absurdly powerful in general. Yet in all my millennium, I'd yet to encounter one. There were tales of a great massacre that happened in a general scope around the second culling of the witches. It's amazing how powerful humans could become when motivated by the masses; sad that, too often, it seemed the only thing that inspired such a collective movement was hatred fueled by misunderstanding. It was the thing that mired them most as a species and seemed to be growing exponentially with each generation. I used to think it was hopeless, yet that vision had shown me a new awakening, a mass collective shift in consciousness that could allow them to achieve what we never dreamed them capable of. I couldn't help but wonder what that would mean on the grander scale of things if we could harness that creativity for the collective good. It was a long shot, but something deep inside me wouldn't rest. It was driving me forward to find the answers still just beyond my reach, the path to redemption that still eluded me.

Joining Eden back at the table where we had been collecting a banquet of different foods, we sat down with the final addition of the variety of Jamaican dishes. The spread was fragrant and colorful, ranging from a vegetarian stir fry that included vegetables even I had never heard of, a massive serving of Korean BBQ chicken skewers smothered in rich sweet sauce, a steaming bowl of ramen noodles and all the toppings from diced pork, fresh veggies, and a half dozen farm fresh eggs, large enough to share with a family and served with serval smaller bowls. Hot green tea by the pot with custom recyclable cups, covered in tiny hand-drawn flowers by the baristas, cold fresh fruit smoothies blended to beautiful shades of orange, pink, and red. Alongside the heaping plates of pineapple jerk chicken and rice and crispy fried empanadas stuffed with sweet and spicy meat served with fresh avocado, sour cream, and hot sauce was a full tray of fresh, deep-fried funnel cake, smothered in powder sugar, still steaming from the fryer. Losing all reservations, we dove into the delights before us, savoring the variety of exotic flavors that could only come from street foods as we devoured our way through serving after serving, washing it all down with several pots of hot tea as the sun shifted from the final warm moments of the afternoon to the crispy cool air of the early evening. The twinkling lights hung across the city, coming to life like tiny galaxies above their heads, lighting up the twilight with a romantic ambiance, soft violins playing somewhere nearby.

With a smile, Eden leaned back in her seat, content and clearly ready to rest after consuming more than her share of the bounty. Noticing a small gathering of people migrating toward the music, crescendoing slowly as the sun faded, I stood bowing once more to Nato, looking up at me with those ever-spooked doe eyes, sparkling, reflecting the twinkling string lights as confusion furrowed her silver brows. "May I have this dance, miss?"

To my surprise, she began giggling uncontrollably. I tried not to let it show in my eyes the damage she was doing to my pride. "I don't exactly consider myself qualified. Coordination isn't my strong suit."

Grinning, I snatched her up by her hand, causing her to gasp in shock as I pulled her close against my chest, releasing the full gravity of my eyes on her. She was trembling ever so slightly. "Leave it all to me, love." I swept her off her feet and in wide swooping circles that sent both our dresses twirling in a circle of sparkly green tulle and lacy white layers of fabric as we parted the crowd and entered the dance floor in a series of synchronized swirls as she twisted effortlessly in my arms, her face alive with sheer joy and wonder as she spun in my strong grasp under the sparkling sky. Shrieking laughter exploded out of her as I lifted her arm and twisted her in faster and faster circles, dipping her in and out in time with the music.

As the upbeat tempo gave way to more somber tones, slowing as the bows pulled across the strings in sad, soft streaks, I took my moment and pulled her in close. I laced my hand in hers as I dropped my other hand further down her waist, swaying her softly as we twirled slowly to the music, our bodies slowly melting together as her tense posture relented, her head sinking into the crevice of my collarbone, a perfect fit. I held her in my arms as the music changed, shifting again from the melancholy cries of the slow pulls of the bow to the upbeat, fast dance tempo of the seesaw motion of a bluegrass fiddle. She didn't even seem to notice as we continued to sway slowly in soft circles, wrapped in each other's arms. Lost in our own little world, several songs passed before she finally lifted her head, gazing up at me with those pleading green eyes. She wanted something from me, and I knew in this moment I would *always* want to give her anything she wanted.

"I just want to *understand* you. What are you even after? What makes you tick? Why you're even here? With me, on a dance floor? You've been evading something. I need to know what you know, what you're looking for."

She was pleading with me, but I thought she'd never ask; I couldn't hide the excitement in my voice as I answered. "I think we can change the world, Nato. You made me see that humans can be so much more."

My eyes were shining. This was my chance; I could convince her and get her to see the truth. I had held back from overwhelming her, waiting for my moment, laying the groundwork so she could truly understand my vision, to trust me enough to open her eyes and really see my grand plan. She was the most important puzzle piece; I needed her more than anyone to make this work, and fate had given me everything I needed to win her over.

Just as I opened my mouth to speak, a jolting sound interrupted my plea, a soft sound that shattered my world as I instantly placed its source.

"Well, this is surprising. Sorry to interrupt." Amil was standing just a few feet away, dressed in a tux, hair smoothed back into a well-tamed ponytail, a cold hard look in his eyes, jaw clenched and arms crossed, a silent rage seeping off him.

CHAPTER 17 – THE COMEBACK KID

Screaming into the void with such a primal rage, the trees shook violently within a one-mile radius, fresh spring flowers falling in soft contrast to my sheer seething anger. How did I let this happen? How could I have been so arrogant? I should have seen through that pathetically obvious trap. I should have crushed her instantly and without mercy. It was just so hard to deny *her* what she wanted when she looked at me with those doe eyes, those same eyes that turned cold and hard as she was whisked away from me. Rage coursed through my veins in a fresh wave attempting to bite back at the heartbreak trying to swallow me whole. My humanly aspects were growing stronger, clearly getting the best of me, yet there was no fighting back the all-consuming tide of a million emotions.

Where had I gone wrong, what sign had I misread, what words had accidentally pushed her out of my grasp and into the hands of that psychopath? I would never forgive myself if I didn't rectify this failure. I *would* find her before that demon could find a portal to the Underworld, and I *would* destroy that demon piece by piece for daring to lay hands on her. Already shedding myself of the pessimistic human emotions I was burdened with in this adapted vessel, my mind was shifting into mission mode, calculating my next step with precision. There was no time for pity; there was only time for action. She needed me more than ever, even if she never wanted me the same way. Even if I had pushed her away somehow in that moment, I would never abandon her completely. That *demon* didn't know what she had coming for her. She had unleashed something inside of me I thought I had overcome long ago, something that had been festering since the Fall, the monster within that I swore I would never untether again. Yet we play the hand fate deals us, and right now, she was forcing mine.

Moving across the yard with near-godly speed, I was back in the house in just a few heartbeats, quickly gathering a bag full of things I needed for the journey ahead. Packing light, I was out the door and heading for the arc in a matter of moments. I reached a small, sleek structure resembling a garage tucked around the corner and nestled in a grove of small trees behind the house. Mind racing, I threw open the arc door while mumbling a mantra angrily, instinctually yet unintentionally crafting an aggressively oversized all-terrain vehicle with massive wheels equipped to handle the wildest roads. Clearly, my anger had gone a bit overboard, but it would get the job done. Grabbing the top bar of the open-aired cabin, I swung into the driver's seat, already revving the hostile engine to life, roaring like a hundred hungry lions as I pushed the gas petal a few times before shifting it into gear and taking off into the day, leaving a wake of crushed grass and wildflowers. Making a mental note to apologize to Hova at some point for the destruction I unleashed on her Keep, I tore across the large meadow and onto an old wagon path, pushing the pedal to the ground as I forced the metallic beast to its limits, racing toward the nearest town as fast as possible.

Beyond lucky that he was close right now, for such a vagabond, it seemed like divine fate, which I never knew if perhaps it was, that he would be at that yoga retreat deep in the woods of Oregon. I barreled through the small town, going at least twice the speed limit and running several red lights as I weaved in and out of the few cars I passed along the tiny streets. I took a sudden turn onto the highway, pushing the pedal all the way down again as the odometer pushed well past 100 miles per hour. I closed the miles between us as fast as possible, desperate for any clue that might help me find her. Oddly enough, a faint pull on my heartstring was calling me in another direction, but I knew better than to listen to that traitor. I had learned that lesson too many times—trust the mind, not the heart, and logic will always prevail. As the afternoon sun gave way to the deep rich red rays of the setting sun, I raced further along the highway, and I was starting to feel the pull of his massive energy on this plane. He couldn't be far now. Instinctually I turned down an unmarked dirt road, leaving a massive cloud of dust in my wake as I tore up the dirt road without letting up my speed a fraction.

For several miles, I bounced along the twisting dirt road, dropping and rising with the rugged topography, cutting closer and closer to the sprawling untamed trees the further I went into the wild woods. Just as the final rays of the sun were falling behind the trees, casting a dark shadow over the woods, the dirt road leveled for a few yards before opening up to a massive clearing in the woods. A huge handmade wood and canvas structure resembling a massive teepee was sparkling with twinkling lights strung, crossing back and forth high above the open-air deck wrapping the entire structure. A million little fires lit up the clearing around him, small campfires burning at tiny individual teepees that littered the clearing. There must have been a few thousand of them, at least. Slamming on the breaks as they squealed to a halt aggressively, a cloud of dust billowed past me, catching up with me and filling the open-air cab as I threw the gear in park and jumped out of the vehicle, my feet already carrying me forward.

He walked out to greet me with arms wide open, a tall tan man with a long mess of dreaded light brown hair piled on top of his head in a loose bun, balanced by a well-groomed thick but short beard and rich blue eyes deep as the sea, flecked with brown, that twinkled brighter than the stars above. "Old friend! It has been too long! Come. Sit. Eat. Drink. Let's share stories and good times." He was striding toward me barefoot, dressed in light linen clothes, loose drawstring pants, and an open robe that showed his bare tan chest and faded geometry that looked like nothing more than old scars now.

Suddenly his warm arms were wrapped around me in a tight hug as he held me close for several moments longer than one would consider normal. I reluctantly patted his back before waiting for him to release me, brows furrowed as I tried to be patient before bombarding him with questions for the answers I sought. Odd how civility still matters to me even now; I should probably work on letting that go. Civility cost me Nato in the first place, and I would be a fool to make that mistake again. However, if I was being honest, context was important too. I needed to play my cards right. He had never been a man to be rushed, and he did everything at his own speed or nothing at all.

As he pulled back and I got a closer look at him, I could see the elaborate layers of embroidered gold in his clothes and the high quality of the material. They might look plain, like something you might see on a homeless person, yet clearly, they were made of the finest fabrics; he always had been something of a conundrum. Turning, I followed in his path as he led the way up the stairs to the open-air twinkling deck and pushed back the massive curtain doorway that welcomed us to a steamy tent full of thousands of half-naked sweating bodies, poised in silent meditation as a large group of barely clad men and women, easily the most beautiful of the bunch, softly played sound drums, flutes, and small complicated-looking guitars with their eyes closed and heads bowed, lost in the trance of the hypnotic music. A soft hum filled the air with an electrostatic current, the harmonious voices of the mediators creating a collective sound wave in unison that filled the room with palpable energy.

Clapping his hands in the air pompously, all heads snapped to attention, fixated on him as they came out of the haze of the music, which had ground to a halt at his signal. Cheerily he held his arms out to the crowd, a warm smile spreading across his tanned features as he projected his voice, a current of authority hiding in the cheery tones.

"Beloveds, what a beautiful meditation. We have opened our hearts and minds to the light, and nothing can separate us when we expand our consciousness to the 5D state. You are me, and I am you. See past the illusions of separation in this world, and you will be granted the wisdom of the eternal within all of you. Now, we gather, feast, dance, and love freely and without boundaries, opening ourselves to the bounty of the earth and each other without limitations. Namaste."

He bowed to them, and in a single gesture, the whole atmosphere of the room changed. The music began again, the tempo picking up in speed for a more upbeat number. Everyone was moving, laughing, talking, hugging, dancing, kissing, the room was alive with energy, and the sexual tension was palpable. Parting the sea of crowded, sweaty bodies, I followed in his wake as we headed for an elaborate set of embroidered cushions scattered across the floor, surrounding a long low table filled with every vegan cuisine you could imagine and several pitchers of rich colored wines, pink, red, purple, and even a rich blue one with an intense fragrance I could smell from here, a soft pulsing glow to it that was off-putting and alluring all at once.

Folding my legs together, I sat on one of the floor pillows across from the smiling man who was staring at me intently with those deep blue eyes, duller and darker than mine but still alive with a current that bore into my soul for several minutes before he broke his stare and opened his hands up, gesturing at everything and everyone around him.

"So what do you think, Amil? It's much better than the cults of the eighties and nineties, with more sex and fewer clothes, although this vegan food is terrible, just the worst. They got rather offended, however, when I tried to explain the plants are just as alive as the animals, so I decided it wasn't a battle worth fighting. I've had to deal with worse over the centuries, after all." He looked off into the distance for several minutes, his sparkling eyes going dull at whatever train of thought had taken hold of his mind.

Turning back to me, the twinkle had returned as quickly as it left. "Lifetimes of spreading the gospel, you see it all, really, right?" He nodded determinedly as if answering his question before blathering on.

"I suppose Hova sent you to check on me? Nothing much to report here. Just doing what I always do. Establishing misguided religions, instilling false prophets, infiltrating anyone close to the truth, and sowing seeds of doubt and misinformation so no one can ever come close to really understanding what's happening here. I spent centuries convoluting every religion under the sun, and now that those are losing popularity and have already been corrupted beyond belief, I've moved on to some of the more fringe factions of truth seekers. Hova should be pleased. Everyone here is so confused and busy fighting each other that they'll never be prepared for what's to come. Not that there's even anything to prepare for, but I still guess it's good to dot your I's and cross your T's, right? Even these new age light workers who think they've surpassed their egos have become more consumed by it than any other group of people I've ever had the pleasure of leading, blinded by their own arrogance and self-righteousness." He rambled on for several more minutes before I finally cut him off.

"Adam, listen, I'm not here about Hova. I'm here about *her.*

I know you know where she is. I need you to tell me where to find her."

His eyes dropped to the floor, and for the first time, the smile vanished from his face. His shoulders sunk as he spoke under his breath in a nervous tone. "You *know* I don't know. I can't know. Hova has been trying to find her this whole time, and if I knew, she'd know. It's for the best that I'm in the dark."

I sighed, my own shoulders dropping, I knew this already, but I had hoped against hope. "There must be something, Adam, *anything*. You know something you've just been trying to deny, even to yourself, *especially* to yourself. I need to find her. She's the only one who can help me now. Please, Adam. I wouldn't ask if I wasn't desperate."

Looking back at me, he bore into my eyes for several moments with those captivating blue and brown eyes, searching for something to convince him he could trust me, I suppose. After a long time, he let out an exasperated breath as he leaned back, looking up at the sky, a twinkle of stars visible through the open circle at the top of the teepee structure. "I can't imagine what you think she can help you with. However, if I was a gambling man, I'd bet that the only sect of worshippers I haven't been able to infiltrate must have something to do with her. It just so happens a massive pagan festival is happening this weekend. It's halfway across the world, so good luck with that, but if you can make it there, I have a feeling you'll find what you're looking for."

Shaking his head as if to erase whatever thought had tried to take root in his mind's eye, the smile spread across his face again as he opened his arms back up to the cluster of bodies around him gloriously. "It's too late for rescue missions. The full moon is almost upon us, and the time to celebrate is now. Join us, Amil, and relish in the pleasures of this realm. You are our honored guest, and we offer you all that you could desire."

As if his words were a command, a cluster of ladies had surrounded me, collapsing around me as they began offering cups of wine, grapes fed still on the cluster, fragrant shiny gold joints lit as soon as they hit my mouth, clouds of bioluminescent smoke escaping my lips as soft hands rubbed away at the overworked muscles of this vessel. I knew I should resist, but the day had been long, and the pull was too tempting for even me. After all, a few drinks couldn't hurt. I could slip away once Adam was preoccupied with his own company. Giving in to the carnal cravings of this body, I melted at their touch, accepting their offerings willingly as one glass of wine gave way to another and another, washing away my worries as liquid warmth spread through my veins and settled deep in my bones.

As the moon rose higher in the sky, slowly making itself visible through the opening in the roof of the tent, joining its twinkling brethren in the heavens above, washing out all but the brightest stars, I lifted my cup to drain the remaining contents. When had I switched from the lush red wines to the ominous glowing blue substance that had caught my eye earlier, the very same substance I had made a mental note to stay far away from when my senses had still been about?

Finding it hard to hold on to that thought with the haze that had suddenly washed over me, infinity more intense than any high the night had brought me previously, a wave whisking away my concerns like grains of sand caught in the tide. One moment I was trapped in the technicalities of tomorrow, trying to pry myself away and back into my vehicle, instinctually plotting even in my daze; the next moment, lips were on mine, pushing me back as hands pulled at my restrained hair, freeing it from its bun as dark purple curls cascaded down my shoulders, fingers running through the silky strands, softly scratching my head, luring me into their siren's snare with sweet whispers. Lips were pressing against mine again, different lips, softer this time, lingering before moving across my body and being replaced with the original hungry, demanding lips that had first pushed me to the floor. More hands were on my body than I had the whereabouts to count at the moment, and despite the little voice inside screaming in the background, I was lost in the symphony of senses. I gave in to the cluster of women around me, melting into their ecstasy, which gave way to mine several times over.

Vaguely I was aware of Adam off in his private corner, surrounded by the hoard of musicians, making out with the beautiful man that had been playing the complicated-looking guitar as the others fawned around him, tending to his every need, and I mean his *every* need, yet it was as if he wasn't really there anymore. All that mattered were the bodies pushing and pulling against mine, seeking out the secret spots only lovers knew as the night gave way to the early morning rays of light. We finally collapsed, in a heap of exhaustion, sleeping in a pile like a pride of lions back from the midnight hunt.

Jolting awake, rage and regret consuming me as soon as I was conscious, I clawed my way out of the pile of nude women collapsed on top of me, tangles of blonde, brown, red, and black hair threatening to pull me back under. Ignoring the displeased groans of my companions, irritated with my rude awakening and callous demeanor after the shared sentiments of the night before, I was already searching the room for the target of my overwhelming anger. Leaning casually against the deck with a steaming cup of coffee in his hand, I spotted him through the folds of the canvas tent. I was on him in less than a second, my hand wrapping around his tanned neck as I lifted him into the air, coffee cup cascading out of his hand, sending a torrent of hot liquid into the cool morning air as a snarl ripped out of my cracked lips, dry as the desert from the night of drinking and smoking.

"You drugged me! What the fuck, man?"

That dumb smile of his stayed in place, reaching all the way to his eyes as he looked down at me, laughter parting his perfect features without a single concern for my massive hand blocking his airways. Crackling under my grasp, his voice came out broken but joyous. "I was only trying to help. It's all about timing, my friend, and you would have never slowed down on your own."

Dropping him as my rage ebbed as quickly as it swelled, the lingering high from the night before was fading fast, and with it, I was gaining more control over my emotions again. These vessels were never easy to master, but I was finding this one more and more unpredictable by the day.

Pushing himself up from the crumbled heap he had crashed down into, he was still smiling as he spread his arms wide. "Let me make it up to you, pal. I think I might have a solution to your problem. Follow me!"

Without further explanation, he turned in a whisk of white linen fabric as he strode off down a stone pathway into the wild woods twisting ominously around the cleared-out meadow, littered with scattered still-sleeping half-clothed bodies and a handful of early risers brewing coffee and making breakfast by their lingering fires. Left with limited options, I followed in his wake, desperation compelling me forward, too aware of the unforgiving flow of time. Each passing moment put her more permanently out of my reach. Last night had made it abundantly clear that I couldn't fail this mission, but more importantly, I couldn't fail *her.*

Pushing my way through the thick tangle of trees closing in on us the further we ventured down the path, I spent several minutes wrestling with a particularly stubborn patch of vines and thorns that finally gave way to another massive open clearing, at least five times the size of the one that housed the canvas structure and collection of matching miniature tents. A surreally massive industrial structure towered above me, several hundred yards of tin and steel pieced together to create the single greatest arc I'd ever seen in my many lifetimes in this realm.

Adam turned to me as casually as if he'd just displayed his novelty plate collection and handed me a crumpled piece of paper. "You'll need these coordinates. I'm sure you're creative enough to figure out the rest."

Turning back to the trail we'd followed, he looked back once more, a longing look hiding behind those murky blue eyes flecked with brown. "Don't tell her you saw me. It's better that way."

Nodding in acknowledgment, I turned to the building, leaving him in his private pain as he walked back toward his followers. Placing my hand on the side of the structure, the mantra flowed from my lips excitedly before I threw open the expansive door, grinning despite myself at the sleek jet plane manifested before me.

CHAPTER 18 – REUNIONS & RAMIFICATIONS

Twirling in her arms, the moment felt like it would have lasted a lifetime—until it all came crashing down instantly. Turning to face him, my heart thudded out a whirlwind of emotions, sheer joy and utter terror all at once, the last thing I had expected when we were finally reunited. I clutched her hand still, harder, actually, out of an unexpected instinct to protect her from him. My feet were moving, and I was suddenly in front of her, blocking his path forward, even if he hadn't actually moved an inch yet.

"Listen, Amil. You don't understand."

His words were cold and cruel as he retorted back at me with venom in his voice. "I think I understand just fine, Nato."

His words shot through me like bullets, and my face crumpled. It took everything not to let my body follow. I wanted to sob in the streets, but I knew better. I needed to be strong to navigate this moment, or I risked losing everything. His words broke my train of thought, softer this time, full of regret.

"Apologies, m'lady. It's not your fault. Just step away, and this can all be over." The end of his sentence hissed out of clenched teeth, and his eyes darkened as I watched him already crouching forward, gaze locked on Mia behind me, who hadn't made a sound, probably busy calculating her next move with that ticking brain of hers. I hoped she was figuring out something fast because I couldn't protect her for long, and the thought of watching them fight it out here in the square made me sick to my stomach.

"Don't be crazy, Amil. *Look at all the people.* This isn't the place." Mia's voice was dry, dull, and passionless as she walked out casually from behind me and a few steps toward him with her arms up. "You want a fight, you've got it, but not here, pal. Have some manners, after all."

I couldn't stifle the soft giggle that escaped my lips, I had a bad habit of laughing when I was nervous, and it was especially difficult to abstain when I was watching a demon lecture an angel on manners. My life was absurd. Amil, however, was tense, unamused by either of us, his eyes moving rapidly between the two of us as the space grew between Mia and I, calculating how quickly he could close the gap and make a break with me, I assumed. Instinctually I took a step closer to Mia, a weird emotion twisting across his face that made my heart throb in a painful sort of way. I was too late, though, as he made his move anyway and was tearing across the small space between us, arms outstretched to grab hold of me and flee. He was just too slow, though, Mia flinging her body at the last moment to block his path to me as I staggered back, falling flat on the hard ground as their bodies slammed together like boulders clashing.

Launching backward, Mia was crouched on all fours in front of me as Amil took a defensive position, his eyes already calculating his next opening. The crowd around had scattered at the sound of the crash, but they hadn't gone far. Watching curiously from the outskirts of the square, the musicians, ever diligent, had even continued to play, upping the tempo a bit and expertly using tritones to match the intensity of the situation. I guess they really did go down with the sinking ship. Before Amil could pursue further, Mia was already pushing herself back up, brushing herself off as she straightened her elaborate gown.

She spoke coyly. "You know you smell like a whore house.

How many women did you bed last night?" A flush brighter than I'd ever seen filled Amil's cheeks as he looked away from me. Was that shame he was trying to hide there? "Angels think they have so much moral high ground. It's sickening. At least I only took one woman to bed last night." She dragged over the end of her sentence, relishing each word.

I couldn't look away from him, and I watched as each word twisted into his heart like a dagger, his eyes darkening further as his fears were confirmed. I didn't regret being with her, but in this moment, I couldn't stop my heart from breaking into a million pieces. What had I done to him? The only man that had ever been kind to me, ever put his hands on me in all the ways I wanted, and I had destroyed everything before it even had the chance to begin.

I couldn't stop myself from stepping forward, reaching my hand out for him. I didn't know what to say, but I had to try and show him how important he was to me. I couldn't stand there watching his heart break and do nothing. Mia was tensing up beside me, and I noticed from the corner of my eye a dark expression twisting across her own eyes. What a mess I had made of the whole situation. Pushing past her, I closed the final gap between Amil and I, grateful that Mia either trusted me enough or wasn't bold enough to stop me at this point. Resting my hand on his chest, I felt a sigh of relief escape our lips synchronously. I didn't realize how much it had felt like a part of me was missing, but now that he was in my arms again, I felt like I had been completely hollow and was suddenly full to the brim. Was this the connection he spoke about when he baptized me? It was an intense, overwhelming sensation that made me realize how painful it would be to be separated again. Curious, I turned to Mia, who watched like a hawk, her normally captivating eyes cold and dead in an attempt to hide whatever emotions were playing behind that poker face. I didn't want to admit it, but I couldn't deny that the pull was there too.

Turning back to Amil, he stared down at me with those intense blue eyes, smoldering me as he pleaded. "I don't care what happened, Nato. You don't belong to me, and you're free to do whatever you need, but we *need* to go now. If it's your command, I won't even harm the demon, but you *must* come with me. The eclipse is almost upon us, and we have a long road ahead of us."

Mia boldly stepped forward, interrupting him. "Of course she's free to do as she pleases, angel. Get off your high horse and stop with the passive-aggressive guilt trip. She made a choice that she *wanted*. Sorry that choice wasn't you."

Amil's grasp on me tightened as he turned to Mia, fuming yet clearly trying to keep his composure. "I know your tricks, demon. I'm sure you made her feel like it was her choice. It's not like she's ever dealt with keeping a seductress at bay before, you want to pretend those eyes don't hold sway over humans, but I know better."

Mia was bristling, stepping even closer. A few more steps and she would be in arms reach of him, which was making me increasingly nervous. "To accuse me of such a thing! Just like a man to assume I need to use some trick to get a girl in bed. Would it be so damaging to your pride to admit that maybe a girl is just better in bed than you are, or would that hurt your poor fragile male ego?"

Amil snapped, pushing past me to reach for her neck, his strong hands finding it instantly and clutching around it as panic crossed Mia's face. Clearly, she had let her guard down, and it was going to cost her her life.

Crying out, I grabbed Amil's muscular arm and tried to pull it away from her to no avail. The crowd around us was murmuring rather loudly now, but not a single soul stood up to help, which honestly, for their sake, was probably for the best.

Closing my eyes, I started chanting out the mantra Mia had taught me, the internal rush of heat coming to me quickly now, the spark of my heart basically a raging fire that I pushed outward in an explosion of fiery energy that threw the tangled duo apart by several feet. Rushing to Mia's side, I was already helping her up and trying to check her injuries, deep red, purple, and blue handprints already bruising her dark neck. As I helped her, I turned back to find Amil seething, the foreboding aura seeping off him once more as he watched our intimate exchange. The soft way I stroked her neck, the emotions I knew he could read, the thudding of my heart that I was sure he could hear, the way my voice cracked when I asked her if she was okay, the way she beamed back at me, thrilled to be my patient as she shrugged off the injuries but relished in the attention.

Dropping my eyes, I pushed myself back up and toward him; his anger made me nervous, but I refused to show it on my face. Hopefully he was too preoccupied to read it in my mood because I wasn't afraid of him, but I wasn't afraid of her either. Closing the gap again, I purposely put my hand back on his chest and looked up at him with the most compelling look I could muster.

"*Please*, Amil, I just want to hear her out. Maybe I'm a fool, but these are my people, and I need to know I tried everything before condemning them to their end."

Staring at me for several minutes with those intense blue eyes, clouded with worry, Amil's shoulders finally dropped as he relinquished to my request, the foreboding aura fading ever so slightly as he continued to watch Mia with untrusting eyes. Mia was still kneeling on the ground, rubbing her neck as she muttered a small mantra under her breath, soft light emitting from her hand as the bruising subsided ever so slightly. She stopped short of healing it fully, a shadow of his handprints remaining on her tattooed neck, gold drips falling from her chin down to the base. Reaching my hand to her, I pulled her surprisingly dense body up in a solid motion, shocked by my strength. *Had it been growing?*

"Please, Mia, you had something to tell me."

She turned to Amil with untrusting eyes before lashing out coldly. "I don't trust *him*. Why would I reveal my plan to someone in Hova's back pocket? What do you take me for, a moron?" She had turned back to me with raised eyebrows and crossed arms, defiant as always. "Mia... I trust him. He is Hova's disciple, but he has made it clear to me that he is *mine*. He was made for me. If we are going to pull this off, I'm sure we will need his help. Please, if you trust me, trust him, at least enough to help me convince him."

Mia's eyes darkened when I called him mine, and I couldn't help but notice in my peripheral vision that Amil seemed to momentarily beam at the title. Sighing, she finally relinquished and continued in a much less excited tone than she had led during our dance.

"Listen, I was there that night, the night you were baptized." My eyebrows shot up on my forehead, and even Amil's mouth dropped open in surprise, followed by a furrowed brow and an incredibly disappointed look that he quickly pushed aside. "A vision came to me that night, and it showed me a future I never thought possible. One where humans can reach the next stage of enlightenment. They could become co-creators. I suppose what you might refer to as demi-gods on this plane. Could you imagine the possibilities? Could you imagine what we could achieve universally if we could learn to enlighten another species below us?" Her eyes were glowing with excitement, but her words were clearly falling short on both of us.

"That sounds lovely and all, *demon*, but you need to get a grip on reality. Humans are breeding stock. How do you create demi-gods out of breeding stock? We've tried in the past, and they still fall victim to their egos, their greatest shortcomings. It's completely unrealistic, and it sounds like you just hit your head too hard and had a little dream about some fantasy you have." He was crossing his arms defiantly as he took a step closer to me again, clearly losing his patience with entertaining Mia's stories.

"It's not a fantasy. I was gifted a vision as real as you or me, and it could work… At least, I think it can." Her confidence wavered ever so slightly at the end but held true in her eyes.

Meanwhile, I was furrowing my brows as I thought back on that night and the vision I had seen myself. Nothing about it had given me any hope for the humans; in fact, it was the exact opposite. Even thinking back on it now, it reconfirmed my convictions that humans were a lost cause, a failed experiment that had reached its expiration date.

"Listen, Mia, I have to agree with Amil here, I had a vision that night too, and it was nothing like yours. I saw the truth, and the reality is they are hopeless. Why are you, of all people, fighting for them?"

A dry laugh escaped her lips unexpectedly. "Trust me, love. No one is more surprised than me. I can't explain it, but my best guess is that Hova was influencing your vision, manipulating it somehow. Showing you bits and pieces of the truth but completely out of context. What I saw was the real truth. I can feel it in my bones."

Now that she mentioned it, I couldn't help but think back to the pool of water that had almost become my grave. The visions there, drifting in the light, fighting what I thought was my last fight, were different from those I had when I awakened that first night. They were trying to tell me something I couldn't understand, but deep down, I knew it was whispering the same truths Mia was screaming at me now, but I still didn't want to hear them. Following a divine purpose for an all-knowing God seemed a lot easier to wrap my head around than some fringe plan to go up against the entire universal system and make a global shift that would forever alter the course of humanity. I wasn't made for revolutions, I was just a tiny piece in a too-big puzzle, and my best move was to quietly take my place and accept it for what it was, even if the small voice inside was scolding me for my complacency.

Taking a step closer to Amil, I shook my head stubbornly. "No, it's too much, Mia. You're talking about going up against a God, and sorry, but I just don't trust *those* odds." I dropped my head, afraid to see the disappointment in her eyes. I was a coward and I always had been. Even my powers weren't enough to change the fundamentals of my personality—weak, afraid, and submissive. How does a girl like that save the world?

Stepping forward, she softly placed her cool hands on my face and tilted my chin upward, gazing deep into my eyes with that intense look as her eyes pulsated. "I know I'm asking a lot of you, love. It's okay to be afraid. Won't you at least trust me enough to try and find the other Riders? I *promise* I'll even help you get to the Kingdom if that's what you choose. Just give me a chance to show you another way. That's all I'm asking."

Trapped in her gaze, I was vaguely aware of how tense Amil was next to me, frozen as he awaited my decision, clearly irritated with the intimate way Mia felt welcome to touch me. Sighing softly, I pulled away from her grasp and dropped my eyes again. I really was so pathetic. "I just don't know, Mia, I want to believe it too, but it just feels like so much."

Mia opened her mouth to speak again, but suddenly Amil was between us, shoving her away from me in the blink of an eye. "You *heard* her, demon. Enough with your lies!"

Staggering back several feet, Mia caught herself, snarling softly under her breath. "She can speak for herself, angel. She doesn't need some *man* controlling her."

"Say what you want, *demon*, but this isn't some petty human sexist thing. She is my everything. I will always protect her. I was *made* for her."

Mia's cackling laughter interrupted his convictions as she continued her cruel attack on him. "Oh, she's your everything? Odd, because I pick up at least a dozen scents on you. Who's really the *demon*, after all?" His face crumbled, his electric eyes going dull as they dropped to the ground in regret.

It broke my heart. It made me want to piece him back together and hold him tight, to take away all the pain and confusion. I had caused this—I had ruined this, just like I ruined everything in life. It's what I was, a ruiner—hell, my destiny as a Rider was even to finally ruin it all for good.

"Amil, I'm sorry, it wasn't supposed to be like this."

Confusion swept across his face. He was already shaking his head as he lunged forward, grabbing both of my shoulders fiercely. "Sorry for what? You don't owe me anything. I already told you that, secondly, none of this is your fault! I let you down when I let her get her hands on you. It's not your fault. She's a seductress by nature." I stared at him, tears biting at the edge of my eyes; he was so pure. I didn't deserve him.

Hissing at the insult, Mia was quick to defend herself against his accusation. "What we shared was more than consensual, angel. To continue to imply otherwise is highly insulting not only to me but also Nato."

Letting go of him softly, I nodded in agreement with a resolute look in my eyes. I would stand by my choices, good or bad, regardless of the consequences. "She's right, Amil. I'm sorry if it hurts to hear it, but the choice was mine to make, and I hope you can respect that. It was something I needed, and I refuse to regret that, even if it was a *one-time* thing." Mia's mood seemed to shift from arrogance to annoyance in a matter of moments as she dropped her gaze away from me, hiding whatever my words had struck there as Amil tilted my chin up himself, a warm look in his eyes.

"Like I said, my lady, no need to explain yourself. You owe me nothing. It is only I who has transgressed you, and that I do regret."

Shaking my head, I couldn't find the words, but I pleaded with my eyes for him to understand there was nothing to forgive, even if I knew I wasn't hiding the crushing pain and jealousy completely as I imagined him surrounded by women much more beautiful than I.

His soft chuckle pulled me out of my spiral. "You are the most stunning creature to ever walk this earth. None of those women could even dream of competing with you." Mia mumbled something about finally agreeing on one thing when a sudden loud bomb-like burst interrupted the emotionally tense moment.

Sizzling in the air, the cyan, yellow, and pink sparks faded into the twinkling night sky, alive with a million stars even with all the sparkling streetlights. The music picked up in volume as another firework whizzed into the air before exploding into an elaborate display of golds and silvers, creating an array of geometric shapes that slowly faded into the night. Two more fireworks whizzed after the first two at once this time, bringing the sky to life with an array of colors and shapes that intermingled with each other as they spread from their epicenter. Three more colorful explosions shot into the air, followed by five more, eight, and finally, a massive eruption of thirteen fireworks set off all at once, creating an astounding display of color, geometry, and frequency that lasted for over ten minutes and reverberated throughout the crowd. Transfixed, we seemed all momentarily hypnotized by the visual arrangement, as if it was embedding something into us. Vaguely I became aware that the fireworks were being set off in a very particular pattern. As the astounding thirteen-shot display finally faded into the night in a cloud of smoke, another outrageous number of fireworks shot into the air. Counting them, I wasn't surprised; twenty-one fireworks in total... Next would be thirty-four, I assumed. How very clever.

Just as I marveled over this spectacular homage to the Fibonacci sequence, the coordination, and the pure creativity of putting on such a show, a cold hand grabbed me by the shoulder. Leaning in, Mia whispered in my ear, "Maicoh is waiting for us, and we are late. *Please*, I need your help, love."

She was pleading with me with those intense gold eyes, breaking down my barriers with a softness I'd only seen there when we shared that night together. I was about to give in to her whims when a warm, strong hand slipped into mine, and leaning in toward my other ear, his whisper was as sweet and pleading as hers.

"It's a trap, my lady. Trust your instincts and come with me. We have a lot of ground to cover in very little time if we are going to get to the nexus point in time. Please, I need you to *trust me*." Frozen in place, I couldn't even breathe as the indecision tore me to pieces internally, silently falling apart as they both kept their hold on me. How do I make such an impossible choice when they both had somehow unintentionally taken such a strong hold on my heart when I wasn't paying attention?

Letting go of my ego and rational mind, the little me inside that was always rambling on about my problems, I drifted into my subconscious. Temporarily leaving my body as I lifted into the astral plane above to seek out the answers I needed most right now, I called out to the void desperately for any sign to follow, any clue that would let me know what to do. The visions came slowly but suddenly flooded me, filling my vessel with light that literally began pouring forth from my eyes and mouth of my discarded body, much to Mia and Amil's alarm. Several lifetimes seemed to pass, and the universe filled me with the knowledge I had requested and then some.

Finally releasing me, I fell back into my human form like a ton of bricks, collapsing out of their arms and hitting the pavement hard, skimming both my knees bad enough that blood trickled down my legs, hidden by my elaborate grown. Both Mia and Amil offered their hands to me to help me up, but I pushed them aside, using my own two hands to get back on my feet, something I needed to do more often, according to some of the messages the universe had shared with me. Looking between them both, I took a deep breath, ready to make my choice.

CHAPTER 19 – JUXTAPOSITION

Clutching the ivory octopus, I couldn't get the image out of my head as her face shattered into a million pieces. She didn't even try to stop me when I took a step away from her and toward Amil. He didn't hesitate for a moment to take his opening. Swooping me into his arms, he was off into the crowded streets of the festival, twisting and turning in case she had awoken from her shock and taken chase. While weaving in and out of the laughing festival goers, panic painted his normally collected features. I tried to smooth some of that panic away, placing my hand softly on his face. His brow only furrowed further as he looked away from me, pushing himself to move even faster as we began to reach the outskirts of the town.

Less and less people were gathered in the darker corners of the ancient town; the music didn't quite reach this far out, and only a few lines of twinkling lights kept the streets bright enough to walk on.

Amil still didn't relent as he pushed passed the final boundaries of the little village and into the surrounding woods, full of small trees rich with blooms of every color. A sleek motorcycle was waiting, hidden in the dense bushes, oddly shaped and all-white with gold hexagonal geometry carved into it. It had almost a spaceship-like quality to it. He loaded me on silently before pressing forward through the woods at full speed for several hours. Accepting that he would speak when he was ready, I rested my head on his back, arms wrapped loosely around him as exhaustion caught up with me.

After tripping most of the night, nearly drowning, not to mention topping it all off with an out-of-body experience to gain a bit of clarity, I could barely keep my eyes open. The rhythmic movement of the motor rumbling beneath me as we tore through the woods was finally too much, and despite my best efforts to hang on to consciousness, I drifted off.

Walking along a beach, the sand was soft between my bare toes, a million stars twinkling in the twilight skies above as the tulle of my dress scratched softly against the surface of the sand while it dragged behind me, damp from the lapping waves that were just barely reaching my feet, wave after wave slowly sweeping in as I walked aimlessly down the shore, searching for something, yet I wasn't sure what. In the distance, a small fire was crackling, dancing with flames of every color as the driftwood burnt with a rich, salty smell, calling me closer.

Slowly I approached the little campfire, alarmed to find a woman passed out on the ground, her face covered by a mess of green curls and her chest barely rising with each shallow breath. Dropping to my knees, I had to use all my effort to roll her over. She was as dense as Amil and nearly impossible to move for a small woman. After much struggling, she finally flipped over, a huge empty glass bottle rolling out of her hand toward the fire. Was she drunk?! My concern ebbed ever so slightly as I began shaking her softly at first. She seemed to come to, mumbling under her breath, so I shook harder until suddenly her eyes snapped open and she jolted up, grabbing me by both shoulders.

"Finally!! I thought you'd never find me, and it was getting hard keeping the demons at bay." She was staring at me with massive green eyes, with streaks of gold sparkling in the firelight. I was too shocked to speak and knew I should be more alarmed about where this place was and what happened to Amil, but something about her seemed so familiar to me, and curiosity was getting the best of me.

"So... you're running from the demons too?" I stumbled over my question as she began laughing rambunctiously.

"No, no, no, dear, not *the* demons, *my* demons. Very different, ya know." She was nodding her head matter-of-factly. "Head demons are the worst demons, much more powerful than those ego-driven children of Hova. They make you think one thing is another and that the things that matter don't matter and that what could never matter is the only thing that matters, if you follow my drift."

I did not. I did not follow her at all, but I needed to know more; she had answers for me if I could unravel her rambling. "Why am I here?" More laughter, bell-like sounds that reminded me of my favorite person, but it couldn't be.

"Only you can answer that question, my dear. It would help if you stopped listening to everyone else."

Staring at her in confusion with my mouth open, I struggled to piece my words together. "I *have* been listening to myself. I've never listened to myself more, to be honest. These visions keep coming to me, and I'm doing my best to follow them."

The woman nodded her head solemnly, curtains of green curls bouncing as she moved. "Yes, it can all be very confusing. We think we are listening to ourselves, but who is this I? The I inside that speaks away, shows us what we think is the truth, guides us down the paths between paths. That is the question you must ask yourself."

I continued to stare at her, trying to will her words to make sense to me, but it still all just seemed like the rantings of a mad woman, drunk and off her rocker.

"Let me simplify it for you, my dear. What you see is not what it seems, and what it seems will never be what you see.

Blocked you are and blocked you will be until you open up your internal eye and *really* see." Before I could react, she was next to me, putting her thumb on my forehead and hand on my heart. "I'm out of time, dear. This is the best I can do for you."

She began chanting that familiar but unknown language, light pouring forth from her eyes, mouth, and hands as she pushed that light into me, filling my vessel till I felt like I was exploding with energy and truth. It was pouring forth from me in torrents of burning hot white light for what felt like an eternity. Abruptly our light burnt out, and everything faded to black.

Jolting awake, I found myself in a dimly lit room in a large four-post bed, a massive window looking out into the starry night, trees swaying in the soft breeze. Amil was sleeping in an oversized chair in the corner of the room, shoulders still stiff as if he was ready for a fight even in his slumber. Looking over at the bedside table, a small digital clock told me it was three thirty three in the morning. Quietly I pushed my way out of the covers, tangled in the folds of my dress from tossing in my sleep. Finally breaking free, I tip-toed silently across the room and out the door. My throat was dry, and my lips were cracked as I followed the familiar layout of a Kingdom Keep toward the kitchen to find a glass of water. Turning the sink on, I let it run cold, splashing my face with the crisp water a few times before filling my glass.

Just as I was taking my first sip of water, a hand softly landed on my shoulder, sending me flying into the air, spitting my water everywhere as I choked, coughing in fits as his strong hands stabilized me. Wiping my face as I turned, he was standing *so* close and looking down at me with those intense electric eyes.

When he spoke, his voice was gravelly with sleep. "Sorry I scared you, m'lady." I was already shaking my head, sighing with relief. The whole thing made me realize how on edge I was. Nothing was what it seemed; I just didn't know who to believe anymore, and the whole thing was rather exhausting. I was actually longing for the days when everything was dull and boring and predictable—everything was messy and confusing now, and it was all too much.

He took a step back, clearly picking up on my mood and how completely overwhelmed I felt, although it didn't have to do with him, and I hated that he thought that, even for a moment. Setting the water down, I took a purposeful step forward, placing my hands on his chest as I looked up into his glowing eyes.

"Thank you for coming back for me."

His hard expression melted like butter as he put his hands on my waist and pulled me closer. "I would *always* come back for you. Nothing in this world or the next could keep me away from *you.*"

A warmth spread over me, and I realized for the first time in my life I felt like I had someone that would truly take care of me, protect me, and it was a surreal feeling. Resting my head against his chest, a smile spread across my face as he wrapped his strong arms around me, cradling me in his grasp as he swayed us back and forth. I felt content for the first time in my life and could have stood there forever, wrapped in his embrace, curled into the perfect grooves of his body that seemed to be made for me. After a long time, he finally broke the silence.

"So... breakfast or bed?"

I couldn't help but giggle at his casual tone during such an intimate moment, and teasingly I pushed him away. "Bed, obviously."

I grinned at him, placing my hand on his chest for a moment more before sliding past him and skipping off to the bedroom. Feeling nervous yet oddly confident at once, I was certain I had ruined things, but maybe they could be salvaged yet. Some small part of me felt a tinge of guilt thinking of Mia, but I pushed it aside. I didn't owe her anything, and I wasn't going to pass up this chance again—if I still had a chance, that is.

Reaching the bedroom several strides ahead of him, I pulled at the straps of my dress. For as much struggle as the thing was to get on, it came off pretty effortlessly, cascading to the floor below me with just a few pulls at the straps, leaving me standing there in teal green lace undies and a matching lace bra that Mia had insisted I wear, going on about some rule about nice undergarments being standard with formal wear. I didn't buy it at the time, but I couldn't say I regretted her choices now. Walking in, Amil paused, immediately dropping his eyes as his cheeks turned red. Mumbling apologies, he turned to leave the room when I called out.

"Please stay..."

He hesitated, back turned toward me. I wished I could see what was going on in those eyes. When he finally turned around, they were closed off and cold, hiding whatever was going on in that mind of his.

Crawling into the bed, he took off just his shirt, leaving on the joggers he had been wearing while sleeping in the chair, before following into the massive soft bed with me. He tensely wrapped his arms around me, letting me curl into his chest, but he was hardly breathing and seemed uncertain of himself, or perhaps me?

I sighed deeply before forcing myself to address the elephant in the room. "I know this must be hard for you. I just hope I didn't ruin what we had for good. If you need time, I get it..." I trailed off, unsure what else to say and afraid to look up at him and see whatever emotions were playing across his face. After several moments of silence, I finally faced my fears and looked up. He was staring down at me with the most intense look.

"I didn't know there *was* something between us to be ruined." I couldn't help but laugh nervously as the tears started biting at the corners of my eyes, rejection already setting in.

"Oh, well... In that case, I guess it doesn't matter anyway. I'm just not very good at reading signs—never mind what I said." I was rambling on, spiraling in my own self-pity, when a soft hand lifted my face up. Suddenly his lips were on me, moving slowly against my own with the sweetest softness as his tongue searched out mine, dancing together in a slow sway for several moments.

When he pulled away, it left me breathless and wanting more. Gazing into his eyes, I held my breath as he opened his mouth to speak. "There's nothing more that I could hope for than to be yours, my lady, I would do anything for you, and if you'd have me, I would always be yours for as long as you wish."

A smile erupted across my face as a rush of confidence swelled within me. I guess sometimes you could have your cake and eat it too. I couldn't remember feeling more elated in my life, and I rode that wave of certainty as I launched myself back at him, our bodies collapsing together like a match set. His lips met mine with the softest kisses that traveled across my body and brought a soft gasp from my lips. He pushed and pulled at all the right parts of my body, gentle and loving, giving in to the sweet surrender of his soft touch. It was so different from the night with Mia, wild and fierce, almost like a fight between lovers to see who could burn with more passion. Tonight was like two souls becoming one, our bodies blending together, unsure where he ended and I began, with each barely-there motion that brought my skin to life and made my flesh burn down to the bones.

He hesitated ever so slightly. I wasn't sure when and how we had lost the remainder of our clothes, but our naked bodies were hovering inches apart, and there was nothing more in the world I wanted than to close that gap. He looked deep into my eyes, reading my emotions, searching out any hesitations or fears from my past life. I realized, somehow, I had moved past that. I had become more than a victim, I had become a survivor, a warrior, and now a savior, and I wanted to reclaim and redeem this body completely, once and for all. Pulling him toward me, he took the invitation willingly, and in one soft swift motion, he was in me, a loud gasp escaping my lips. The next several hours were nothing more than a blur of intense ecstasy that made time meaningless as I lost ourselves in our shared pleasure.

As the sun rose in the storybook window, bringing the flowering trees to life in an array of bright pinks, yellows, oranges, and purples, we rested peacefully in each other's arms, drifting in and out of consciousness. Vivid images played behind my eyes as I was sinking between this world and dreamland, brightly colored visions of a different future, humans working in harmony, nature flourishing as the balance was restored, technologies beyond anything I could have imagined building great cities that bought about new ages for mankind, the visions folding in and out of themselves in geometric patterns as they revealed one possibility after the next. They showed me things straight from my wildest dreams—Mia and Amil standing hand in hand on a cliff, overlooking a raging sea, and then I knew my fantasies had really gone overboard, as their lips touched, an implosion of fire and ice. The jarring juxtaposition between the dream versions of my two lovers and the reality of their mutual hatred was enough to pull me out of my ridiculous semi-lucid dream state and back to the warm grasp of Amil's arms cradling around me.

The late morning sun shining through the window made it hard to open my eyes as I sleepily pushed myself up, looking back down at his still-sleeping form, resting peacefully for the first time since I had met him. Softly I traced the lines of his tattoos with my fingertips as a small smile spread across his face, refusing to open his eyes as he relished in my feathery touch, content to be the recipient of my affections as long as possible. Grinning, I eventually pushed myself up and sauntered to the closet to find clothes. I heard him sit up, yawning as he stretched, groaning as his bones popped loudly. It made me wonder how badly he had pushed himself to find me. I knew he had limited ether on this plane; it crossed my mind that he could run out before we reached our destination, and I'd be screwed. The time with Mia may have cost us everything, but what I shared with her was hard to stop thinking about even now.

Immediately an intense wave of regret for the little detour I took swelled over me, but I quickly shook my head, telling myself I was only worried about lost time, nothing at all to do with the night with Mia. Pushing her out of my mind, I began sifting through the clothes, trying not to think about what absurd outfit she would have picked out for me, and instead going for a comfortable looking pair of mustard yellow corduroy overalls and a deep blue cropped long sleeve shirt in an absurdly soft, thin cotton.

When I walked back into the room, Amil was already gone, the smell of bacon wafting in from the kitchen and drawing my grumbling stomach in. As I reached the familiar-looking breakfast bar, I began to notice small details of this Keep that were different than the last, the view, the type of marble of the countertop, and the orientation of the fireplace, but it was clear that it was still a part of a set. Amil, shirtless and back in his joggers, with a far too satisfied grin plastered across his face, was already working on a variety of dishes. Bacon sizzled and crackled in a large pan on the back burner while scrambled eggs were just setting in the pan, and the batter was being poured into an already hot waffle iron.

He honestly worked impressively quickly, or I was just terribly slow when it came to getting dressed. Indecision had always made that particularly simple task complicated for me, hence why I just wore the same things all the time when I was at home. It was easier that way. Amil flipped the bacon before whisking the eggs again in the pan and rotating the waffle maker before resetting the little timer that had chimed at him. Moving fluidly as if his steps were choreographed, he placed piping hot maple bacon, perfectly scrambled eggs, and a toasty brown waffle smothered in butter on a gorgeous crystal plate that he placed on the table in front of me. Ravenous, I silently consumed the entire plate within moments, much to Amil's amusement.

After breakfast, he told me about his plans to reach a place I never thought I'd be seeing in my life but was more than familiar with, Stonehenge. Amil explained it was one of the oldest known nexus points, something beyond time and space itself. Even during a small celestial event, such as a meteor shower, when travel between most nexus points was difficult at best and more often impossible, it would still be more than simple enough to make the jump from this realm to the next. I couldn't help but wonder what it would be like to be on the other side of the veil, how different the Kingdom must be from this world. Amil nodded his head solemnly, picking up on my apprehensive mood.

"It will be overwhelming at first. Our worlds are nothing alike, the very makeup of reality is different, and if we allowed you to see it in its pure potential, there is a risk you would lose your mind and, at very best, you would never be able to return to this plane. Fortunately, Hova has designed a filter for your human eyes. She developed it on some of the original Riders after, er... We had some issues with the first couple of batches when we tried to transfer them for training. Now there is little risk, though, and in many ways, you will perceive our spiritual bodies much in the same way you would see them in this physical form, which, trust me... It's for the best." I stared at him, mouth agape. It never occurred to me to really think about the fact that Amil might have a different form than the one he occupied here. I couldn't help but wonder what his pure soul manifested must look like, even if I had no chance of seeing it anytime soon.

Moving through the house, he was quickly packing bags for our journey as I sat pensively on the couch, toying with the ivory octopus I had yet to take off, mostly because I was afraid the tattoo would leave with it, but if I was being truly honest, the reasons were deeper than that. The morning passed quickly as I watched him load up the large intimidating jet with our stuff from the window. I was incredibly uncertain about flying; it was something I had never done before and honestly had never had any desire to do. Something about trusting my life to a massive metal object that propels through the sky at hundreds of miles an hour seemed insane to me. Although, I guess, of all planes, this one wasn't crafted by mere mortals, so perhaps I could put a little more faith in this machine. As he loaded the last bag into the jet and closed the luggage compartment, my heart started beating rapidly as the impending reality began closing in on me that soon I'd have to actually get on that *thing*. Frozen to the couch, I clutched the necklace so hard it was digging into my palms almost to the point of them bleeding. Amil stepped through the door, looking at me with a confused look.

"Are you okay?! What's wrong?" Panic poured over his face as he picked up on my thundering heart, sweaty skin, and nauseating mood shift as a panic attack washed over me. Dropping to his knees, he placed both hands firmly on my shoulders, insisting I look at him. After several moments, I was finally able to gain enough control of my shaking body to turn toward him and force my eyes up to his own.

Stuttering, my teeth chattered, and I was shaking so badly as I forced the words out through hyperventilated breaths. "I'm. Afraid. Of. Flying."

How absurd, everything I'd been through in the past few days, spending literally the previous forty-eight hours with a real-life demon. How could I possibly be this pathetic? Yet all the same, I was trapped in the terrors of this vessel as my body convulsed uncontrollably no matter how much my rational mind tried to fight back this physical assault on my entire being.

Shaking me out of my own self-sabotage, Amil moved his face inches from mine, staring intensely into my panicked eyes. "*Nato*! It's okay, you've got me, and I would *never* let something happen to you. Not again." He looked away momentarily, but I caught the shame in his eyes regardless. It seemed he still had not forgiven himself for letting me go with Mia. "That plane could fall out of the sky, and I promise you, you'd get to see those wings I told you about. It could catch fire, and I would wrap myself around you and parachute out of there. It could crash into a side of the mountain, and I would still barrel roll out of there with you. Literally *nothing* bad can happen to you in there, trust me, *please.*"

He was purposefully smoldering me with those captivating eyes, and it was working. My body was calming, my heart slowing, the shaking subsiding, and before I knew what was happening, I was nodding, letting him take me by the hand and out the door and onto that big jet plane.

CHAPTER 20 – FROM ON HIGH

Nato gladly accepted the little blue pill I offered to help with her anxiety and was currently dozing in her chair in the back of the small passenger jet plane. I had offered to allow her to sit in the cockpit, but the whole thing seemed to totally overwhelm her, so I didn't push it. Amazing how someone with so much power and potential could be so delicate, fragile, and breakable like the porcelain doll she resembled. Moments from the night before flashed before my eyes as I remembered her ivory skin glowing in the moonlight, exposed in its entirety, rivaling the nearly full moon for the brightest thing in the room.

After our little rendezvous in the bedroom, I felt an intense shift in my entire being. I had always wanted to protect her, to serve her, to even love her if she'd have me, but now it was an insatiable urge to be at her every beck and call. I wanted to bow down at her temple and worship at her very feet, although I held back as I had a feeling it might creep her out a bit. I didn't care to admit how many women I had been with over the millennia, but not one could ever begin to compare to the connection forged in my bones last night. Pushing on the throttle, I came back to reality as I began edging the plane downward toward the small, unmarked stretch of grass I planned to use as a makeshift airport outside of one of the most sacred Kingdom Keeps, hidden in the hills just beyond Stonehenge.

I landed with ease, but considering I hadn't actually done that much physical flying of planes in my lifetimes, something I hadn't wanted to admit to Nato, I wondered if it possibly had something to do with the way the autopilot was designed—even I wasn't *this* much of a savant. After a few small bumps and a stretch of the wheels slowly catching on the mossy ground below, the plane slowly rolled to a stop. After clicking a few buttons, I was up and walking toward Nato, semi-conscious from our touchdown; she was mumbling on and on. Mia's name was mentioned several times, much to my disappointment, but I pushed it aside, reminding myself it was me she spent the night with last night, not her. Shaking her softly, she jolted awake, looking up at me with big sleepy eyes as a smile spread across her face.

"Morning again… We're here already?" She was yawning and stretching, clearly having a hard time shaking off the effects of the medication. I couldn't stifle the small laugh; I had given her the smallest dose I could.

"We are, my lady. Shall I carry you through the threshold?" I grinned unabashedly at the idea, fully aware of its human implications.

She pushed me playfully at my teasing but leaned against me all the same. "Perhaps it *would* be for the best. Shame to make it all this way and die because I trip on a rock." She looked up at me with those doe eyes, and it was clear to me she was playing it up, but she didn't have to ask me twice. I swooped her up in my arms in one fluid motion, giggles erupting from her perfect lips as I swept her off the plane and across the small patch of grass toward the Keep.

Reaching the doorway, I kicked it open with my leg and tucked her head in as we walked through the threshold of our final home on this plane. At least this time around, I couldn't deny how natural it felt as I twirled her to her feet just inside the house. Looking up at me dreamily, she leaned forward on her tiptoes and kissed me, softly restrained, her tongue searching out mine in a timid sort of way. I didn't push more than she was willing to pull, still afraid of chasing her off. She dropped back down on her feet, grinning ear to ear as she stared up at me for several minutes before her stomach grumbled loudly, causing us both to laugh and wander off toward the kitchen to make lunch.

Smothering fresh caught Alaskan Salmon I found in the fridge in a thick yellow homemade coconut mango sauce, I roasted the slabs of fish in the oven while pouring white rice into boiling water and covering it on low to simmer while the fish cooked. I pulled out a guilty pleasure of mine of the human world, a classic box of mac n' cheese that I started in another pot, along with some broccoli steaming on the back burner. The whole meal came together quickly. Still sleepy, Nato sat silently at the counter, gazing at me as I moved through the kitchen with ease and grace. It was one of my favorite things to do in the human world. There was something amazing in the art of food, the delicate creation that lasted but a few moments. Plating out the dish, I poured us both a small glass of white wine to compliment the fish and took my seat next to her. She hadn't wasted any time in already shoveling several mouthfuls of food in her face by the time I sat down, much to my delight and humor.

As I stifled my laugh, she slowed down with a small grin. "Sorry, I couldn't help myself." She shoved several more bites in as I laughed and shrugged.

"I take it as a compliment."

I joined her in rejoicing in good food and drink, the sweet sauce on the salmon paired perfectly with the savory fish, and one glass of wine turned into two and then three as the plates cleared. We shared stories, passions, and dreams we had of the future. I could tell I had spent too much time on this plane because my human imagination was starting to run wild, to dream of possibilities where we could always be like this, just a boy and a girl, in love in a simple world. That was a dangerous thought, though. No matter how connected I felt, I needed to remember the mission. Things wouldn't be the same once we reached the Kingdom. I wasn't prepared for them to change, but there was no avoiding what tomorrow brought. I needed to warn Nato how different it would be when we transitioned, but I couldn't find the words to make her understand. By the look on her face when I grew quiet, she seemed to come to the same conclusion that these dreams would never be now—the future would be a different place on this plane.

Pushing aside these dark thoughts and the wine glass while I was at it, Nato suddenly jumped up, hands on her hips, a look of determination in her eyes. "You were teaching me about my powers before, and I want to learn more. *Please.*" She pleaded needlessly with me. It was an easy request; besides, I would give her just about anything she asked, at least for now, while I could.

Reaching my hand out, she wrapped hers in mine, walking as one toward the back door, down the patio stairs, and to the all-too-familiar patch of soft mossy grass next to the iridescent pool of water. Even a hemisphere away, it was part of a symmetrical set that spread the world over, like a cookie-cutter neighborhood sprinkled over the earth.

"Your element is water, so this is the perfect place to practice. You don't always need a water source, but it's easier to manipulate water than make it, so it's a good starting point. Water is made of icosahedrons. It aligns with your sacral and third eye synods. You need to see the icosahedrons in your mind, bending the water at its core, feeling it in your gut as you follow through, pushing and pulling the water at your will."

Closing my eyes, I placed my hands together and began chanting under my breath, reaching out to the body of water, bending it through the angles of its geometry as I pulled at the tide, pulling it all the way up to our feet, soaking our bare toes. Nato shrieked and giggled as I let the water flow back to its original shore.

"See? It's not much, I'm tempted to conserve my ether just in case, but it gets the point across. If you use your imagination, I'm sure you can see how it would come in handy."

Eager to show off, she was already closing her eyes, palms together, as she mimicked my chant. Several times over, she had to repeat it, yet all of a sudden, a massive wave swelled up, washing over us, soaking us completely as we both collapsed under the pressure to the mossy ground below, laughing loudly as the water subsided. I was impressed with her raw talent, and I couldn't imagine what proper training would do for her—or to her. I didn't want to think about what they had put the other Riders through to pull out their pure potential. I wanted to believe it would be different this time, that *she* was different, but would it be enough? Shaking my head, I pushed myself off the drenched ground and offered her my hand, a soft grin playing across my face, determined to make the most of tonight while I still could.

"You know, there's a little town nearby. I'd be honored if you'd let me take you out for coffee and cake."

Beaming at me, Nato jumped up from the ground excitedly, shoving my hand aside. "Are you asking me out on a date?" Her eyes were sparkling, something I had rarely seen, and I stumbled over my words.

"Well...yes, yes, I suppose I am." Much to my surprise, she literally jumped in the air for joy and then did a little dance. I couldn't help but laugh. "It's not that big of a deal, you know, just coffee."

She began shaking her head, waving her finger at me matter-of-factly. "Oh no, my good sir. See, I have never been on a date, and here I thought I would leave the human world behind without one. Now you really have a lot to live up to. I heard these things are supposed to be pretty special after all." She was clearly giving me a hard time, and I loved it.

Rolling my eyes at her little speech, I suggested we go get more presentable for a first date, which seemed to put a damper on her mood, but even she couldn't deny *wet* overalls wasn't the best date attire as we strolled hand in hand back into the house.

Walking into the oversized closet of the second bedroom, I quickly found an acceptable pair of dark wash jeans and a lavender batiked floral button-up. Cuffing the sleeves a couple of times, I left the shirt untucked before sliding on some casual dress shoes that resembled if sneakers had a baby with an oxford in a perfectly matched hue of purple. I stopped by the mirror to re-twist my bun, smooth out my beard, dab on a spritz of cologne, and put on an understated silver Rolex with a purple face and metallic white hands reading out the time. Strolling back into the main room, I found myself pacing nervously, much to my surprise, as I waited anxiously for her to finish getting dressed. I was beginning to feel the pressure of her earlier statement; I actually *was* determined to make this the best first date possible under the current circumstances. I might not have fate or fancy on my side, but I would show her just what I could see in her and what she meant to me before she had to face her destiny tomorrow and everything changed. Perhaps if I was lucky, it would be enough to hold on to herself even during the dark days ahead.

Stepping out timidly from the room, she had really outdone herself this time. Her hair was smoothed into two high buns, perfectly wrapped and sleek as could be. A few loose strands cascaded down, framing her face perfectly, her eyes and lips softly enhanced with the smallest dab of makeup, so subtle you almost couldn't tell if you weren't looking for it. Layers of blue and green lace and tulle cut into odd angles that draped around her thighs playfully, sparkling folds of fabric that weaved in and out of itself as it spiraled out from the waist where it met a tight-fitting top, the same forest green, wrapping itself tastefully around her petite figure, strappy sleeves showing off her porcelain shoulders. There was magic sparkling in her usually listless green eyes, and she had never reminded me more of a mythical creature, although I would say more Fae than Rider of the Apocalypse. Twirling around playfully, she looked at me, insecurity momentarily crossing those twinkling eyes.

"Is it too much?"

Stepping forward, I was shaking my head as I grabbed her face in my hands. "It's perfect. *You're* perfect." With that, I bent down and kissed her softly at first, pushing her boundaries as my tongue fought relentlessly against hers, passion getting the better of me as I swooped her up and pushed her against the wall. Soft moans escaped her lips as I ground against her, pulling back on her lip softly with my teeth as I saw a hunger in those eyes as deep as mine, and before I knew it, we were tangled as one, pushing and pulling the soft cries from those perfect lips.

Pulling away as we peaked together in synchronized cries of passion, I delicately set her back on the ground, grinning as I fixed my ruffled outfit. Blushing intensely, she was still breathing heavily as she tried to compose herself. I had knocked her perfect buns loose, causing several strands of hair to escape, which seemed more suited to her anyway. Finally getting a hold of herself, she laughed nervously.

"Well, that was pleasantly unexpected. I guess it *is* a nice outfit."

Laughing at her nonchalance, I reached my hand out for hers. She hesitated, pulling at her dress and the loose strands of her hair, looking uncertain. "You *still* look perfect. Let's go! The date night has only just begun."

Standing straight in her newfound confidence, she beamed up at me. "I think you've got the order of events down wrong, but I'm excited nonetheless."

Rolling my eyes at her playfully, I shrugged while grabbing her hand forcefully. "What can I say? I'm not *always* one for the rules." Pulling her along, I headed out the door and down the small cobblestone path that led to the arc hidden in a grotto of trees behind the cabin. Turning toward Nato, I couldn't suppress my excitement. "I want to see if I can teach you something else, if you're open to trying."

Eagerly she shook her head. I loved that about her; for someone absolutely terrified of the world in general, she was always down to try her hand at a new skill.

"These arcs exist across the world. They are at Kingdom Keeps and sometimes even in places you would least expect. I believe even the demons have mimicked our technology and created something similar at their little Underpost that they think we don't know about. They are interesting little buildings embedded with a special geometry that allow you to manifest whatever type of vehicle you can conjure up in that imaginative brain of yours. I'll teach you the mantra, but the rest is up to you."

Quickly reciting the spell for her, she repeated it to me for clarification before hesitantly walking up to the arc and placing her hands on the door. Closing her eyes, she spent several minutes focusing before she chanted out the words and, with a coy smile, flung the door open. The cutest little scooter in bright sparkly purple awaited behind the door, and she seemed unabashedly humored that I would be the one driving it.

Happy to humor her, I jumped on unashamedly and patted the small seat behind me for her to join. Impressed by my nonchalance or irritated that it didn't bother me more, her smug grin disappeared, replaced by a genuine smile of excitement as she jumped on and wrapped her arms around my waist, calling out enthusiastically. "Onward, trusty steed!"

Laughing at her childlike joy, something I didn't know she still possessed after what she had seen in this world, I revved the tiny four-cylinder engine several times, more a cat's meow than a lion's roar, before taking off down the dirt road, wind blowing in our hair as Nato squealed in sheer delight. Leaning in further as we picked up speed, she tucked her head against my back. I enjoyed the soft weight resting against me as we cruised along the old cobblestone streets that led into the ancient town that sat in the shadows of Stonehenge. Just minutes after entering the small town, we were pulling into a parking spot in front of the cutest little cafe this side of the world had to offer.

Tiny little tables scattered across a stone patio, covered in trellises blooming with every rose known to mankind. Twinkling lights were draped across the flowers, bringing them to life even in the afternoon light, not that there was much of it in this cloudy, dreary town. Walking hand in hand under the arched trellis of flowers that marked the entrance to the patio, Nato was eagerly looking around the patio at the scattered guests, seated at an eclectic array of tables that all looked like they had been up-cycled by hand by a rather eccentric artist.

Reaching the doorway to the cafe, I stepped forward swiftly to open the door for her. "My lady." I bowed, swooping my hand forward to indicate she should step in.

Blushing and giggling at my formal attitude, she curtsied back to me before skipping delightfully into the building. Following her, I found the inside surprisingly larger than you would expect from the street. The cafe seemed to stretch on for miles past the expansive counter, equipped with at least a dozen espresso machines and every tea imaginable in see thru boxes on the wall. There was another batch, larger this time, of eclectic seating sprawled out in an atrium covered in plants of every type, little trees in pots, blooming bushes lining the dining area, vines and wisteria draping from the ceiling—the whole space seemed so alive.

Beyond the dining area, rows upon rows of books stretched as far as the eye could see. Nato's eyes widened as she took in the marvelous sight. I had heard good things about this place from the other angels but never actually visited myself. The real marvel was right in front of me, though, the way those large green eyes sparkled at the sight of so much knowledge, the slight flush in her too-pale porcelain cheeks, the loose strands hanging out of her space buns that I had knocked out of place, the way her tiny hands fit perfectly in mine—it was almost too much to bear. Stepping back into the moment, I pulled her toward the counter and ordered us both their specialty mocha and a slice of every cake they had. Nato looked at me like I was insane, and I just shrugged as the cashier hustled off to start collecting cakes.

"You said it had to be perfect, so you get *all* the cake." Giggling, she rolled her eyes before sauntering off to find the perfect table. I followed after when the two mochas came up, steaming hot and rich with the fragrant smell of fresh espresso. Following after me came an army of waiters that seemed to have been conjured out of thin air to carry trays upon trays of tiny, sliced cakes. They filled up not only our table with cakes but several of the surrounding tables, too, before bowing away and leaving us in a fit of laughter at the expressions of the other patrons. Looking at us indignantly, one fellow cafe-goer was so offended by our display that she jumped up and left in a huff, clutching her pocketbook as she stormed out the door.

Fresh bouts of laughter followed her departure before we finally calmed down enough to take sips of the hot coffee, sweet but not too sweet, the rich salted dark chocolate blending perfectly with the strong but not too bitter espresso, just the right amount of foam on top paired with a dollop of in-house whipped cream and a sprinkle of fresh cocoa. It was honestly the best cup of coffee I'd had in all my lifetimes, and it made me regret not coming to this place sooner, although also grateful that we would always have the Cafe of the Angels as our special place.

This was one of the few public places on this plane that was created by Hova, a rare gem of a cafe that was absurdly popular with travelers and locals alike, so caught up in its beauty they didn't even seem to notice the physical impossibilities of this place, although a few fringe conspiracy theorists had often scrutinized this restaurant in wild YouTube videos but never to much mainstream success. Gorging ourselves on cakes of every flavor, Nato was excitedly taking tiny bites of every single one to ensure she got the full experience. Finally, when we felt like we would explode with cake and coffee, Nato pushed herself up from the table and urged me to follow her as she frolicked off to the rows upon rows upon rows of books.

We lost ourselves for hours in those books. Nato was sprawled out on the ground, flipping through several different volumes at once, eyes sparkling as she absorbed the ancient words of several original one-of-a-kind copies of books saved from the folds of time. The one she was most fascinated with, a history of the world up to that point, was a relic of the great fire that destroyed Alexandria. I remember it was one of the only books we actually recovered from what we expected was a demon cover-up to steal sacred knowledge of Hova's.

As the light began shifting, the afternoon fog clearing just enough for some rays of the setting sun to sneak through the windows of the atrium, a grin spread across my face. "It's nearly time!" Offering her my hand, I lifted her from her pile of books and began helping her put them back in their place. She was very particular that each went in the right space before I grabbed her hand again and towed her toward the back of the building.

"Where are we going? The exits that way." She was pointing back toward the front of the building, but I was already shaking my head.

"You didn't think that was the sum of our date, did you?" Looking confused, she shrugged and followed me in silence as we walked for what felt like miles, finally arriving at a small nondescript door at the very back of the oversized building. Tapping out a jazzy little rhythm on the ancient wood, the door swung open, and off we went into the dimly lit room alive with old-timely music.

CHAPTER 21 – SACRED SPEAKEASY

Walking into that room was like walking into someone's living daydream. Colorfully clad patrons of every mythical background filled the room, a brighter brood than what I found in the Under-wonderlands. Fae from the trees, the earth, the winds, and the waves, with sprawling tattoos and unexpected attributes that hinted at their origins from vines of leaves crawling up their arms to roots and rocks growing up their legs, feathery features erupting from their shoulders, and even gills on the necks of some of them. Pixies floated in the air scattered across the place, sprinkling dust on various patrons, causing them to lift in the air for several minutes as they joyously flew across the vaulted space. Gnomes sat drinking at the counter in a cute little row with a dark-haired maiden who seemed too familiar, sharing a drink with them while enjoying a crisp red apple. Somewhere in the dark corners of the room, I could just catch a glimpse of a unicorn stamping his feet, his soft whinnies on time with the beat of the music, upbeat jazzy music from a band with a ton of horns, and one unreal piano player. A beautiful young woman with tight curls was dancing around on the stage in a sparkly white flapper dress as she belted out with so much soul you could feel it moving your very own.

We took a seat at the bar, and Amil ordered us two drinks as I stared out at the dance floor, trying to place as many faces as I could. As impossible as it might seem, all of these fantastical creatures gathered in one place, and more than just Hova's, I knew from the stories Eden had told me that most of the creatures in this room were actually descendants of the Earthly Plane and were beyond her reach. Perhaps that was why they felt so emboldened to make a speakeasy right in the back of her cafe; it was brilliant, really. There seemed to be a few minglers, though, a handsomely dressed vampire with a charming smile despite the fangs twirling around a young woman in an elaborate ball gown with more love in his eyes than lust. A real-life werewolf, in all his full moon glory, controlled and stable, holding a nice conversation with some sort of sea captain about a fabled beast of the sea. A leprechaun several seats down who seemed like he'd had too many drinks already but was rolling with it pretty well as he did a little jig to show the bartender he was good for one more. A rowdy group of pirates led by a short but fierce-looking young woman with dark brown hair and even darker eyes entered the room after us, approaching the dance floor and bowing to a gang of princesses that reminded me of the movies I watched growing up. The leader of the group broke off and came to sit a few seats down from me, ordering a scotch on the rocks as she made eye contact with me and gave me a little salute. Blushing, embarrassed that she caught me staring, I nodded timidly back before turning back to Amil and the drinks that had just arrived.

Chugging the first one down like a fish out of water, he had a second on the way before I even had to ask. The flavors were overwhelming, a rich blend of berries with a sour tang at the end, but at this point, I was starting to get used to everything from *his* world being so spectacular. It made me wonder what exactly he could find so interesting about me because, clearly, he was *very* interested. Since our night together, it felt like he never took his eyes off me. Even when he pretended to, I would always catch him watching me from the corners of his eyes. I told myself he was just worried about losing me again, but it seemed like something more, something behind those eyes that I couldn't quite decipher.

The second drink arrived not a moment too late. My curious thoughts had turned darker as anxiety crept in; the doubts about my choices deciding to voice their opinions loudly were quickly drowned out by the second drink washing down my throat and racing through my bloodstream, giving me a very heady feeling. Amil ordered a third drink for me without a word, despite still being on his first beverage. Of course, he was picking up on my mood and wanted to push this date in the right direction.

Finishing the third drink as quickly as the first two, the liquid courage began to seep in as I jumped to my feet and turned toward the breathtakingly beautiful man at the counter that somehow was mine for the night, and maybe longer if I wanted him. The thought made my heart flutter, a dangerous reaction.

Bowing to him, I reach my hand out for his. "May I have this dance, good sir?"

A slow, sultry song had just begun, and the young woman on stage was moaning out low long notes that pulled at your heartstrings and raised the hair on your arms. Grinning from ear to ear, Amil swallowed the rest of his drink in one giant gulp and was on his toes immediately, taking my hand and sweeping me off to the dance floor. I didn't know a thing about dancing, but that didn't seem to bother Amil as he led the way, dragging me along in his wake with each elaborate move that cut paths through the dance floor and made several of the other dancers stop completely to watch us. With each swooping move, we cleared the dance floor more until I became hyper-aware that we were the only ones left dancing on the brightly lit dance floor, a crowd of onlookers surrounding us and cheering as they watched Amil swoop me low to the ground, toss me high in the air, and spin me around and around until my nerves couldn't hold on anymore. I let go of all the self-consciousness I felt with all these eyes on me. Suddenly I was giggling, releasing my need for control as I let him toss me this way and that way, the fascinated crowds applauding with each extravagant move.

Lost in the moment, I could have stayed there in his arms forever, tossing and turning to the music, but time waits for no one, and the song changed, causing Amil to pull me in close, swaying me in his arms slowly despite the upbeat tempo of the new tune, the onlooking crowd merging back onto the dance floor, moving their bodies in sync with the music. As we drifted into the sea of sweaty creatures, like two clouds caught in the breeze, a loud crash brought me abruptly back down to earth, the flames of fear already tearing through my body as my little bubble of happiness burst. Tumbling through the door, a mass of burly bodies piled into the room, led by a tall, handsome man that I recognized all too well with his mess of blue ringlet curls.

The men who had captured me in the bar had returned with a vengeance, their features twisted in anger and frustration as they scanned the room for us, clearly uncomfortable in this Sacred Speakeasy. I suppose they didn't spend so much time mingling with the more ethereal creatures of the mystic world. Already reacting to the intruders, Amil pushed me behind his tensed body as he crouched down defensively, eyes flickering from one demon to the next as he tried to count them all. At least a dozen had come tumbling in after Levi, and several more were flanking in from two other entrances I hadn't noticed before. Despite my fear, I couldn't help but wonder where those doors must have come from because there had clearly only been one entrance from the way we came. Could they be portals like the door that took us to Eden's kitchen?

My curiosity was cut short as the gang of demons began closing in on us. I struggled to count them as they moved in and out of the oblivious crowd. There had to be two dozen of them at least; I couldn't imagine that Amil would be powerful enough to take them all, even with his advantages as an angel. I know he'd been trying to hide it, but it was clear his ether was more limited than he wanted to let on, and even at full strength, their sheer numbers seemed more than enough to overwhelm him. His face was determined, set to defend me to the end regardless of the impossible odds, but I could see the trace of fear deep in those electric eyes as they shifted from one target to the next, desperately trying to calculate a way to take out enough of them for me to attempt an escape. I wouldn't run this time, though; I wouldn't be the damsel in distress who froze in the face of danger. I would stand by his side and fight hand in hand, even if I was more likely to trip on my own feet than actually land a hit. I would do everything in my power to protect Amil the same way he wanted to protect me. Just as I was moving toward his side to stand with him, full-on panic taking over his face as he picked up on my intentions to fight instead of flea, the most unexpected thing happened, taking even Amil by surprise.

Stepping forward casually from the bar, the tiny girl with fierce brown eyes pulled her oversized captain's hat back on and walked toward the group of demons who towered over her, hand resting on the hilt of her sword. Tossing her curtain of dark brown hair back, she was suddenly backed by the entire posse of pirates that had been entertaining damsels on the dance floor, beckoned by some secret signal from their comically small leader.

Pulling her sword from her sheath, she held it idly near Levi's heart as she spoke in a rather bored voice. "A long time ago, I got a fortune that told me to be here at this particular bar at this particular time. It seems like I finally know why." Turning toward us with an expression as bored as her voice, she motioned for us to run. "Take your leave, fair lady. Leave these scoundrels to me."

With another nod, she turned, lifting her sword and going for the first strike. Levi responded instantly with a dodge to the left, his eyes still set on me, cold and calculating, clearly driven to catch me if it was the last thing he did. Without a moment's hesitation, Amil whipped around, wrapping his arms around me as he lifted me and ran with all of his might toward the back door, an extravagant arched wooden doorway covered in geometry and hidden in shadows.

Pausing just long enough to chant a small mantra at the door, I caught a glimpse over his shoulder of the scuffle going down between the pirates and the demons. It was hard to tell who was beating who; both parties were holding their ground ferociously. As Amil swung the door open, a spiraling vortex lay beyond, alive with light and calling out to us in a mystical voice that spoke in tongues. Traveling through a portal like this for the second time in my life, I pressed my face against his chest, bracing myself for the impact as the light began pulling at my very being, tearing me apart at a cellular level and building me back again on the other side. As the final pieces came into place and my consciousness caught up with my vessel, I found myself just outside the little cottage we were calling home for the night. Just as Amil turned to close the gateway, a hand reached through, followed by the twisted furious face draped in vivid blue curls, his eyes mad with determination as he grabbed Amil by the throat and slammed him to the ground with the full force of his body. Several more bodies came tumbling after him, a mess of brightly colored hair crashing upon him with everything they had, tearing into his flesh with their hungry teeth and pulling at him from every angle.

Erupting in a ball of lightning, Amil emerged damaged but not yet defeated as the wild, angry energy pushed back everyone except me forcefully. Panting heavily, he rushed to my side to try and run with me again, but it was already too late. Levi was the first on his feet, pulling a massive wave with him from the nearby pool of water, cascading it on top of Amil as another demon he called out to by the name of Pho, a beautifully androgynous being with a deep magenta pixie cut twisted into two distinct horn-like spikes began raining down literal hail fire on top of the deluge of water pouring down on Amil. My heart skipped a beat as I watched him falter beneath the power of the attack, his body eventually going limp as he was relentlessly pounded into the ground with the unreal display of force. More demons were gathering around him, some recovering from the attack and preparing to launch their own assaults should he manage to survive the current deluge, while more still poured forth from the open portal. I was about to watch him die, I could feel it in my bones, and I would be swept off to do some demon bidding in bringing about the eternal apocalypse here on Earth. I needed to do something. I needed to do *anything.*

Closing my eyes, the gravity of the situation rushed over me, the fear, the panic, the pain of watching someone I loved—and I did love him, I was sure of it now—die before my very eyes. Even if, logically, I knew it was only his temporary vessel that would be destroyed, it was still too much to bear. It let loose the floodgates I had been subconsciously holding back my entire life. Every ounce of torment, frustration, and hopelessness came bubbling to the surface all at once. It suddenly was gushing from me, manifesting in the form of pure ether rushing to escape from my entire being. Floating into the air, the energy pushed past the boundaries of my vessel and exploded out of me in a burst of pure cosmic energy, sending the demons flying back again and dissolving several of the weaker ones completely, their smoke trail dissipating in the rush of wind that followed my initial attack. Now that the power was flowing through me, it seemed like it was impossible to stop it. Another wave of cosmic energy rushed out, pushing the demons further back as I instinctually called out to the water. It answered my call willingly, like a dog ready to please its master, crashing in a massive wave toward the remaining demons and sweeping them away in a tsunami of bioluminescent water.

Falling to the ground in a heap, exhausted from the sheer force of the power that had been flowing through me, I had to use all of my remaining strength to push myself back to my feet that were already moving, one in front of the other as fast as they could to take me to Amil's limp body. Dropping to the ground next to him, I place my hand on his heart. I could just feel it beating, weak but fighting, nonetheless. I took the shreds of energy left in my depleted body and began softly chanting the mantra of healing I had used before on Mia. I didn't have the strength to restore his body fully like I did before, but I managed to give him enough ether to wake him up, his eyes cracking open slowly as he looked at me with a weak grin.

"I'm the one who's supposed to be saving you, you know." He chuckled softly, a movement that made him grimace as I gingerly helped him sit back up. "Take me to the lagoon. It won't help much, but it may be enough that we can still get out of here in one piece."

After a lot of struggle, I was able to get him to his feet, wrapping his arm around my shoulder so he could lean on me for support. We walked slowly toward the water's edge. I was trying to be strong, but my body was tapped out, and I barely made it there before we both collapsed in a pile of heavy breathing at the shore. Laying at the edge of the shore, half submerged in the water, Amil began chanting a new mantra that brought the water to life, slowly wrapping its way around his body, creating a liquid shell around him that began pulsating. I watched in utter amazement as the water seemed to feed itself into his body through his tattoos.

He sat up slowly, breath steadied and eyes determined. Standing, he reached down, offering his hand to me to help me up. My legs felt like noodles as I stood, and I had to lean on him for support. "Could you try that little water trick on me?"

He furrowed his brow, looking down at me sympathetically. "Sorry, my lady, that trick only works on angels. Besides… we are out of time. They are already on their way back."

Looking up, I could see Levi leading the remaining demons, paused on a hillside looking down at us with utter hatred in his eyes. He knew he had us in check, and now he just needed to make his final move to end the game. Pushing me behind him, Amil crouched again, determined to use whatever strength he had left to protect me from what remained of Levi's little posse.

"I don't need to buy much more time, my lady. The gate opens at midnight when the moon is at the peak of its eclipse."

He pointed up to the sky. I hadn't noticed, but more than half the full moon had gone red as the earth slowly blocked its view of the sun. "When the nexus point opens, I want you to go, despite what is happening here. Promise me you'll jump, and you won't look back." Every ounce of me was screaming not to leave his side, but I couldn't argue with the look in his eyes, so slowly and silently, I nodded my head yes.

Suddenly the demons were descending, rushing at Amil with the full force of a stampede of wild animals. He smiled at me, soft and sweet, before turning to take his position to fight an impossible fight. Pho was the fastest, on him already as they exchanged hit after hit, blocking and striking at each other faster than my eyes could follow. Levi was the second on him, trying to flank him and take advantage of his battle with Pho to find a weak spot and land a strike. Amil was quick enough to keep them both at bay, but it was only a matter of moments before the handful of demons that had survived my explosive display of force were on top of him, striking from every direction at once.

Amazingly he danced in and out of them, dodging left and right, but his power was fading quickly, and Levi managed to land the first strike, leading to a second and a third. Shaking his head, he managed to push back the horde of demons again, protecting his ground as he got a second wind and was able to dodge their attacks and land a few of his own. Several of the demons backed up a few feet after several well-placed hits on his part, but it wasn't stopping Levi and Pho from closing in, using every opening they had to land a hit on him, hits that seemed to be getting stronger and more well placed as his grunts of pain transformed to screams of agony. There was no denying that he was losing this battle, and there was nothing left I could do to help him. The only question was, could he hold out long enough for me to get out of here, or would this all be for nothing?

Calling on his final reserves of power, Amil closed his eyes and began lifting into the air, bringing all the surrounding earth with him as he floated up at least fifteen feet before he sent the ground crashing back down, burying Levi and his crew at least ten feet beneath the rubble and rocks. Dropping back down, his chest was heaving up and down with each labored breath he took. I ran to his side to help support him; he was crumbling against me, leaning completely into me to the point where I could barely even stand myself.

Between shallow breaths, he whispered, "You need to leave me now. I can hear them underground, and it won't take them long to escape. I can hold them off for just a bit longer, but you need to get to the gate now." We both looked up to the skies above. The moon was nearly all red now, with just a sliver of white left. "If you start running now, you'll make it just in time. The gateway opens at Stonehenge. It won't remain open long, so you must go on without me. I will find my own way back quickly enough, I'm sure, and we will be reunited in the Kingdom."

I was staring up at him, tears biting the corners of my eyes. I wasn't prepared to do this on my own. I wasn't prepared to leave him. I wasn't prepared to let him die to protect me. Even if he did come back, it felt too real and too painful to lose him.

He could tell I was faltering. He could tell that I wasn't going to run. He could tell that I would stay and fight by his side even if it meant my own death or, worse, becoming a pawn of the ultimate evil. He looked down at me with those intense blue eyes and bore into me with everything he had, the weight of his gaze causing my resolve to buckle as he pleaded with his honey-sweet voice.

"Please, Nato, I need you to trust me. I will be okay if you're okay. Please run. *Now.*"

A crumpled hand burst forth from the ground at our feet, followed by a muddy mess of tangled hair, just barely blue under all the red dirt. Levi crawled his way out of the earth like some B-rate zombie movie, his body crushed and contorted in unnatural ways. Slowly his bones were popping back into place as he dragged his shattered body across the ground, grasping desperately for Amil. Despite everything, I wavered ever so slightly in my resolve, succumbing to his pleading eyes as suddenly I found my feet taking me away from him, one foot crashing in front of the other as I ran, blinded by the tears streaking from my eyes, trying to ignore the heart-wrenching sounds of Amil's screams as I refused to turn back and see what my heart already knew.

CHAPTER 22 – HAIL MARY

Standing there, suddenly hollow, every inch of me screamed to go after her as my heart unexpectedly shattered into a thousand pieces. It was a strange empty feeling that I had never experienced before. I couldn't understand, my instincts had never let me down before, and I was certain after everything we had been through that I would be able to convince her to join my cause. I was out of time now, though. The firework show was drawing to an end with an absurd display of fifty-five fireworks rocketing upwards at once, lighting up the skies with the most intense series of explosive colors, and I had a date with destiny.

Turning my attention to the massive clocktower that dominated the center of the town, I was already moving, my feet pushing hard against the cobblestone streets as I moved fast enough to be nothing more than a blur to those around me, too impatient to conserve my limited ether anymore. Time was almost up anyway, and it wouldn't matter anymore if I didn't succeed. She would be gone, whisked away to the Kingdom, and the war would be lost, humans would be eradicated, and this plane would never be the same again.

Stalking my way into the tower, my ears perked, listening for any trace of movement in the dark brick hallways. A soft touch on my shoulder sent me flying like a cat into the air, hair on end as I stiffened for battle, whipping myself around, crouched and growling as I hit the floor facing my opponent. Maicoh was standing there bemused, leaning casually against the wall, arms crossed, clearly unintimidated by my hostile display, a large smile spread across his dark tan face as he chuckled softly.

"Calm down there, kitty cat. I didn't mean to startle you." Standing up straight, he opened his arms apologetically as I glowered at him.

"How did you do that? Sneak up on me like that?"

He chuckled again, shrugging his shoulders in a frustratingly casual way. "I'm a quiet guy. What can I say?"

Glaring at him for several more moments, I finally accepted that was the only answer I was getting from him and moved on. "So, you're the one that asked me here. So here I am. What now?"

An excited grin crept across his face, just inches from mine, some weird glint in his unnerving two-toned eyes. "Follow me. There is so much to tell."

Silently he began plodding along in front of me, leading me deeper into the confines of the clocktower. After several turns, we found ourselves in a stunning little garden, alive with a million blooms of every color, a small sparkling fountain sprung forth from the flowers, a goddess with lamb-like features carved into the stone, pouring water from her open chalice to the small pond below her, full of sparkling coins. Several stone benches surrounded the little wishing well, and Maicoh encouraged me to take the seat next to him as he tossed a coin into the water, muttering under his breath. Turning to me, he handed me a tiny gold coin. "Make your offering, utter a wish—perhaps if your intentions are true, it will be granted." I thought for several moments before softly uttering my deepest desires under my breath with the flick of a coin that splashed resolutely into the emerald waters.

Turning to him with a newfound wave of conviction, I squinted my eyes. "Spill it. Why did you bring me here? What do you know about me?"

He grinned as he leaned back in his chair. "Ever perceptive,

I expected nothing less. I'll tell you everything I know, but first, I need to tell you a bit about myself."

Impatiently I shifted in my chair as I glared at him once more. "Make it quick."

He laughed, a warm sound that lured you in as he sat up. "Yes, ma'am. Long story short, it is… Many moons ago, my people were a nomadic tribe traveling the coast, moving with the tides. We were one with the land and the sea, and she shared her magic with us, the natural order of things. So dedicated were we to the cycles of the earth that she gifted us with our own magic, a deep connection with our spirit animal could be channeled into the ability to shift and harness the power of that animal."

He paused, eyeing me as I looked at him skeptically. "You mean like a werewolf, right? You're a werewolf? I've heard of those. Hova made those."

He shook his head, clearly irritated. "Well, no, actually, a Jackal. Much cooler than a wolf if you ask me, and definitely not *a* werewolf. We come in all sorts of forms, and have walked this earth for many millennia. We are of this plane, not something of Hova's doing, but inspired by the teachings of the original mother." *The original mother—he must be talking about Eve.* "She spoke of a prophecy, a tale as old as time, about a new God that would unite the Riders and bring light to the people of Earth. Something tells me you'll lead me to them."

Cutting him off rudely, I laughed obnoxiously, doubled over in fits of hard-to-breath, gut-wrenching laughter. A *New God.* As if, what an absurd proposition. After several more bouts of laughter, I finally composed myself enough to form a rebuttal.

"Listen, I don't know where you got your wires crossed, but there's only one God. Your *'mother'* was just a rebel in over her head."

He shrugged casually, still beaming at me with reverence.

"Believe what you want. Either way, I've got nothing better to do right now, and you seem to be down a companion. Let me at least help you in the meantime, and maybe you'll lead me to my God." He raised his eyebrows, pleading with those oddly ominous yet somehow comforting heterochromatic eyes.

Huffing, I dropped my shoulders in defeat. I didn't know this guy, but he wasn't wrong. I needed help, and who was I to look a gift horse in the mouth? Standing up, I held my arms out impatiently. "Well, do you know which way we should go, at least?"

As he stood, lumbering over me, another massive grin spread across his face. "Lucky for you, I'm a tracker, so finding your girl will be no problem."

My cheeks burned bright red despite myself, and I hissed under my breath. "I'd hardly call her mine. Don't pretend you didn't see the choice she made."

He shrugged casually again. "Bad choice, in my opinion, if it matters at all."

I couldn't help but smile, my confidence had taken a hit, and I didn't mind the compliment after such a crushing defeat. Moving swiftly out of the labyrinth of hallways that made up the clock tower with his long legs, I rushed to keep up in his wake.

When we left the confines of the building, he suddenly shifted, becoming ghost-like before solidifying again in the form of a massive, tricolored jackal, covered in glowing white and gold geometric symbols, a whole collection of platonic solids scattered across his body, weaving in and out of each other. I couldn't suppress the shocked exclamation that escaped my lips at the unexpected sight. Turning, he gave me a toothy grin before barking and taking off into the night.

I raced after him all through the night and into the morning, exhaustion weighing on me as the early rays of rising sunshine glared into my sleep-deprived eyes. Funny how these vessels had so many trivial human needs; it made me miss the ease of being in my ethereal form. He pushed himself even harder, paws beating against the hard ground, and I focused all of my energy on staying right on his tail, literally. Just when we started to let up, his stride slowing to a trot as we reached a massive open field of wildflowers with a small cabin square in the middle, an engine roared to life, reverberating across the field like a dragon coming alive after a several-year slumber. Before we could move another inch, a sleek jet streaked off into the air above the cabin. My angered screech was drowned out by the engine erupting as the jet took off into the sky and disappeared from sight in a matter of moments. Collapsing to the ground in a fit of rage, I slammed my fist down, a shockwave of power erupting out that Maicoh just managed to dodge. Turning to him, he had transformed back into his human form and was slowly inching closer to me, arms outstretched.

"Sorry about that, miss. Would you like a hug or something?" Growling, I shoved him away and stalked off, already calculating my next move.

Marching my way across the field and past the house, I looked around for several minutes before finding what I was looking for. An unsuspecting-looking garage tucked in a grotto of trees, as common as any garage to an unsuspecting eye—I knew it was anything but. Walking up to the door, I placed my hand on the cool wood, closed my eyes, and chanted out a soft mantra while envisioning a beast of a dirt bike that would take me across this country and to the next in no time. Excitedly I pulled the door open, expecting to find my creation, yet it was empty, void of anything except a few dust bunnies and a tiny mouse scurrying away at the sight of me. Frustrated, I closed the door and repeated the mantra, clearly focusing on pulling at the pentagonal geometry out of the ether to create my mechanical steed. Pulling the door open once more, it was empty again, much to my dismay. Puzzled, perplexed, and downright irritated, I stood there for several minutes pondering the possibilities of what I could be doing wrong. After several long moments of deep thought, an idea struck me—it was so *obvious*.

Thinking back to the dreams of awakening I had, what felt like lifetimes ago now, when I was first hunting Nato for all the wrong reasons, I remembered becoming trapped in the folds of the universe because I was moving in all the wrong angles. If logic prevailed, the Keeps must be crafted using the same geometry the angels move in, and their arcs would be as well. Moving forward, uncertain if this would even work but determined to try, I placed my hand on the door and began repeating the mantra for a third time, but this time I envisioned pulling at the ether in hexagonal angles, bending and folding the geometries into the metallic bike I had originally envisioned. Once more, I pulled open the door, a smile creeping across my face as I stared down at the beautifully sleek bike, dark and streaked with silver, carved in a mix of pentagonal and hexagonal geometry. Jumping onto the dirt bike, I revved the engine several times before peeling out and sliding to a halt in front of Maicoh, a grin on my face as I patted the back seat.

Shrugging casually without a worry in those earnest eyes— either he was just coy, or he really did just lack the toxic masculinity that plagued most of his kind—he jumped onto the back seat without a moment's hesitation. Unabashedly wrapping his arms around my waist as I took off, I tore across the screeching flowers on purpose as I fishtailed my bike several times before taking off into the misty morning sun in the direction I watched the plane take off in. Pushing the throttle all the way down, the bike engine screamed as we raced across the countryside, the morning sun giving way to afternoon rays as we put as many miles behind us as possible. We traveled through small country towns and extravagant sprawling cities, the entire time not letting up even a fraction as Maicoh directed us in the right direction, and I pushed the bike as fast as I possibly could. Night finally descended upon us, and I didn't need a tracker now to know she was getting close. I could feel her, feel the pull that had been drawing me toward her this entire time, the very pull that had made it feel like I was being pulled into a million pieces when she walked away; my heart ached just thinking about it. I pushed the thoughts aside as I leaned forward against the handlebars and coaxed even more speed out of the machine as I raced in and out of the back roads, desperate to be reunited with a girl who didn't even want me.

As the moon rose above us, I could already see the sliver of red beginning to block out her bright light. I was running out of time; when the full moon reached the peak of its eclipse, the nexus point would open, and she would be gone forever. Demons could travel pretty freely from our plane to this one. We didn't need sacred sites for our portals or even much of a cosmic event, a shooting star and any spiritually charged land could be enough for our kind to enter this dimension, but no demon had ever managed to enter a nexus point and travel back to the Kingdom once they had fallen from grace.

I often wondered about those times, about the great Fall. Every original demon I knew could remember it, but I had no recollection of it for some reason. Mother had always told me I was gravely injured in the final battle, and it took all of her strength to restore me, leaving her weakened, trapped in the Underworld forever more. There was something about that story that just wasn't enough for me anymore. There was some truth I needed to know that was hiding just beyond the other side of the veil. I was certain if this Hail Mary was successful by some stroke of luck, Nato could help me find the other Riders and perhaps the truth along with them. I had one last shot at convincing her, which was a long shot at that, but I had to try everything, considering humanity was counting on me. I never saw myself as much of a savior, but suddenly, I just couldn't let them down.

Time passed quickly, and the red streak was turning into nearly half the moon when Maicoh instructed me to take a sudden turn onto a dirt path, proudly declaring it was a shortcut, one that my bike was fortunately able to handle. Bumping along the hilly path, I pushed the machine to its limits, the engine beginning to whine under the pressure and strain I had put it under for hours upon hours. Even angel technology couldn't last forever, I suppose. Watching the moon, I could feel the pit in my stomach growing as the slice of red shifted well past the halfway mark. The closer I got to *her*, the more I could tell something was deeply wrong. She needed my help, and despite the choice she made, I would still lay it all on the line for her—what a strange feeling. I should be bitter, I should be resentful, I should want vengeance—these are feelings I was used to dealing with, but this devotion... It was unlike anything I had ever experienced. She should mean nothing to me, a mere pawn in my own agenda, but somehow, she had crept her way into the cold confines of my heart, and now I was certain there was no turning back. I had never been a believer in love, but I wasn't foolish enough to pretend I didn't know what this feeling was.

"Just ahead now." Maicoh's voice was heavy with his own worries. Perhaps tracking wasn't his only ability because his brow was already furrowed, as if he knew the trouble we were about to run into. The tires tore across the damp mossy earth as we climbed one last massive hill before the whole scene before me changed. Amil barely stood against an army of demons bearing down on him with Levi in the lead. Nato was nowhere to be seen, but I could feel that she must be very close and in an immeasurable amount of pain. Had she left him to sacrifice himself so she could make it to the nexus point? I was torn, every part of me wanted to chase after her, to use my last chance to convince her while I still *had* a chance, yet my intuition was pulling me toward Amil, the last person in the world I ever thought I'd want to save. I should leave him to die there, chase down the woman I love, and convince her to come with me. I should do anything except what I was about to do.

Revving the engine, I turned to Maicoh. "Prepare yourself for the worst." He grinned, clearly unafraid of a challenge. I raced toward the gang of demons at full speed, launching myself off the bike, Maicoh following my lead at the last moment, sending the machine crashing into the attacking horde, all metallic squeals and anguished screams. Landing on all fours like a cat, I was back on my feet instantly, Maicoh landing much less gracefully but right behind me as we took our stand next to Amil. The look on his face was absolutely priceless, but I didn't have long to relish in his shock and confusion. The bike had been but a temporary distraction. Levi was back on two legs again, fury twisting his face as he saw me standing next to the angel.

He pointed his finger at me aggressively as he screamed out his accusations. "Traitor!"

I just grinned and shrugged, no longer phased by his opinion of me, I thought what we had shared once was love, but now I knew what real love was, the blinding bliss of binding myself completely to someone for the first time in my life, even if the string could only ever be pulled one way. I would drown in my devotion for her, but I was eager for the waves to wash over me regardless.

"Call me what you want. I know who I am and what I'm trying to accomplish, and you're the last person I'm concerned with convincing. You mean *nothing* to me, so either get out of my way or prepare for me to move you out of my way."

Crouching down, he charged at me at full speed, rage seeping off him as he crashed into me. I used his own force against him and redirected his attack, sending him flying backward as I began pulling the fire within my heart into a massive ball that fed on all the fear and worry eating at my soul right now as every cell in my body begged to be reunited with *her*. Yet here I was, defending the very man who had stolen her away from me, attacking the only friends I had ever known. Erupting out of me all at once, a massive wave of fire, fanned by the turmoil and confusion gripping my heart, tore across the field, consuming everything it touched, including several demons. Even I was shocked by the sheer display of force. Levi and Pho both managed to dodge the rapture of flames along with a few other demons that were falling further back, clearly intimidated by the power seething off of me. Levi launched another attack, smarter this time as he barreled forward while signaling for Pho to flank me from the side. Maicoh was already on it, though. Jumping into the air, he disappeared in a blast of skin and flesh before coming out on the other side as a rabid jackal, tricolored fur on end, covered in gold and white geometry of every type, fangs exposed as he dove for Pho's neck, pinning them to the ground as he tore into their flesh relentlessly.

Growing desperate as he watched his comrade fall to Maicoh, Levi screamed for the remaining demons to rush forward all at once. Maicoh was preoccupied with wrestling with Pho, who was still clinging to life as they tried to fight the savage beast off of them to little avail. Amil had collapsed back to the ground, puffing and panting as his soul struggled to hang on to his beaten vessel, and nothing stood between him and certain death besides me. Reaching into my coat pocket, I pulled out my final explosive, tossing it with precision toward the row of angry demons raining down upon me. A massive explosion morphed into a vortex below their very feet, eating them up and taking them somewhere halfway across the world. Levi screamed as he watched the last of his companions fall into the portal and disappear, leaving him alone in the misty field, looking at me with pure hatred in his golden eyes. I looked to my companions, Maicoh bloodied and limping, Pho's body fading in a puff of shadows, Amil struggling to barely breathe, and I knew I was the final hope, even if my own ether reserves were nearly depleted. Pulling out the dual pistols I had been saving for the worst-case scenario, I pointed them directly at Levi and opened fire, one round after another.

He was fast, faster than any of the other demons as he moved like water, fluid as he dove in and out of the line of fire, one bullet after another whizzing past him, exploding behind him as they made impact with various trees and rocks, creating a glorious backdrop of flames as he closed in on me. His blue ringlet curls were a tangled mess of blood and mud, the flames reflecting in his eyes, making him look absolutely mad as he finally reached me despite taking all my best shots.

Closing his hands around my throat, he slammed me to the ground in one effortless motion. I knew I wasn't a match for him in hand-to-hand combat. Hitting the ground, one of my guns flew out of my hand, but I managed to grasp the other at the last minute, clinging to it desperately as he tried to use his free hand to wrestle it away from me as his other hand closed tighter and tighter around my throat, making my head spin, stars starting to appear in my eyes as the blackness began to settle in. I was doing everything I could to turn the gun on him and use my last bullet, but I was losing the battle and fast.

Suddenly Amil was on top of him, ripping him off me with the last of his strength as they tumbled into the grass together. Even weak, he was still a worthy opponent, wrestling Levi to the ground where Maicoh began taking bites, pulling bits of flesh off

Levi as he screamed and riled against his captures, trying his best to throw them off him.

There was no time to hesitate. I jumped to my feet and ran to their side; lifting the gun I had managed to hold on to, I aimed it squarely between his eyes. Screaming, he used the rest of his strength to try and call the water to him again, a last-ditch effort to drown us all together, but before he could even lift the wave, I pulled the trigger, the bullet ripping out of the chamber and spiraling toward his face. It planted itself squarely in his forehead, exploding as it made contact, throwing us all backward in a blinding wave of light as a fresh wave of demons poured through the open portal.

CHAPTER 23 – PORTAL PURGATORY

My feet pounded rhythmically against the soft damp ground, tearing up the earth beneath me with each step as I ran faster than I ever had in my entire life. I honestly wasn't sure if my strength was growing still or if my adrenaline had just kicked into high gear. Tears flowed freely as I tried to drown out the shrill screams behind me, tearing at my heartstrings and trying to pull me back with all their might.

Guilt was already eating away at me. How could I have just left him there? Why was I like this—pathetic, weak, afraid, pitiful? I was filled with self-loathing that was growing with each step. It wasn't supposed to be like this; he should be by my side right now, taking the next step in this journey together. If only I had listened from the beginning, we could have avoided all of this. If I hadn't been off with Mia, everything would have been different. Thinking about her only made my heart hurt worst. How had things become so complicated? How did I let her get under my skin when I should have been focused on the mission at hand, at fulfilling my destiny, at reaching the Kingdom *with* Amil, hand in hand? I would never forgive myself for abandoning him, even if he somehow made it out alive, even if he did have another vessel waiting for him in the Kingdom, even if we could spend eternity together in the afterlife. I would always remember this moment.

Reaching the large stone structure, there was an eerie glow about the place, almost like it was alive with energy. Looking up at the sky, the moon was nearly all red, and I knew I was almost out of time. Standing there, the moments felt like lifetimes, trapped in the purgatory of uncertainty. I knew I needed to stay, to actually listen to Amil this time and take the leap of faith, yet every cell in my body was screaming at me to go back, to try and save him even if it seemed impossible. Isn't that what real heroes did? Faced the impossible, overcoming challenges despite the overwhelming odds. Squirming in my own skin, the urge to turn back was starting to win as I racked my mind for some solution, some way to save the only man I'd ever loved. There had to be something I could do, *anything* that might be enough to be his saving grace. Some parlor trick with water wasn't going to cut it, though. It needed to be grander than that.

An idea hit me like a ton of bricks as I gasped, shocked at how stupid I had been. The Pandora's box, the fortune teller, it suddenly all made sense. Searching through the folds of the dress I had on, I found the one hidden pocket where I had stashed the little icosahedral pearl-colored box. I had taken it everywhere with me since I found it out of an abundance of caution. I also pulled out a tiny silk bag, iridescent and full of tiny crystal shapes; I grabbed the corresponding icosahedron and put them both in my hands, clasped tightly together as I whispered a mantra instinctually, envisioning the shapes folding in and out of each other through their shared symmetries.

Pulsating in my hand, the bright hot spectral glow was escaping through the cracks in my fingers, pushing against the boundaries of my hands with intense power and force. When it became too much for me to hold back anymore, I finally opened my palms to two having become one, the tiny box slowly unfolding, more blinding light pouring forth from the inside, the familiar thudding beat that had originally called me to it growing louder as it opened. Twisting and turning, the box began expanding out, contorting in and out of itself as it shaped its way into muscle and veins, blood and flesh, skin and bones, all forming before my very eyes. Piece by piece, I watched a surreal horse take shape, a pale, too-skinny body filled with raging seas and stormy clouds swirling relentlessly below his ghostly semitransparent skin, deep, hollow sockets swirling into dark whirlpools where his eyes should have been, giving him a soulless look, like living death, as he hoofed the ground and shook his liquid mane with impatience. He should terrify me. He should make my soul uneasy with those lifeless eyes. He should, at the very least, make me incredibly nervous, yet something deep inside me recognized him like an old friend from a life I couldn't remember. Stepping forward, I placed my hand on his face, and he whined softly, dropping his head and pushing it against my chest in a soft sweet hello as the words escaped my lips in barely more than a whisper. "Kai"

Running my hand along his side, I stroked his odd jelly-like skin several times before he knelt at my feet, whinnying again as he tossed his head back, motioning for me to jump on. I hesitated for a fraction of a second before throwing caution to the wind and hitching my leg over his lowered back onto a geometry-engraved saddle. Standing in his towering glory, I suddenly felt like I was on top of the world, perched on my steed, towering over my problems even if the undercurrent of my own inner turmoil and anxiety still threatened to sweep me away.

Looking back to the sky once more, the moon looked to be entirely red now; the energy around the stone structure was ramping up, becoming palpable, an electric buzz in the air that was causing the hair on my arms to stand up. Any moment now, the nexus point would open, and who knows how long it would stay open, yet I knew deep in my heart that I had to do something, and I had to do it *now*. Leaning against his neck, I wrapped my hands around the understated silver and gold gilded reins and gave him the softest nudge with the heels of my feet. Seeming to respond more to my thoughts than my actions, Kai was already taking off at full speed into the night before I was even finished nudging him onward. Holding on to the reins tightly, he pushed himself, hoofs stamping that same familiar rhythm against the ground as he tore across the earth and closed the distance between Amil and I, hopefully before it was too late.

It took just a few minutes for my steed to traverse the short path that had taken what felt like hours for me to run in my sheer terror and heartbreak. I couldn't help but notice that the closer I got to the field where I had abandoned him, the more I could feel another familiar pull, but I didn't want to believe it—couldn't believe it, in fact. If *she* was here, nothing good could come of it, but I couldn't deny that every cell in my body wanted it to be true, wanted to be reunited with her despite everything.

It was a sickening feeling. It made me furious with myself, I was a fool, and she was playing me, and I had fallen for it. I was still falling for it. Was I really so desperate for affection and attention after a lifetime of neglect that I would take it even from the most toxic of sources? That I would fall for a girl who so clearly had her own agenda and wanted to capture me as nothing more than a pawn? Sure, she spun a good story about wanting to save the human race, but even I wasn't *that* foolish. Of course Cifer would want me to believe that some good could come of joining their crusade, a desperate attempt to try and convince me that there was even anything worth saving here, but I just couldn't believe it, even if I wanted to more than anything in my life. The fact remained this world was a dark place, and it was time to shed some light on it once and for all. Free choice sounded nice in theory, but humans, and demons for that matter, clearly couldn't handle the responsibility.

Riding past the final cropping of bushes keeping the field

out of view, I burst into the battlefield, shocked to find Amil, Mia, and the stranger from the festival crumpled together around Levi's fading body. A swarm of demons was pouring forth from the gate, hundreds of them now taking advantage of the full moon eclipse energy to shift through the ether into this world and jump from gates, all connected to this one open portal.

Standing tall and proud, my horse stared at the incoming army with a deep sense of calm. Meanwhile, I was squirming in my seat, fear gripping my heart as I watched the hoard of demons descend upon not one but two people I loved. Closing my eyes, I reached deep into my mind's eye, connecting with the steed on a spiritual level. We shared our thought space for an infinite moment, collaborating on our next move. When I opened my eyes, they were alive, glowing with streaks of blue, determined and focused. Leaning forward, I softly nudged the horse once more with my ankles, and with that, he was off, flying across the ground with unrelenting force as we barreled straight toward the oncoming army of demons.

As we approached, I could hear a soft cry calling out to me. Turning, momentarily distracted, Mia was the first to regain consciousness. Still trying to push herself up from the ground, she was looking at me with pure panic in her eyes as she pleaded silently with me not to sacrifice myself for them. Content in my choices and happy to face the consequences, I simply smiled softly at her before turning back to my mission at hand. It was too late, though; the fastest of the demons were already on top of me, half of them ripping me away from my steed while the others struggled in an already intense battle with Kai, kicking and stomping every chance he had, outright crushing several demons who disappeared in a cloud of smoke.

With Mia fresh on my mind, I called to the spark in my heart that answered instantly, erupting out of me in a fan of flames that consumed everything it touched, eating up all the demons within a ten-foot radius, several just out of that circle backing up a few feet as they recalculated their attack. Jumping back onto my horse while I still could, we were off, running toward the lagoon at top speed as the demons took chase, emboldened by our perceived attempt to flee.

Abruptly we whipped back around as we reached the water's edge, and I called out to it, visualizing the icosahedral cells of the water bending and blending into one massive wave that I pulled forth and sent cascading down on the nearest demons, crushing them beneath the sheer weight of the water as another dozen or so dissipated into thin air. Hundreds more were still behind them, and I was already panting. Each attack took so much out of me, and I wasn't sure how long I could hold out.

Pushing Kai forward, we charged the oncoming demons again, pulling another wave of water with me that was larger this time but harder to control. I missed my mark, washing away a small handful of demons while allowing several of the closer ones to still barrel forward, eyes wild as they desperately searched for an opening to knock me off my horse. As they descended upon us, my horse began bucking wildly, flailing his legs around and landing well-placed kicks that sent demons flying left and right. Modifying the ability Mia had taught me, I focused the spark from my heart into my hands and began shooting out intense balls of boiling liquid, demons screaming as the scorching hot liquid consumed their vessels, leaving nothing but smoke and ash in their place. I was growing confident despite my dampening powers. Another wave of demons crashed down on us, and I reached inside, tapping into the healing light I had used on Amil and Mia. I began twisting it, distorting it to have the opposite effect. After toying with the energy for a fraction of a moment, I pushed it out of me in a giant shockwave of death, the light spreading far and wide, but instead of healing, it began sucking the life out of the demons and feeding it to me, replenishing my depleted power source.

Running for their lives, the tides had turned as I barreled after them on my sea-filled steed. Growing more in sync with my beast by the moment, we moved in unison as I flew off his back just in time for him to morph into a massive wave, one that would rival some of the worst tsunamis this world has seen. Raging and consuming, it crashed onto the remaining demons, tossing and turning them relentlessly, drowning some, crushing others, washing over the land, and taking away their bodies along with most of the trees and rocks in the surrounding area. Even I stood in shock at the pure raw energy, unrelenting as the water searched out every last demon and wiped them clean off the face of this earth, leaving nothing behind except for the small pocket of light that protected my fallen companions. Rushing for the portal like my life depended on it, but demons were still slowly trickling out of the gateway. I sliced through them by channeling the tainted light ability into a transparent sword, each hit draining them of their life force, feeding their ether to me, their bodies dropping instantly before their ashes drifted away in the wind. Using all of my remaining strength, I fought with the door and began pushing and pulling while still using my free hand to parley with several demons who were attempting to overpower me and stop me from closing the portal.

The amount of energy I had consumed was suddenly beginning to backfire. It was becoming too much for my vessel to handle, and I had started to shake uncontrollably. An unexpected consequence suddenly had me on my back foot again. The light sword was becoming too hard to control and growing beyond what I could contain. Letting go of the gate in an attempt to steady myself, the demons began pouring forth freely once more. My arrogance was going to cost me this fight, my entire being was trying to hold on to the sword, but I was shaking so violently that I thought I would fall to pieces right then and there.

Just as they closed the final gap that separated us, a familiar face came charging through, throwing herself between the demons and myself in a last-ditch effort to protect me with her own flesh and bones. They were nearly on her, eyes livid and hungry—they would tear her to pieces in a heartbeat, and I was helpless to stop them. The anger, fear, and sadness welled up inside of me like a storm and came pouring out all at once. With a primal scream, I gathered what strength wasn't dedicated to clinging to a sword of deadly light that was still growing uncontrollably, and in a roar of frustration and heartbreak, a swell of water erupted from within me, bioluminescent like the water from the Keeps, but angry and thrashing like the seas that made up my steed. It knocked the onslaught of demons back several yards as I finally lost control of the sword, and it erupted, consuming everything in a hundred-yard radius, including Mia.

Barely clinging to life, even now, she impressed me with her strength, outliving what hundreds of other demons could not, even in her weakened state. I dropped to her side, tears welling up in the corners of my eyes as I looked at her broken body. She had been trying to save me, and I had destroyed her, just like I had destroyed everything.

Looking at me with dim eyes, she smiled softly as she reached up weakly and placed her cool hand on my face. "You really are incredible, you know."

I couldn't help but laugh a bit, an uncomfortable sound followed by sniffling as the tears boiled over and turned into full-on sobs. I needed to save her. I needed to untwist the ether and give her back her life force. I needed to save her vessel because if she went back to the Underworld now and by some small chance this had been a genuine attempt to save my life, and perhaps even save this world, and not just some ruse, I was certain I would never see her again. After all, I didn't imagine demons were the most forgiving type. Just as I was closing my eyes to try to untangle the ether and twist it back into a geometry of regeneration instead of degeneration, a massively bright light caused them to fly open again.

Looking in the direction I had come from, a gigantic beam of light was shooting up from Stonehenge. It had begun, the nexus point was open, and I was out of time. Turning back to Mia, she looked at me with desperate eyes, searching for some answer she needed. Suddenly, her broken body collapsed in defeat.

"I see you've made your choice." Looking her in the eyes, I willed her to understand it wasn't that I didn't love her; I loved her too much, and I knew it was too good to be true. I didn't want to let her go, but I had to if I was going to fulfill my destiny, and I wouldn't make the same mistake twice; I wouldn't fail Amil again.

Standing up, she watched me with a strained smile, her eyes cold and fading fast. "Take this at least, won't you?"

She was holding something weakly in her hand. I knelt back down, my heart breaking all over again as my resolve wavered ever so slightly. I wanted to save her; I wanted her to know I wanted to save her. I wanted her to know I loved her. Dropping a small crinkly parcel into my hand, I looked down to find the small fortune cookie, the second token the fortune teller had exchanged her from her precious explosive, an explosive that might have saved her life in this fight.

"This is yours. You should keep it." She smiled softly again, using my close proximity to her advantage. She used the last of her strength to grab me and pull me in close. "Everything I have has always been yours. I just didn't know it. Try not to forget about me up there." Suddenly her lips were on mine, fierce and demanding as her tongue pushed against mine, searching out the last sweet moments before, in an instant, she was gone, nothing but a cloud of smoke.

Tears still flowing freely, I pushed myself to my feet and turned to find Amil awake, sitting up and staring at me with a strange look on his face. Blushing, I dropped my eyes as I stashed away the cookie in the folds of my dress and rushed to his side, dropping to my knees as I began fretting over him.

"Are you okay?" He shook his head, irritation painting his broken features.

"Not at all! Why did you come back for… us? What were you thinking?!"

I laughed nervously, happy to have him back even if he was furious with me. "A girl's gotta do what a girl's gotta do. Are you going to get me to that nexus point or what?" I easily helped him to his feet and then began looking around, searching for the familiar companion from the street fair, Maicoh, I believe was his name. He seemed to have disappeared in the chaos and was nowhere to be found, and I didn't really have the time to worry about where he could have gone.

Whistling, the raging seas still tearing across the land finally subsided and reformed into the sickly pale horse that came galloping toward me joyfully, shaking his head proudly at the damage he had caused. Patting Kai softly on his head as he approached, I cooed praises to him before using my abundance of strength from draining the demons to toss Amil easily onto the horse. Fortunately, the energy was draining fast, fast enough that I was no longer shaking and had regained most of my control over this vessel. Regret was filling the void it left behind as the vision of Mia being blown away by my own hand played on repeat in my head. The broken look in her eyes as I abandoned her, the intensity of our last kiss, her final parting gift to me—it all left me feeling confused, my insides twisting and contorting as I jumped up next to Amil and rode off into the night toward my destiny.

Pushing the steed as fast as he would go, we made it to the stone structure in a matter of moments. It was alive with bright spectral light, shooting up to the sky in a pillar of pure cosmic power, swirling and spinning, folding and funneling into itself infinitely. The moon was completely red now, and the earth and the heavens seemed connected by the massive nexus, calling out to me in an ethereal voice that sounded like a thousand angels singing in perfect harmony.

It felt surreal, I couldn't believe the moment had arrived, and somehow, I was here, with Amil, his warm lanky arms wrapped tightly around my waist as my horse pounded across the final pathway between me and eternity. Amil had told me once my destiny was fulfilled, I would be granted an eternal afterlife, one I could share with him, one where we would never be faced with the pain of being parted again. Now that the moment was here, it was hard to ignore the pit in my stomach, the little *I* that always sabotaged everything by telling me I didn't deserve this, I didn't deserve to be happy, that this was all too good to be true. I shoved those feelings deep down as I leaned forward and pushed the horse to close the distance between me and my future before I turned into the yellow-bellied coward I was. It was time to face the future. It was time to make the leap. It was time to finally have some faith.

Jumping off the steed, with a final neigh, he dissolved instantly, leaving behind just the small crystal icosahedron the fortune teller had gifted me. Picking it up, Amil unwrapped a small leather cord from around his wrist and unraveled it, fed it through the small hole in the shape before tying it around my neck. I could still feel the slight rhythmic pulse, ever so slightly rumbling against my chest where the crystal icosahedron was resting, just below the ivory octopus that served as another painful reminder of the girl I left behind that I couldn't seem to part with. Amil reached out for my hand, and I took it willingly, looking him in the eyes for several minutes. We had a long unspoken conversation before turning toward the spectral nexus pulsating with power. He leaned over and kissed me softly on the forehead while whispering reassurances to me.

Tears were still flowing quietly as I thought about all the things I was about the leave behind, the people I had forsaken, the unfinished business, the debts unsettled, the lovers crossed, and the family abandoned, everything that was fighting and clinging to keep me here, to convince me to try another way. I was done being held back, though. I was done standing in my own way. I was done being my own worst enemy.

With one final deep breath, I let go of my earthly tethers and stepped forward into the light.

www.ingramcontent.com/pod-product-compliance
Lightning Source LLC
Chambersburg PA
CBHW030859060726
47591CB00005B/1350